DEN
OF
LIONS

DEN OF LIONS

A Church Street Kirk Mystery

Daniel K. Miller

Chapter One

Dark clouds rolled across the night sky as the wind howled through the Scottish Highlands city of Inverness. The waters of the Moray Firth churned and roiled, hammering the rocky shore. In the distance, a blood-curdling scream pierced the air. The following splash was barely perceptible amidst the crashing waves.

The next morning, a curious crowd had gathered at the edge of the beach. Sirens soon filled the air, and two police cars pulled up near the crowd. Four officers got out and pushed their way through to find the lifeless body of a young man lying on the rocks. Sea water lapped calmly at the man's boots—a far cry from the angry waves of the night before.

"Oi, get these people back," one officer shouted. Two others spread their arms, motioning for the crowd to disperse. The curious onlookers stepped back, but only a few actually left the morbid scene. Another police officer kneeled beside the body and checked for a pulse—a mere formality, she knew. Everyone could easily tell the body had washed ashore a long while ago. The question was, how long ago?

"Who was he?" the first officer asked.

His colleague checked the soaked jeans pockets. She looked up and shook her head. The first officer pulled out a pad of paper and began writing. "No identification. Deceased is male, about, eh, mid-thirties, appears to be of African or Middle Eastern descent," he mumbled as he wrote. "Cause of death?" he asked.

His partner furrowed her brow. "Hard to say. I don't see any obvious lacerations or wounds." She glanced behind her at the shadow of the Kessock

Bridge, which spanned the water and connected Inverness and the Black Isle peninsula. "Jumper? There seems to be a lot of bruising on this side—possibly from when he hit the water?"

The first officer grumbled and wrote more in his notepad. "We'll have to wait and see what the boys at the morgue say. Make sure you get pictures before we load him into the van."

His partner nodded and pulled a camera from her pocket. As she took pictures of the body, the first officer stared out across the sea. His eyes focused on the silver spire of a partially constructed wind turbine looming in the distance. "That the new wind energy farm they're building?" he asked.

His partner looked up. "You kin it has something to do with him?" she asked.

He shrugged. "Come on. If you're done, let's get him loaded and out of here. This crowd's getting more unruly, and I think I see a press van pulling up."

* * *

Eliza MacGillivray sat at a small round table in the kirk hall. She placed her palms on the table to steady herself and stop the tremors. She had felt unsettled all morning. The singing from the choir hadn't helped. Church Street Kirk had been without a proper choir director for six months. Young Reverend Darrow had tried to fill in, but he had no ear for hymn arrangements. He could hardly carry a tune himself, much less wrangle the discordant voices of the choir into a harmonious unity. He was also American, so he didn't know many of the traditional Scottish songs, and his pronunciations were all wrong.

This morning's attempt at Psalm 23, *E'en as a Shepherd Tents His Sheep*, had made Eliza feel dizzy, so she had left the service before the benediction. She entered the large gathering hall, snuck a few biscuits from the serving table, and sat at her usual table in the corner. She took several slow breaths. Her heart was racing.

She tried a biscuit to settle her stomach. It was sweet, but dry. She should have thought to pour herself a cup of tea before she sat down. Crumbs fell onto her lap. She attempted to brush them off her black dress, but some got stuck in the lacing. The large handbag she had placed on the table began to shake at the sound of her crunching. She unclasped the top and two furry gray ears popped out. A furry head followed, with two black eyes and a furiously twitching nose. Eliza broke off a piece of biscuit and offered it to the rabbit. It nibbled and then attempted to grab the rest of the sweet pastry with its paws.

Eliza pulled her hand back and scolded it. "Ah, you greedy thing. We must watch our weight, mustn't we?" She put the biscuit down and patted the rabbit's head. One of its ears turned toward the door. Eliza could hear it, too. Off-key notes, too loud and out of sync, echoed through the room. The church service was coming to a close. Soon, parishioners, hungry for tea, pastries, and gossip, would enter the kirk hall and disrupt their calm silence.

A wave of dizziness came over her again. Her mind felt like sea foam left churned up on the shore by an angry tide. The lace collar of her dress felt suddenly constricting. Her fingers fumbled with the button. She brushed aside her necklace. It was the same necklace that had hung around her neck since she was a young girl—a simple gold chain supporting a smooth donut-shaped stone. The familiar stone called to her, and she reached for it. She hoped the talisman would steady her in a way that the biscuit had not. But it had the opposite effect. She gasped and her eyes glossed over. The rabbit in her purse sat up on its hind legs. It was used to these episodes, though it had never witnessed one so severe. It leaped out and nuzzled its owner's other hand.

But Eliza MacGillivray was already gone. She was transported away from Church Street, away from the city of Inverness. She floated above the North Sea on air currents like a gull. Her vertigo only increased the farther up she floated. Was she actually spinning? Then everything stopped. She hung, suspended for several seconds. In the distance, she could see the shore. She could make out the bustling port and the Kessock Bridge, reaching across the Beauly and Moray Firths. Eliza watched as cars drove back and forth across it, but her eyes focused on a single figure who stood at the railing in the center of the bridge.

She squinted, trying to make him out. He wore black clerical robes and, from her great height, he appeared as small as a wee doll. He raised his arms as if he were about to jump. Eliza opened her mouth to shout "Stop!", but no sound came out. The man's arms waved back and forth, and Eliza realized he wasn't preparing to jump. No, he was shouting at her. Whatever invisible strings that held her snapped, and she fell. Her body rushed toward the water; her eyes teared up at the speed. Then, just as suddenly as she had begun, her fall was interrupted.

"My lord seems to have little thought of you, or of his children, or of his Highland home."

The voice was male and had gravel in it. It surrounded her, but also felt distant, like an echo. She knew this voice.

Eliza awoke on the hardwood floor of the kirk hall. Her chest ached, and her head pounded. Many figures were standing over her. She couldn't make out who they were or what they were saying. She blinked several times.

"Eliza?"

"She's awake."

Eliza touched her head. It stung and felt damp. She looked at her fingers, red and wet. She blinked again. Where was she? Who were these people?

"Stand back. Give her some air."

"Ms. MacGillivray, are you okay?"

Eliza tried to sit up, but she felt too dizzy and weak.

"Don't try to move, dear. The paramedics are on their way."

"Sara?" Eliza whispered.

"Yes, it's me, Sarah. Looks like you had quite a fall. Hit your head on the table," Rev. Sarah Calder said. She placed a cloth on the older woman's head to stop the bleeding.

Eliza glanced around her. She was on the floor, surrounded by what seemed like half the congregation. Her right hand still held tight to the stone of her necklace. She willed her fingers to release it. "Where is Reverend Darrow?" she asked.

"Shh, shh, try to stay calm," Rev. Calder said.

"Darrow," Eliza repeated.

"I'm right here," Rev. Daniel Darrow said. He kneeled beside her and took her hand.

"Reverend Darrow, there you are, back from the sea. I received a message for you."

Chapter Two

Odhar stood atop the grassy hill, her gaze fixed on the church burial grounds below. She pulled her woolen shawl around her shoulders to fight off the chill in the air. Thick clouds hid the moon, causing eerie shadows to be cast over the gravestones. Her young son, Coinneach, followed her gaze. Cattle milled around them, chewing their cud and munching on the dewy grass. Their breath escaped in hot, visible wisps. Odhar listened for other people, but the night was silent except for the distant sound of crashing waves and the peaceful chewing of the cattle.

"Mum," Coinneach whispered, his voice tinged with curiosity and fear, "why do we graze the herd so late at night?"

"Shush, laddie," Odhar replied, her eyes never leaving the church or the graveyard. "Ye kin the richest grass in the county grows on these grounds. God is generous and shares his bounty wi' all his children, but the laird and his priest are not so benevolent."

As midnight approached, Odhar's face contorted with worry. Several of the cows had wandered down the hill to the edge of the graveyard. She glanced at Coinneach. "Ye must hurry back home, Coinneach," she said with an urgency in her voice. "I fear there be worse things than a miserly priest out tonight."

"What's wrong?" he asked, his small hands gripping the hem of her skirt.

"There's no time tae explain," she said, pushing him gently but firmly away from her. "The veil between the living and the dead grows too thin. 'Tis dangerous for weans tae be out now." She hesitated, then added, "Take these cattle and hurry home. Don't look back. I'll gather those wanderers and be right behind ye."

Coinneach saw the fear in his mother's eyes. He didn't want to leave her, but he was an obedient child. He nodded and shouted, "Yah!" to drive the cattle toward their home on the other side of the hill. His heart pounded in his ears louder than the sound of their many hooves thudding on the damp ground. The dark sky loomed overhead, and a chill wind whipped through the tall, wet grass that slapped against his legs as he drove them on. Just before descending the hill, Coinneach couldn't help but glance back at the graveyard, despite his mother's warning.

He saw strange wisps of smoke rising from the ground all around the churchyard. His blood ran cold when he realized what they were—spirits rising from their graves, spreading out in all directions like a terrible fog. He stumbled, catching himself before he fell, and forced his legs to move faster. His breath came in ragged gasps as he raced towards the safety of home.

When he reached their small cottage, Coinneach hurried the cattle into their pen and shut the gate without checking to see if it locked. He flung open the cottage door and collapsed inside, his heart hammering in his chest. He leaned against the rough wooden wall, trying to catch his breath. With a trembling hand, he made the sign of the cross over his chest and closed his eyes, praying for his mother's safe return.

"Please, Lord," he whispered, "keep Mum safe from the spirits."

On the other side of the grassy hill, Odhar snuck up close to the few cattle that had strayed to the edge of the cemetery. An eerie mist slowly covered the ground, and she whistled for the cattle to come near to her. The heat from their breath and hairy bodies surrounded her like a comfortable blanket. She waited there, hidden amongst the cattle, while she watched with horror as shadowy apparitions rose from their graves. Odhar held her breath and tried to calm her thudding heart, as the spirits floated on the mist all around her. To her great relief, they passed by the small group of cows, unaware of her presence.

An hour passed before the spirits began to return to their graves. One by one, they slipped back into the earth like smoky tendrils, leaving the burial ground seemingly undisturbed. Odhar rose, ready to leave that fearful place. Her back ached from crouching so long amongst her protective ring of cattle. She made a mental note to give them all an extra helping of grain in the morning. She was about to lead them home when she noticed that one grave remained open—a dark, gaping maw amidst the shadows.

Her curiosity piqued, Odhar crept cautiously toward the still-open grave. She clutched her wooden staff protectively in her hand. As she neared the edge, she stumbled, losing her grip on the staff. It fell with a soft thud across the grave. She reached out a trembling hand, but before she could retrieve it, she noticed the mist rising around her once again.

Odhar froze as a spirit appeared before her. The specter was both terrifying and beautiful—a young woman with pale, luminescent skin that seemed to shimmer in the moonlight.

"Remove your staff so I may reenter my grave," the ghost demanded. Her voice echoed eerily through the darkness.

Though she was frightened, Odhar hesitated to obey. She realized that her clumsiness had inadvertently given her some strange power over the spirit. "Why did ye no return with the others?" she asked, her voice wavering slightly.

The spirit sighed, her ethereal form flickering like a candle flame. "I had a farther journey than the rest," she said. "I had to fly all the way to Norway, for I am the daughter of the king."

"And how did ye come tae be buried here?" Odhar couldn't help but ask, her curiosity once again getting the better of her.

The spirit's glassy blue eyes filled with sorrow. "I died whilst bathing in the sea one day. After weeks adrift in the North Sea, my body washed ashore here. I was found and buried in this unmarked grave."

"Is there anything I can do for ye?" Odhar asked softly, her fear momentarily forgotten as she listened to the spirit's sad tale.

"Remove your staff so that I may rest tonight," the spirit repeated. "Return tomorrow and place a stone on my grave to remember me, Fryja, daughter of King Harold. If you do this, I will bless you with a gift."

Swallowing hard, Odhar nodded. She lifted her staff from the grave and stepped aside to allow the spirit to pass back into the earth. Alone in the graveyard, Odhar breathed a heavy sigh of relief. She quickly gathered her cattle and drove them back up the hill toward home. All the while, her mind raced with thoughts of the fantastic riches the spirit would bless her with once she completed its request.

The next morning, Odhar awoke with the memory of the ghostly encounter still fresh in her mind. As she was preparing breakfast, her son approached her. "Mum?" Coinneach asked, "What happened last night? I ken I saw spirits rising from their graves. Is it because we trespassed on the kirk grounds?"

"Och, it was nothing but a wee mist rolling off the sea. No need to worry yerself," Odhar replied, not wanting to frighten him. Their mortal lives were difficult enough without having to burden the poor child with worries of the spirit realm. *However,* she thought with a sly smile, *our fortunes could change for the better very soon.*

"Forget yer chores, I've got a more important task for ye today. There's an unmarked grave needs tending. Go fetch a flat wood slab from the barn and carve a marker for it. Fryja, daughter of King Harold, it should say."

"Who's that?" Coinneach asked.

"Never ye mind. I'll help ye draw the letters if ye need."

"Should it not be of stone instead of wood?"

"Aye, but take a look around ye. We canna afford a fine stone nor a stonemason to carve it. Now go do as I say and hurry. It must be completed this day," Odhar said. She watched her son run outside to find a suitable piece of scrap wood. Stone or wood? What difference should that make to a spirit? She would fulfill her part of the bargain, and soon she and her son would have enough money to hire a thousand stonemasons if they so desired.

Wee Coinneach spent the better part of the day carefully carving the name of the ancient Norse princess into a large wooden slab. He carried it to the church graveyard and hammered it into the ground exactly where his mother had instructed him. The installation didn't take as long as he'd imagined, so he decided to take the long way home. He had about an hour before sunset and hadn't enjoyed a walk along the shores of Loch Ussie in a long time.

As he skipped along the rocky shore, he stumbled upon a smooth, round stone with a hole in the middle. He picked it up and was about to see how far he could skip it across the water when another idea struck him. He held the stone up to his eye and peered through the hole.

"Holy Lord!" he exclaimed, startled by what he saw. The distant village of Inverness had transformed before his eyes into a sprawling city with massive ships, magnificent stone buildings, and more people than he had ever seen in his young life. Fire and water seemed to run together in streams through the streets and lanes, giving light to the buildings. He had never before seen such a fascinating or frightening vision.

"What in heaven's name?" he muttered, unable to tear his eye away from the stone. When he finally lowered it, he gasped in horror as he realized that he could no longer see out of the eye that had been looking through the stone. Coinneach cried, clutching the stone tightly in his hand as he raced back home.

"Mum! Mum!" Coinneach screamed. He burst through the door of their small cottage, tears streaming down his pale cheeks. "I've had a frightful vision! And…and I cannae see with one eye!"

Odhar rushed to her son's side, her heart pounding in her chest as she examined his eye. All color had disappeared from it, as if it had been covered in a pearly sheath. "Blessed saints," she whispered. "What's happened?"

Coinneach opened his hand to reveal the stone he had found. "When I peered through it, I saw Inverness, but changed and terrible. Then I lowered the stone and…" His voice trailed off, overcome with tears.

Odhar held her son until he calmed down. "Stay here, Coinneach," she said firmly, hiding the fear and anger she felt inside. She grabbed her shawl and staff and hurried out the door. She ran the entire way to the church and fell panting at the grave of the Norse princess. With a shaking finger, she traced the crudely carved letters on the wooden grave marker.

"Cruel spirit, why would ye do this to my boy?" she cried. "Show yerself! Ye promised a blessing. I did what ye asked and ye've repaid me with a curse!"

The surrounding temperature suddenly dropped, and mist snaked along the ground. A young woman appeared. The spirit wore an expression of sadness mixed with anger. "You broke your promise," Fryja said, her voice cold as a winter's wind. "This wooden marker will weather and fade, leaving me forgotten once more."

"Forgive me," Odhar pleaded, her hands clasped together in desperation. "I'm but a poor woman, and I cannae afford a stone. My son meant no harm. I beg ye; show mercy on him."

"As this marker will fade, I have taken the sight from one of your son's eyes. But in its place, I have given him the gift of second sight," the spirit replied, her words tinged with bitterness. "It is both a blessing and a curse, one that he must bear for his mother's broken promise."

"Please, restore him tae what he was," Odhar begged, tears streaming down her cheeks. But the spirit was already gone, faded back into the mist, leaving Odhar alone in the graveyard. She stood and, with a heavy heart, walked slowly back home to the uncertain future that awaited her and her son.

Chapter Three

"Today's the big day, is it?" Rev. Sarah Calder asked. Rev. Daniel Darrow nodded. "Are you nervous?" she asked. Daniel nodded again. "Don't be." Rev. Calder placed a reassuring hand on her young protégé's shoulder. She had to reach up, as he was a full head taller than her. "I've known wee Ellie Gray her whole life. She's had a rough time these past several years, with her da dying and then her mum's imprisonment, but she's got a strong heart and she's stubborn. When she sets her sights on something, she usually finds a way to get it. And I've seen the way she looks at you. In fact, I'm surprised it's taken this long."

Daniel laughed a nervous laugh. "Thanks for the pep talk."

"Of course, she could think you're just asking her to marry you because your immigration papers are due for renewal soon."

Daniel's eyes grew wide. "You don't think? I hadn't thought of that."

Rev. Calder shook her head and laughed. "You *are* nervous, poor lad. It'll be fine. Do you think she suspects?"

"I don't think so. I told her to meet me at Urquhart Castle on Loch Ness—that's where we had our first kiss. Then we'll have dinner at a little pub in Invermoriston that she likes."

"How romantic. Ellie's sure to say, 'Yes,'" Rev. Calder said. She held her purse, pausing before the coat rack near the door of her office. She nodded to herself and grabbed a light waterproof jacket. "You never know this time of year."

Daniel looked at his own attire. He'd changed out of his clerical robes into a new pair of jeans and a button-down shirt that Ellie had once said brought out his eyes. He hadn't thought to bring a rain jacket on such a nice June day. Then again, he also didn't have the benefit of having lived a lifetime with Inverness's capricious weather. "Are you sure you don't want me to tag along? I'm sure I could still make it in time," Daniel said.

"Not if you're relying on public transport," Rev. Calder said with a smirk. "I'll be fine on my own. We don't want to overwhelm Eliza with too many visitors just now. Though you should check in on her tomorrow. She did seem rather insistent on talking with you before the paramedics arrived."

"I'll go see her first thing in the morning," Daniel said.

"Don't you have that radio interview tomorrow morning?"

"Right, I'll go see her second thing in the morning!" Daniel grabbed his own satchel and followed her out the door and down the hallway. "It's actually a podcast interview, not radio."

"Hmm, like those true crime stories? I love those. But wouldn't radio be better?" Rev. Calder asked.

"Not exactly. This one's more of a topical news program. They have quite a large subscriber base."

When the two reverends reached the door leading to the church sanctuary, they went through, and Rev. Calder locked it behind them. Sunlight radiated brightly through the stained-glass windows behind the altar, illuminating the room with colorful speckles of light, like a very slow disco ball. They took a quick pass through the pews, picking up any left-behind items from the morning's service. A hat, candy wrappers, a newspaper, and a plastic baggie with cat treats—so that's why they hadn't seen Sir Walter Scott, the kirk cat, roaming the pews as was his usual Sunday morning routine. The discarded newspaper on the back row likely belonged to Hugh Macpherson, Daniel's landlord and occupant of the flat adjoining his own in the nearby neighborhood of Bellfield Park. Hugh Macpherson always brought the Sunday edition to keep him occupied while his wife, Marjory, helped arrange flowers for the service.

Reverends Calder and Darrow reached the kirk's main entrance. Daniel pulled open one of the two doors. The doors were large and made of heavy wood from a tree felled long before either one of them had been born. Each door was adorned in simple, symmetrical carvings—mostly geometric lines with a few floral embellishments. They met at their peaks to form a single massive arch that complemented the simple arched ceiling inside and the stonework of the kirk's single steepled bell tower outside.

"Good luck with the podcast. It will be nice for the kirk to be in the news for something other than arson or murder," Rev. Calder said with a laugh that betrayed just a hint more shame than humor.

"Yeah, those pesky things tend to overshadow the good work we actually do," Daniel joked. Then, reading his boss's face, he added, "But seriously, this new wind farm wouldn't be happening without local support, and Church Street has played a big part in that. I know we don't do it for the recognition, but like you said, it'll be nice to get a little positive press, anyway."

They left the large wooden front doors unlocked and went their separate ways. Rev. Calder to her car and Daniel to the public bus stop. They often left the main doors to the kirk unlocked during daylight hours for passersby who needed a quiet place to pray or simply wanted a calm refuge from the bustle of the city.

Daniel got on a bus that, with one transfer, would take him past Loch Ness. It was a forty-five-minute ride on a good day. With the pleasant weather, many people were out, and traffic was slow. Rev. Calder had been right, squeezing in a hospital visit before meeting Ellie at Urquhart Castle would've been impossible. Daniel opened his bag and dug in a pocket that was sewn into the inner lining. He pulled out a small velvet-covered box. The box opened to reveal a ring. Sunlight glinted off the modest diamond in the ring's center. *Modest* was the word the jeweler had used to describe the diamond's size, but Daniel knew that was an optimistic phrasing. The jeweler had wanted a sale, and Daniel had wanted something that wouldn't put him too far into debt.

He returned the ring box to his bag and placed the bag on the empty seat beside him. He retrieved a small notepad so he could review the talking points for his interview in the morning. It was hard to concentrate, though. He was anxious over his date with Ellie, and the excitement that morning hadn't helped. Eliza MacGillivray was one of the eldest members of Church

Street Kirk, but she had never seemed in poor health before. Daniel often saw her walking around the neighborhood, always with her rabbit on its leash. Sometimes she led the rabbit, sometimes the rabbit seemed to lead her, but she never had trouble getting around. What had precipitated her episode in the kirk hall? Stroke? Heart attack? Malnourishment? Her hands, with their thin skin, appeared skeletal in the right light. Perhaps she was frailer than she let on. Wild animals were like that—putting up a healthy façade despite growing illness, not wanting to appear weak to predators.

And why had she been so insistent on talking to me? Daniel wondered. She had said she had a message for him? Daniel shuddered. Eliza MacGillivray's *messages* were not like other people's messages. She fancied herself the heir of Coinneach Odhar, the Brahan Seer, Scotland's own seventeenth-century Nostradamus. Though she was not related to him, at least not as far as anyone knew, she claimed to possess his donut-shaped seeing stone and, with it, his spiritual legacy. Like Coinneach, most of Eliza's visions were limited in scope to the Highlands, Inverness most specifically. Some prophesies she had lifted from the Seer himself; some were Eliza originals. All, according to Eliza, had come true.

While Daniel had initially met her supposed gift with skepticism, he had come to accept the power of her words—if not for their prophetic truth, at least for the impact they had on others. Everyone at Church Street had received a message, or prophecy, from Eliza at some point during their tenure at the kirk. Ellie claimed to owe her acceptance into the University of Edinburgh's veterinary school to one of Eliza's visions. Eliza had foreseen Daniel's arrival at Church Street, or as she had put it: "From across the sea shall a shepherd come." She had seemingly predicted the motives, if not the actual assailants, of two murders in as many years.

Daniel flipped through his notebook and landed on a page where he had written Eliza's last message. He checked the date—six months ago. He chuckled to himself. On the surface, the prophecy seemed to be about the best time to fish the Beauly River, but, when read a certain way, it could be seen to predict his imminent proposal to Ellie Gray. When Eliza eventually heard about the proposal, she would inevitably read it that way and congratulate herself on another vision successfully fulfilled.

Daniel reached to the seat beside him to return the notebook. He was too distracted to think about tomorrow's interview. His hand fell empty upon the seat. Where was his bag? He looked under the seat, but nothing had fallen down there. A cold panic swept through him. His phone was in that bag. Ellie's ring was in that bag! He glanced up and down the aisle. The bus had come to a stop. Passengers were disembarking, and a minute later, others would board and take their place.

"There was a bag here. Did you see it?" Daniel asked the woman sitting near him. She shook her head and returned her attention to her phone. "My bag, it's missing!" Daniel said, frantically.

A man sitting two rows back answered. "Likely one of 'em two what just left. Crime in Inverness has skyrocketed since we've opened our borders to those people."

"What?" Daniel asked.

"Hurry if you intend to catch 'em," the man said, pointing to the exit.

Without thinking, Daniel raced off the bus. He had to push through people that were trying to board. Outside, pedestrians crowded the sidewalk. His eyes flitted in every direction, but he did not see his bag. He heard a shout several yards from the bus stop. He couldn't make out what it was, but with no other leads, he ran toward the noise. People crowded the sidewalk. Regardless of the direction they were walking, most of their heads had turned toward the shout. Daniel picked his way down a quickly fading path, as if someone had already broken a way through the crowd only moments earlier. When he reached the source of the shout, Daniel found a woman and a man both on the ground. Someone was helping the woman to her feet.

"Are you okay, luv?" someone asked the woman. The woman nodded. She stood on shaky legs and held her shoulder.

"You should be ashamed of yourself, shoving this poor woman down. No one needs to be in that much of a hurry," another person said to the man on the ground. The man pulled the hood of his sweatshirt further over his head and crawled away. He attempted to stand, but he had clearly hurt his foot.

"Wait," Daniel shouted. "That's my bag!"

The man leaped up and ran, but the crowd and his hurt foot slowed him down. Daniel followed him. He made up enough ground so that when the man turned a corner onto a less crowded street, Daniel was nearly upon him. Before he could break away, Daniel reached out and grabbed the man's hoodie. The unexpected force spun the man around and dislodged the hood over his head. He was not a man at all, but a frightened teenager with wide blue eyes, acne, and a shock of blonde hair. The boy twisted free and ran smack into the backs of two men walking together.

"Watch where you are going!" one man said.

"Stop! Thief!" Daniel shouted.

The boy attempted to dart away, but one of the men held his arm. "Lemme go!" The boy shouted.

"Thank you," Daniel said. He approached them, out of breath. He reached for the bag.

"Wait, what's going on?" the man said. He was dressed in a suit that was slightly too large, had black curly hair, a short beard, and spoke with an accent that Daniel could not place.

"This boy, he stole my bag," Daniel said.

"This is mine!" the boy shouted. "Let go of me!"

The two men looked at each other, then back at Daniel.

"Open it up. You'll find my phone, a water bottle, sunglasses, and, um," Daniel said, trying to remember what else he'd left in there.

"Whatever, take your stupid bag. Just let me go!" the boy said. He shoved the bag at Daniel.

"Should we let him go?" one of the men asked. Daniel nodded. "You should thank this man. In my country, a thief would lose his hand," the man said. He made a chopping motion on the boy's wrist. The boy's eyes grew wide. He ran off when the man released him.

"Thank you," Daniel said. He checked the inside pocket of the bag and let out a sigh of relief. The small velvet-covered box was still there. "You wouldn't really cut off the kid's hand?" Daniel asked.

The two men laughed. "No," the man in the too-big suit said. "But perhaps that will make the boy think twice before stealing again."

"Where are you from, if you don't mind me asking?" Daniel said.

"Afghanistan," the other man said.

Daniel nodded. He thought of the old man on the bus and cringed. He had been so panicked about losing Ellie's ring, he hadn't taken even a second to question the old man's assumptions. "It's always nice to meet another immigrant. I'm from America," Daniel said. They shook hands. Having experienced plenty of his own cultural missteps in his new Scottish home, he should have known better. "Y'all really saved the day for me," Daniel said, shaking the two men's hands. "If you ever need anything, look me up. I'm a reverend at Church Street Kirk."

Chapter Four

Daniel held his bag close as he walked back to the bus stop. He didn't have to wait long before catching another bus to Loch Ness. When he finally arrived at Urquhart Castle, which sat near the center of the northern shore of the loch, he didn't see Ellie's car in the carpark. He checked his bag again. The ring was still there. Daniel glanced at his phone and breathed a sigh of relief. His unexpected detour hadn't made him late, but he did notice a missed call notification.

The call was from Young Hugh Macpherson, Daniel's past flatmate and the son of his landlords, Hugh and Margory Macpherson. Daniel clicked the button to FaceTime his old friend. Young Hugh answered on the third ring. Usually clean-shaven and with at least a two-to-one ration of hair to gel on his head, Daniel hardly recognized him. Daniel blinked, surprised at the young man with a woolly beard an unkempt hair blowing in the sea breeze.

"Oi, mate. You're a hard one to get hold of," Young Hugh said.

"Sorry, it's been a long day and I haven't even had lunch yet," Daniel replied. "What's up?"

"So, you haven't done it yet?" Young Hugh asked.

"Done what?" Daniel asked, struggling to hear him over the sound of the wind. He must be outside wherever he was.

"Done what? Popped the question, of course! Have you made our wee Ellie an honest woman yet?"

"No," Daniel chuckled. "I'm actually waiting on her to arrive right now."

"You still going the Urquhart route?" Young Hugh asked. Daniel nodded.

"That's proper romantic. I just called earlier to wish you luck. I don't know how you landed a lass like Ellie."

"Thanks, I don't know how I managed it either."

"Now, that fellow, Cameron, her old boyfriend from uni—I thought for certain they'd end up together. He was a handsome one that, and a doctor," Young Hugh said.

Daniel scoffed. "Thanks for the pep talk. I wasn't already nervous or anything."

"Have you prayed for a bit of divine intervention? You might need it," Young Hugh said with a sly grin.

"Remind me why I return your calls?" Daniel asked.

"Just saying, you saved me when I was falsely accused of murder last year—God owes you one."

"I don't think it works that way, but thanks for thinking of me," Daniel said. "What time is it wherever you are, anyway? It still looks dark."

Young Hugh glanced around as if surprised by Daniel's observation. "Oh, it's about seven in the morning here. We'll be leaving port this afternoon."

"So, you're still in South America? Your parents mentioned Brazil last time I saw them."

"Aye. And I suppose they're telling people I'm still trying to find myself—out on an extended gap year. How long will it take for them to realize that I'm not lost? This is me," Young Hugh said with a huff of frustration.

"Your folks are good people. They just miss you, I think," Daniel said, consolingly.

"Sure, and they wish I'd follow in their footsteps—do something proper and boring with my life. Like you."

"Hey, I'm not boring," Daniel objected.

"True, but not for lack of trying. How did you spend last Friday night?"

"I don't want to say," Daniel equivocated. He'd spent last Friday night with Ellie comparing a recent Agatha Christie television adaptation to the original book. They'd had fun, but he knew Young Hugh would turn his nose up at the idea.

"Exactly! And I bet it didn't involve music, or dancing, or even leaving the flat. That's why you need to come join me here. Last Friday night, some boys from the boat and I truly lit up São Paulo. I've got to tell you, mate, no place knows how to blow off steam like they do in São Paulo," Young Hugh said wistfully. In the distance, a bell rang. "Oh, that's me. Best of luck today. Give my love to Ellie."

"Thanks, will do. You try to stay out of trouble," Daniel said.

"And you try to get into some," Young Hugh said. "Ta."

"Bye."

Daniel ended the call, shook his head, and laughed. He turned around and gazed at Urquhart Castle and the vast, blue expanse of Loch Ness. The castle was more crowded than the last time he had visited. That was in the winter. It was now the height of the summer tourism season. Daniel waited near the entrance of the visitor center. He watched tour buses drop off and pick up passengers. He walked to the side of the building to get a better view of the castle. It was ancient, several hundred years old. In that time, Urquhart Castle had seen countless battles—all of which had left their scars on its stone walls. Over the centuries, many of those walls had crumbled to mere outlines, measuring only a few feet high. The main gate and drawbridge still stood, or had been rebuilt, when the castle transitioned from its role as military defense to civilian tourism. The tower would keep no one safe from enemy arrows or cannon fire now. Its southeast side had long ago collapsed, exposing its inner rooms. Daniel couldn't see the spot well from where he stood, but it was there on the second floor that he and Ellie had once sheltered from a surprise winter storm and shared their first kiss. And it was there that Daniel now intended to ask her to marry him.

Chapter Five

Daniel felt a tap on his shoulder and turned sharply. Ellie stood behind him, smiling. Her cinnamon hair was tied back in its usual ponytail. She wore jeans and a light green blouse. "Ellie, when did you get here?"

"I could ask you the same thing. I've been here for at least a minute or two. I wondered if you would notice, but you were off somewhere else."

"Sorry, I was looking at the castle. Reminiscing," Daniel said.

Ellie smiled again. "Well, we're both here now. Let's go in." She gave him a quick kiss and put her arm through his. They walked into the visitor's center, paid the entrance fee, and exited on the other side to a winding path that led to the castle. Its ancient stones rose from the green lawn at the water's edge, a broken skeleton of the once great structure. The sky was clear with a few white clouds that reflected off the deep blue surface of the loch. An occasional tour boat passed by, leaving wide ripples in its wake, disrupting the mirrored sky. Daniel and Ellie reached the end of the walking path and stepped onto the drawbridge. The moat below held no water, just a semicircular indentation in the earth.

"Doesn't look like it'll rain today," Ellie said. They crossed the wooden planks and felt the temperature drop several degrees in the shade of the great arched entry. "I said, it looks like nice weather. You picked a lucky day for a wee trip out of the city. Daniel?" Ellie stopped walking, but held his arm tightly.

"Sorry, what?" Daniel asked.

"What's with you today?"

"I'm just—" *Nervous* was what he wanted to say, or *anxious.* He settled on "distracted." It was warm and rather humid out, but he perspired more than the weather called for. He was glad Ellie held his arm and not his hand. He knew his palms were sweaty. But he felt cool. Any other day, he would think he was coming down with a cold. His free hand felt the outside of his bag, over the place where the ring was hidden. "Um, we had a minor emergency after the church service this morning. You know Eliza MacGillivray?" Daniel said to change the topic. He told her of Eliza's fall and how the paramedics had taken her to the hospital.

"Oh, poor Eliza. Is she at Raigmore? I'll ask Cameron if he's heard anything," Ellie said.

"That's okay. Reverend Calder is with her now, and I'll stop by tomorrow," Daniel said. He didn't need Ellie calling up old college sweethearts—especially not one as handsome and successful as Cameron. To change the subject again, he asked her how her mother was doing. It had been a while since he'd gone with her for visiting hours at the prison. He then asked how her work at the Kinmylies Veterinary Clinic was going.

"I actually have some news about that," Ellie said. "Now that I've graduated, they're going to hire me on as a full-time vet at the end of the summer, once Doctor Patel retires."

"What? That's great news! I'm so proud of you!" Daniel said. He hugged her, lifting her off the ground.

"Put me down!" she laughed. "We should go out tonight and celebrate. My treat!"

"We might have one more thing to celebrate," Daniel said. Ellie gave him a questioning look. "Wait, not here." He led her across the grounds of the castle, past waist-high remains of ancient stone walls, to the tower. There was a small queue, or line, at the tower's entrance.

"What else would we celebrate? Did you get a promotion too?" Ellie asked while they waited.

Daniel shook his head. "I don't think Reverend Calder is going anywhere for a long time. Actually, I wouldn't mind a demotion. Filling in as choir director had added a lot to my plate. Plus, I'm terrible at it."

"Mr. Fisher left big shoes to fill. But this time, try hiring someone who isn't a murderer."

"Believe me, I'm trying, but not many folks want a part-time job that takes up one's weekend and has other unusual hours."

The afternoon sun beat down, causing both Daniel and Ellie to sweat. They let out a mutual sigh of relief once they were able to move under the shelter of the tower's entryway. Though, with so many people lining the stairwell, the air remained thick. "Perhaps we should skip the tower today. It's hot and you promised me a drink at the pub in Invermoriston," Ellie said.

"We're nearly there," Daniel said. He took two steps up the narrow, winding stairs.

"You seem rather insistent about this."

He shrugged and took another step before stopping to wait again. Why were there so many people here today? He had a plan and, with as much trouble as he'd gone through getting himself and the ring here safely, he was going to stick to it. He only hoped that the queue would speed up before Ellie's good spirits and his own nerves gave out.

They finally reached the second floor of the tower and stepped out into the spacious open room. Part of the wall and ceiling had fallen away long ago. Daniel and Ellie walked to the edge of the room and breathed in the fresh air. From here, they had a grand view of the castle grounds and the loch.

"Well, we're here. What was so important that we had to suffer through that stuffy stairwell?" Ellie asked.

Daniel reached into his bag and felt for the small velvet-covered box. He kneeled on one knee and held it up to her like an offering. Ellie gasped and put both hands over her mouth. Daniel opened the box to reveal the ring. He was glad for the lack of a ceiling because the sun's light glinted off the ring's stone, distracted from its small size. "It's not much, but I hope it was worth the wait," Daniel said. Ellie remained in place, speechless. "When I first moved to Inverness two years ago, I never imagined that I would meet my best friend here, much less fall in love with her. I can't imagine living here without you. Ellie Gray, will you make me the happiest American in

Scotland and be my wife?"

By now, several people had taken notice. Ahhs and Ohhs sounded from the small crowd that had formed around them. Ellie reached for the ring, but said nothing. Her silence made Daniel even more nervous. These were the longest few seconds he had ever experienced.

"Come on, lass, say 'Aye,'" someone shouted from the crowd.

"Aye," Ellie laughed. "Of course, I'll marry you!" she said. She held Daniel's hand and pulled him up off his knee.

"Oh, thank God!" Daniel laughed. They embraced. The crowd clapped, and a few cheered. "Kiss her!" someone shouted. Daniel complied. More cheers.

"Can we get out of here and get some drinks now?" she asked, blushing.

"Yes, please," Daniel said. He waved to the crowd and led Ellie out of the tower.

They arrived at the pub a little early for dinner service, so they got their pick of a table. Like most of the buildings in the small town of Invermoriston, which was located near the northern shore of Loch Ness, the pub had white walls and a dark gray roof. It was small and had a cozy atmosphere inside. In winter, a fire in the stone hearth that was built into one wall would keep the place warm. It stood cool and empty now. Daniel ordered drinks while they waited for the kitchen to open. When he returned to their table, Ellie was admiring her ring. "You shouldn't have," she said.

"I know it's small, but it's the best I could do."

"No, you really shouldn't have. Diamonds are sweet and traditional and all, but they take a terrible toll on the environment and the workers that mine them," Ellie said. Daniel laughed. Ellie raised her eyebrows in confusion.

"Well, I wasn't going to say anything, but it's actually a recycled stone—upcycled? It was reset in this ring from someone who had sold it back to the store." Daniel said. He shrugged sheepishly. "I wish I could say I chose it for purely ethical reasons, but honestly, it was less expensive. I love Church Street and all, but the pay isn't much. The Macphersons were gracious enough to let me skip a couple months' rent while Young Hugh was staying with me last Christmas."

"It's perfect," Ellie said. She leaned across the narrow table and kissed him. "Once I'm a full doctor at the clinic, I'll be your sugar momma!" They both laughed.

"In that case, the next round is on you!" Daniel said.

Chapter Six

Daniel sat in a crowded room on the third floor of an office building. The podcast's two co-hosts sat across a small round table from him. "Can you say something into your mic?" the woman asked. Daniel said hello and his name into his microphone. A man surrounded by computer screens gave the host a thumbs-up. "Camera?" Another thumbs up. "Right, I think we're all set. We'll upload the video for this episode later this afternoon. Are you ready?" she asked. Daniel nodded.

"Hello, Scotland, I'm Chester Grant," the male host said.

"And I'm Lexi Campbell. Welcome to The Highlands Bulletin, your source for breaking and in-depth coverage of all the news worth knowing in the North," the female host said. A quick and intense theme music played from the computer console.

"Our first story for the day involves the new offshore wind farm in the Moray Firth. This is a project at the top of the minds of many of us here in Inverness, as it's located just off our northeastern shore," Chester said.

"Some call it an eyesore. Some call it a vital tool in our fight against climate change," Lexi said.

"And some call it an inappropriate and overreaching waste of government funds," Chester said. "To help sort out the controversy surrounding this renewable energy scheme, we have with us in the studio today, special guest Reverend Daniel Darrow of Church Street Kirk.

"Reverend Darrow, welcome," Lexi said.

"Thanks for inviting me. I want to start out by thanking you for bringing attention to this important project. A lot of folks have worked very hard at the grassroots level to make the wind farm a reality. I know it's still in construction, but whenever I look out and see those first columns rising from the sea, I'm filled with pride to know that Church Street Kirk had a small part to play in bringing jobs and renewable energy to Inverness. God calls us to care for the earth and—"

"Sorry, let me cut in for a moment," Chester interrupted. "You said your kirk had a small part to play in the project, but in fact, you, Reverend Darrow, were one of its loudest supporters. Would it be safe to say that the involvement of your parish might never have occurred without you?"

"I wouldn't say that. Yes, I have strongly advocated for it, but I like to think the kirk would have done the right thing even without my prodding. We care about this land, and we want it to be a healthy and prosperous place where future generations will continue to thrive. Homegrown, renewable energy is a part of that, especially after–" Daniel stopped himself. He was getting off script, or at least away from the talking points he had wanted to mention. "Well, I like to think that the church is on the right side of history on this one."

"You paused for a moment there. You said, 'especially after,' Especially after what?" Chester asked.

"Nothing, I was just saying we are proud of the progress being made on the wind farm."

"Were you going to say, 'Especially after Broonburn House?" Lexi asked.

Daniel shifted his weight in his chair. He'd hoped Broonburn House wouldn't come up. Nearly two years had passed since then.

"Would you say that your support of the wind farm is an attempt to atone for that rather grim incident, or perhaps draw the public's attention away from it entirely?" Chester asked.

"No, um, no, I wouldn't say that at all," Daniel stammered. How had this interview taken such a turn so quickly?

"For those of you unfamiliar with Broonburn House, though I can't imagine many are unless you're listening from outside the Highlands, Broonburn House was an Inverness landmark for centuries. Ancient as the town itself. About two years ago, it was undergoing a conversion from a private castle to a public tourism hub," Lexi explained.

"That project also promised many jobs to the region," Chester added.

"Aye, but right in the middle of renovations, Broonburn House burned to the ground. Nothing left but a few charred, broken stone walls and the body of a university student, Tom Shaw."

"And if memory serves, the fire was set by one of your own, Reverend?" Chester said.

Daniel didn't know what to say. Why would they dredge this all back up? He had agreed to do this interview in order to talk about clean energy and caring for the Earth. This was supposed to be a nice, fluffy interview, a bit of good press for the kirk after the recent incident with its former choir director, Mr. Fisher. Daniel hoped they wouldn't want to get into that as well.

"Reverend Darrow?" Lexi asked.

"The fire was caused by a member of my church, yes, but not the death of Tom Shaw. If your memory really does serve you, I hope you would recall that as well," Daniel said, defensively. His response was more biting than he had intended, but they had caught him off guard. "The real criminal there was Alec Harrow, former CEO of Philaguria Energy. Tom had uncovered his scheme to buy up the land around Inverness for fracking. I've actually spoken to Tom's parents, and they've endorsed the wind farm. They say Tom would've approved."

"Hmm," Chester said, "Interesting you should say that, considering the news out this morning. Wind energy may be considered clean, but it has proved just as deadly."

"What are you talking about?" Daniel asked. He and Ellie had stayed out late celebrating last night, and he'd overslept. He hadn't turned on his TV or even browsed any news updates on his phone in his rush to get to the interview on time.

"You haven't heard?" Lexi asked. Daniel shook his head. "A body washed up on the shore near the site yesterday. Police haven't released a name yet, but they've speculated that he might have been part of the construction crew."

"I'm—" Daniel stammered. He didn't know what to say. The news struck him like a brick wall. "I'm so sorry. That's terrible."

"Will you retract your support of the wind farm, given its now dodgy safety practices? Or are you and your kirk too invested in it to turn back, despite the loss of an innocent life?" Chester asked.

"I, um…We care about all life, and my heart and prayers go out to the family of the deceased. Are they sure he was—do the police know what happened? I mean, you said this was a construction accident?"

"I'm sorry, I'm going to have to cut you off there. We've got to put in a word from our sponsors. Keep listening and we'll be right back with more from Reverend Darrow about the Moray Firth Wind Farm and the tragic death of one of its construction workers," Chester said.

The sound operator held up his hand for a second and then nodded. "Okay, we've got two minutes. Would you like a water or tea?" Lexi asked.

Daniel leaned back in his chair. He didn't know what to think. This interview had gone from friendly to hostile to sensational so quickly that he felt like he had whiplash. "What was that?" he asked. "Are you actually accusing me of having something to do with a man's death? You said police thought he *might* have been a construction worker. Do you even know if he had any connection to the wind farm at all?"

"Well, it's still breaking news," Chester admitted.

"I read the guy jumped off the Kessock Bridge. Should we mention that?" Lexi asked.

"Hmm, it's a little dark for our audience. I like the construction accident angle better. People want someone to blame," Chester said.

"Suicide? Angle? Are you just making this up as you go?" Daniel asked incredulously.

"We're reporting on breaking news. We're telling a compelling story that our audience wants to hear," Chester said. "You did a nice job of sounding surprised, by the way."

"I am surprised," Daniel said.

"Either way, it should be great for ratings. I'll admit I thought a reverend talking about wind energy was going to be a bit boring, but this has really turned around!" Chester said enthusiastically.

Daniel shuddered. "Someone died, and you're excited about ratings? I don't think—"

The sound engineer held up his hand to silence them. "We're back on in three, two," *one*, he mouthed.

Chapter Seven

Daniel stood outside the building and replayed the podcast interview in his head. *Once again,* he thought, *I should've listened to Sarah and gone with regular old radio or TV. Or at least listened to a few more of their podcasts to get a better idea of what kind of show it was.* He hadn't been at all prepared for Chester's gotcha-style of questioning. Daniel should've assumed the host might broach the topics of Broonburn House or even Mr. Fisher, but how could he have prepared for another dead body? Who could have predicted that?

His mind flashed to Eliza MacGillivray. She had a penchant for morbidly accurate prophecies. And didn't she say she had a message for him just before the paramedics wheeled her away? Perhaps he should have visited her before rather than after the interview. *No, Daniel thought, I'm done with all that. I finally feel accepted by the members of the kirk. I'm getting married. I finally know what I want in life, and it's time to settle down and put enigmatic prophecies behind me. Didn't the other host, Lexi, say it was a suicide, anyway?*

Daniel leaned against the warm stone wall and closed his eyes. He tried to focus his thoughts on the sun's heat. *Enjoy the little things,* he told himself. *Who knows how long this relaxing sunshine will last?* But like a dark cloud, the thought of the unknown body crept back into his mind. If the death did have anything to do with the wind farm, Daniel could think of only one person in all of Inverness who would know—besides the dead man himself.

Mr. Tweed, or George Fraser, besides being the most sharply dressed member of Church Street Kirk, had an ear for the latest town gossip—often knowing things days before they made the local news cycle. Daniel also knew that Mr. Tweed had invested a large sum of his own money in the energy project. He was even on the board of GlenBreeze Dynamics, the company in charge of the project. If anyone had the inside scoop, it would be George Fraser. Daniel made a mental note to catch up with him the next chance he got.

Just then, Ellie pulled up in her car and rolled down the passenger window. "Oi, good lookin'. Fancy a good time?" she said with a coy eyebrow raise.

Daniel leaned through the window. "I don't usually get involved with married women, but…"

"Oh, this ol' thing?" Ellie said, holding her left hand up so that the small diamond shimmered in the sunlight. "I'm only engaged. We haven't even set a date yet."

"Well, in that case," Daniel said, opening the door and sliding into the seat beside her. He leaned over and gave her a quick kiss. He then held up her hand. "Looks good on you."

"I know," Ellie said as she rotated her hand in the sun. "It's a driving hazard. I should be wearing sunglasses so I don't get blinded by the reflection."

"Now I feel like you're mocking me," Daniel said. They both laughed.

Ellie put the car into gear and pulled back into traffic. "Raigmore?"

Daniel nodded. "Are you sure you want to come on this visit with me?"

"Of course! Eliza's practically family. I've known her my whole life. She and my mum go way back. Other than you and Reverend Calder, she's one of the few people from Church Street that still visit Mum since she's been in prison," Ellie said.

"Speaking of your mom, have you told her about us yet? The engagement?" Daniel asked.

"Have you told your parents?"

"Fair enough."

Ellie glanced at him and grinned. "It's only been a day. I'll tell her when I visit later this week. Let's just enjoy it ourselves for a bit. The rest of the world can find out soon enough."

"Well…" Daniel said sheepishly.

"What? Who did you tell?"

"Reverend Calder. I needed a pep talk. I was nervous," Daniel said.

"Once one of them knows, it'll spread through the kirk like a viral post. That place is like social media, with every privacy setting turned completely off." Ellie rolled her eyes, but the smile on her face said she didn't really mind.

As they drove towards Raigmore Hospital, they chatted about their upcoming wedding and tried to settle on a date. Ellie wanted to wait until her mother's next parole hearing, or at least until she could file for a supervised outing. With no living grandparents and her father deceased, she wanted at least one member of her family standing beside her on the big day.

Ellie's fingers tapped nervously on the steering wheel as the conversation moved towards Daniel's parents and whether they would be willing to fly to Scotland for the wedding.

"Don't worry about them," Daniel tried to console her. "They wouldn't miss their only son getting married. And besides, my dad has talked about visiting Scotland for ages to research his family history. He'll be able to check two things off his bucket list at once."

"We could just elope. It would make things a lot easier," Ellie said.

"Are you nervous about meeting my folks?"

"I'm afraid they won't think I'm good enough for you. That they'll look down on me because of my mum being in prison and all," she said, her voice wavering slightly.

"No mother thinks another woman is good enough for her son."

"That's not as reassuring as you think it sounds," Ellie said.

"You know what I mean. I love you, and they'll just have to love you too," Daniel said. He gave her hand an affectionate squeeze. "And as a back-up plan, we'll invite William McCrivag so he can get 'em good and liquored up before the wedding!"

Ellie laughed and squeezed his hand before letting go to wipe the corners of her eyes. "That man would sneak a bottle into an open bar!"

A few minutes later, they pulled into the parking lot of Raigmore Hospital. "Here we are," Ellie said as she found a parking spot.

"You might want to hide your ring if you don't want Eliza finding out just yet," Daniel said.

"She's the one person we don't have to tell. She already prophesied it."

"Not you too. That prophecy was about fishing in the Beauly River," Daniel said.

Ellie laughed. "Not the way she interpreted it!"

Chapter Eight

As Daniel and Ellie stepped into the bustling hospital, the sterile scent of disinfectant stung their nostrils. They made their way to the information desk, where a harried-looking nurse pointed them in the direction of Eliza MacGillivray's room.

"Remember that time we snuck into the morgue here?" Ellie asked with a mischievous grin once they had gotten out of earshot of the nurse.

Daniel chuckled, recalling the daring episode in their attempt to clear Ellie's mother's name in the Broonburn House murder. "How could I forget? I thought for sure we were going to get caught and I'd get kicked out of the country, or worse."

"I wonder if my old mate Cameron's working today," Ellie said. Cameron was Ellie's old boyfriend from university and now worked at the hospital. He had been only too eager to help them sneak around that day.

"Did you hear about the body that washed ashore yesterday near the Kessock Bridge?" Daniel asked to change the subject. "The hosts interviewing me earlier were weirdly obsessed with it."

Ellie shook her head. "No. Who? What happened?"

"I don't know. One of them thought the guy jumped from the bridge. The other said he was a victim of a construction accident at the wind farm. I guess police are still investigating."

"Why do you bring it up? Did you want to have another wee snoop in the morgue while we're here?" Ellie teased.

"Oh, no. Once was enough for me!" Daniel said. "Hey, I'm all turned around. Do you know where the room is?"

"Should be right up here," Ellie said. They turned a corner and counted down the numbers on the rooms. "Ah, here we are."

"I hope she's awake," Daniel said and knocked on the door. "Ms. MacGillivray? Eliza?" he called, opening the door slowly. He was surprised by the sight that greeted them. Eliza, once an indomitable figure, now appeared frail and vulnerable in her hospital gown and hooked up to an IV and monitor. Despite her frail appearance, her eyes sparkled when she saw them, and she sat up with an air of confidence.

"Ah, there you are!" Eliza exclaimed, as if she were expecting them. "Come in, come in!"

"Eliza," Ellie said softly as she approached the bed, taking Eliza's hand in hers. "How are you feeling?"

"Never better, dear," Eliza replied with a wide grin, though her pale complexion said otherwise. Eliza noticed the ring on Ellie's finger. "Now what's this? Did you bring me some happy news for once?"

"We're engaged!" Daniel chimed in, beaming at Ellie. "It just happened yesterday. You're actually the first person we've told."

"Ah, happy news indeed." Eliza's eyes twinkled with delight, and she let out a hearty laugh. "Of course, I already knew it. Didn't I say so six months ago, Ellie, my luv?"

Ellie laughed and nodded. "Aye, that you did. Once again, your vision was spot on."

"Congratulations to you both," Eliza said warmly, her gaze shifting between Daniel and Ellie. "I cannae wait to see what the future holds for you two." Then, with a wry smile, she added, "Though perhaps I already know!"

Daniel shot a glance at Ellie and shook his head. He turned to Eliza. "Now that our news is out of the way, I want to hear about you. Are you really doing okay? What do the doctors say?"

"Ach, these doctors," Eliza scoffed. "They run their tests and pump me full of fluids and lord knows what else. Makes me feel sleepy or like I'm floating on a cloud. I keep telling them what ails me isn't physical, though it may manifest as such."

"What do you mean?" Daniel asked. He pulled two chairs beside the bed for Ellie and himself. "Does this have anything to do with what you said before the paramedics took you away? You said you received a *message*. Did you have another vision?"

"Another one?" Ellie asked with both concern and curiosity in her voice.

Eliza's eyes darkened, and her expression turned grave. She hesitated for a moment, then nodded. "Twas more than a mere vision. I've never experienced the like." Eliza's voice trembled as she recounted her experience. "It hit me like a tempest. Though...," she hesitated, "I should have recognized the early signs. I think it started sometime during your rendition of a hymn, if you can call it that. It was like a drop in pressure just before a storm."

Daniel cringed and glanced away from her at the floor. He knew he was a poor substitute choir director, but he didn't think his performance was seizure-inducing.

"So, I left for the kirk hall," Eliza continued. "I thought perhaps some air and a wee biscuit would calm my nerves. I sat down and shared a bite with my rabbit. Oh, you will check in on him, won't you?"

"Sure, where is he?" Daniel asked.

"I was talking to Ellie. I'm sure you mean well, Reverend, but I've seen your rapport with the kirk cat and, well, Ellie is the expert in these matters. Sarah, em, Reverend Calder promised to feed him, though I would feel better if you checked in on him while I'm stuck here."

Ellie smiled compassionately. "Of course. I can even keep him with me at the house if you'd like?"

"That'd be lovely. And don't feed him too many biscuits, even if he begs. He's on a diet," Eliza said. Ellie nodded.

"So, I reached for my Seeing Stone," Eliza continued her story. "I felt it pulling at me and, suddenly, I found myself floating above the ocean. I saw a man dressed in clerical robes standing on the Kessock Bridge." She squinted and looked hard at Daniel's face. "I ken he was you, Reverend Darrow."

"Me?" Daniel asked.

"Aye, you were waving your arms, trying to tell me something, but I couldn't hear you. Then I fell. The rush or air stung my eyes. Yet just before I hit the water, a voice held me still."

"Daniel's? What did he say?" Ellie asked, leaning closer to Eliza.

"No, this was a deep, rasping voice ripped through time. It was Coinneach Odhar himself that spoke to me," Eliza answered, her eyes wide with fear.

"Who?" Daniel asked.

"The Brahan Seer?" Ellie asked.

Eliza nodded. "You know that ever since I found his Seeing Stone when I was a young lass, I've borne the burden of second sight. At times, I've even felt his spirit channeled through me like a vessel. But I've never actually heard his voice. He's never spoken to me directly."

"What did he say?" Ellie asked.

"He warned of betrayal and death," Eliza said. She closed her eyes and furrowed her brow, trying to recall the Seer's exact words. *"My lord seems to have little thought of you, or of his children, or of his Highland home,"* she repeated.

Daniel exchanged a worried glance with Ellie, feeling a chill run down his spine at Eliza's ominous words. "What does that mean?" he asked.

Eliza opened her eyes and shook her head. "The vision was interrupted. I awakened before I received the full message."

Eliza touched the place on her neck where her necklace usually lay, but it was empty. Her disposition changed from serious to despondent. "My purse," she said, motioning to the tray table beside her bed. Ellie retrieved the bag, large enough to hold a rabbit, and placed it on Eliza's lap. Eliza rummaged around inside before pulling out her hand to reveal her necklace. The smooth, donut-shaped stone, which had hung around her neck since she was a girl, now lay broken in two pieces.

"Oh, Eliza, I'm so sorry. I know how much that necklace meant to you," Ellie said.

"This is what the doctors don't understand," Eliza said. "When the stone broke, so did I."

Chapter Nine

As they left Eliza's room, Daniel couldn't help but feel a heavy weight upon his shoulders. He knew his off-key choir directing couldn't have caused her sudden illness—that was impossible, right? Still, he cared for her and couldn't shake a feeling of responsibility. He did feature in her last vision, after all.

Daniel glanced at Ellie as they walked back to the car. Her face was a picture of concern and uncertainty. He could feel his own expression mirroring hers. The last thing he wanted was to get them involved in another one of Eliza's mysterious prophecies. He wanted to focus on their future, planning their wedding, and trying to navigate the minefield of meeting each other's parents—surely that would be harrowing enough.

"Poor Eliza," Ellie finally said to break the awkward silence.

"Yeah, I've never seen her looking so frail before," Daniel agreed.

"And her Seeing Stone broken. Do you think that might really have something to do with her being sick?"

"I think she thinks it does," Daniel said.

"So, it's all in her head, is it?"

"I didn't say that. I just think there could be a more scientific explanation. Maybe she had a minor stroke or drop in blood sugar that would cause her to faint. We should've thought to ask a nurse before we left."

"After all this time, all the visions she's had that you've seen come to pass, and you're still skeptical of her gift? Aren't you the one who spent years studying things you can't see with your eyes?" Ellie asked.

"Hmm," Daniel thought. She had him there. Who was he, a supposed spiritual advisor, to question someone's connection to a world beyond the physical?

"And what if I did believe her? What am I supposed to make of her latest vision? Me, standing on a bridge waving as she falls from the sky into the ocean? It sounds like I'm a helpless bystander in this one," Daniel said.

"When have you ever just stood back and watched? You sneak into morgues and aboard smugglers' ships. You confront murderous thieves and CEOs. You chase teenagers through the park on Bonfire Night."

Daniel rolled his eyes. "I'm never going to live that one down, am I?"

Ellie smiled and shook her head. "My point is, you've never been a helpless bystander. That's not the man I fell in love with, and that's not the man I intend to marry."

"I couldn't have done any of that without you," Daniel said.

"Hey, I know the difference between an arsonist and a friendly Bonfire celebration," Ellie joked.

"Okay, I couldn't have done most of those things without you."

"So, it's settled. We're in this together. Whatever Eliza's vision means, we'll figure it out together. She's always been dear to me. I want to help her just as much as you," Ellie said.

Daniel nodded and took her hand. *She really is something special*, he thought as they walked the rest of the way to her car. Once inside, he pulled out the little pocket notebook that he always kept with him for keeping track of appointments and sermon ideas and other notes. He'd written Eliza's previous prophecies in its early pages. Now he wrote her last one.

"All right," Daniel said. "If we're solving this together, our first step needs to be figuring out if there's a connection between the Kessock Bridge and the original Brahan Seer. Eliza said she saw me standing on that bridge, and then she heard the Seer's voice. That's got to mean something."

"Right. Also, what she said sounded familiar. Remember, her vision of us getting engaged was lifted from one of the Brahan Seer's actual prophecies. This one might be too," Ellie said.

"Good point. I'll look into it," Daniel said, writing furiously in his notebook.

"Oh, this is fun. Too bad Young Hugh's off in South America somewhere and isn't here to join us. It'd be just like old times. Hey, I just had a thought," Ellie said excitedly. "You mentioned a body washed ashore near the Kessock Bridge yesterday—the day after Eliza's vision. That can't just be a coincidence, can it?"

"Maybe. She did say her vision was one of betrayal and death. A dead body certainly ticks off the *death* part," Daniel admitted. He didn't like where this was going. Chester, the podcaster from earlier that morning, had already all but implicated him in the man's death. And now Eliza MacGillivray had had a vision of him at the scene of the crime.

"What's the second?" Ellie asked.

"Huh?"

"You said the first step was looking into the bridge. A first step implies a second."

"Oh, right. I guess the second thing would be repairing Eliza's necklace, or at least replacing it," Daniel said. "Whether that broken stone is actually responsible for her illness or if she's just latched onto it as a psychological scapegoat, I'm worried that she won't get better without it."

"I can ask around at some jewelers, but I don't know of any of them that would want to bother with trying to put an old river rock back together."

Daniel closed his notebook with a satisfied clip. Their visit with Eliza had rattled him, but now that they had a plan, he felt better.

"You forgot the third step," Ellie said.

"I did?" Daniel asked, reopening his notebook.

"Eliza's rabbit! She asked us to take care of him. That little furry critter's just as important to her as the Seeing Stone."

"If I recall, she asked *you* to check in on the rabbit," Daniel said.

"I thought we were in this together. For better, for worse, for sickness, for bunny health, and all that," Ellie said.

"I don't think that's how it goes exactly," Daniel laughed.

Chapter Ten

Daniel stood in the nave of Church Street Kirk, staring at the empty choir pews, and listening to the steady pattering of rain against the roof and stained-glass windows. His recent hospital visit with Eliza MacGillivray consumed his thoughts. She had appeared so frail and morose with her broken Seeing Stone. And her vision—a warning of betrayal and death? He much preferred the Eliza from six months ago, who had happily foretold his engagement to Ellie.

Eliza had alluded that her hospitalization was partly due to his shortcomings as a musician and choir director, and, although he knew that couldn't possibly be true, it still gnawed at him. Daniel had never claimed a beautiful singing voice or an understanding of musical composition. He had only accepted the position on an interim basis because the kirk was in a bind to replace the former director, Mr. Fisher. But that was six months ago, and the longer it went on, the more Daniel worried the interim title would become permanent.

The Church Street Kirk choir had always been an unruly bunch, and it had become even more so under his direction—too many divas, not enough stage. How Mr. Fisher had wrangled them all into a mostly harmonious unity, Daniel couldn't begin to fathom. The extra responsibilities of being both a reverend and choir director had stretched him thin. Now, he couldn't help but wonder if he would have noticed any early signs of Eliza's condition had he not been so preoccupied. And now he had a wedding to plan and a potential murder to investigate.

"Enough is enough," Daniel muttered to himself, resolved to bring up the matter with Rev. Calder. He found her in her office, surrounded by stacks of old reference books and paperwork.

Daniel let himself in. "I think it's high time we found ourselves a new choir director," Daniel blurted out, barely waiting for her to look up from her desk.

Rev. Calder raised an eyebrow, her reading glasses perched precariously on the tip of her nose. "Do you now? And what brought about this sudden epiphany?"

"Eliza MacGillivray. I went to check in on her yesterday, and she wasn't very subtle about her feeling that it was one of my hymns last Sunday that put her in the hospital."

Rev. Calder let out a burst of laughter. "I'm sorry, you're serious?" she asked when she looked up at his somber expression.

Daniel nodded. "I know that's a bit of an exaggeration. But I also know she can't be the only one thinking similar thoughts. Whenever I mention the music to anyone outside of the choir, people clam up pretty quickly. Also, I can't help but feel like my other ministerial duties have suffered since I've taken on this additional role."

Rev. Calder sighed and nodded. "I appreciate you stepping up after Fisher was arrested. I think folk were willing to give you the benefit of the doubt because, well, at least you hadn't killed anyone."

Not yet, Daniel thought, recalling Eliza MacGillivray's portentous vision.

"But perhaps you're right," Rev. Calder continued. "This was only meant to be a temporary arrangement. Very well, let's put out an ad and see if we get any bites."

* * *

The following week, Daniel and Sarah Calder sat down for the first round of interviews. The kirk couldn't afford more than a part-time position, so their applicant pool hadn't been huge. *Still*, Daniel thought, *anyone would be better than what've we've had: a convicted murderer and, well, me. Not a very high bar.*

"All right, let's see our first candidate, shall we?" Rev. Calder said, flipping through her notes. "Here we are. Mr. Malcolm McDougal."

A tall, broad-shouldered man entered the room, wearing a kilt and a tight-fitting button-down shirt. A mane of light auburn hair fell haphazardly over his shoulders as if tousled by a sudden sea breeze. His calves were like two stones chiseled from whatever rugged craig this giant of a man had wandered in from.

"Ah! Good day to ye both," Malcolm said with a flourish and slight bow. Rev. Calder exhaled an audible sigh and sat up straighter in her chair when he approached them. He stared at them in silence for an awkward minute.

"Right. Mr. McDougal, can you tell us about your experience in leading a choir?" Daniel finally asked, taking the lead from his boss.

"Yes, em, sorry," Rev. Calder jumped in, blinking as if she'd just awoken from a trance. "Your experience, yes?"

Were her cheeks actually flushed? Daniel suppressed a chuckle. Now he knew what she'd had to put up for the past two years of him mooning over Ellie.

"Of course!" Malcolm exclaimed. "I've led choirs from Edinburgh to Skye, and everywhere in between. Why, there's nary a music hall in Scotland I haven't directed or visited."

"Nary a gym," Daniel scoffed.

"What's that?" Malcolm asked.

"Oh, I said *hymn*," Daniel said hastily. "Can you sign a hymn for us? As a demonstration, I mean."

Malcolm proceeded to belt out a pitchy, though enthusiastic, rendition of *Thine Be the Glory*. As he sang, he pretended to direct an invisible choir. His arms moved up and down like they were more familiar with lifting dumbbells than a baton. Daniel leaned back in his chair, hoping to avoid a pop in the eye should one of the buttons on Malcolm's shirt go flying from the stress of his flexing muscles. Once he had finished, Malcolm gave another slight bow toward Rev. Calder.

"Thank you, Mr. McDougal. We'll be in touch," Rev. Calder said. After he had left, she turned to Daniel and added. "I quite liked him."

"I'm sure you did," Daniel laughed. "Who's next?"

The interviews continued throughout the afternoon, each candidate stranger than the last. There was Mrs. Agnes Campbell, a plump woman with glasses the size of saucers, who claimed she could communicate with angels through song. Then there was young Colin Abernathy, who thought that bagpipes were the only instrument required for a choir. Daniel had never seen such a dirty look as the one Colin threw their way when Rev. Calder asked him to take a crack at the kirk's piano.

"I'm beginning to worry I'll be interim choir director forever," Daniel sighed, rubbing his temples wearily.

"There's always Malcolm McDougal," Rev. Calder said with a mischievous grin.

"The songs may not sound much better, but at least the people would have something pretty to look at," Daniel said. "Do we have any more candidates today?"

"Just one more," she replied, glancing at her watch. "And I suppose this would be him now."

A man with black curly hair and a short beard walked into the room. He wore a suit that was slightly too large. Daniel couldn't believe his eyes. This was one of the two men that had helped him catch the thief who had stolen his bag on the bus. Daniel exchanged a surprised glance with Rev. Calder.

"Do you two know each other?" she asked.

"We met a few days ago, but I never got your name," Daniel said.

"Amir Nazar," the man said, flashing a warm smile. "Hello again. Mr. Darrow, yes? I remembered the name of your church from our last encounter, and when I saw your advertisement for a choir director, I knew it was like a prophecy."

"Prophecy?" Daniel asked, slightly alarmed. He didn't know if he could take another mysterious vision.

"No, that's not the word." Amir thought for a moment. "Fate—it was like fate," he said.

"Please, have a seat," Rev. Calder gestured towards the chair opposite them. "Tell us about yourself, Mr. Nazar."

Chapter Eleven

Amir Nazar settled into the chair opposite Daniel and Rev. Calder. "As you may remember, I am from Afghanistan. My family and I were forced to flee after the Taliban retook control of the country. We had to sneak across the border and leave behind everything we knew. We've moved around from one refugee camp to another until we just recently got our status approved by the UK government and relocated to Inverness."

Daniel couldn't help but be stirred and humbled by Amir's story. He also felt a pang of guilt for complaining about his own comparatively minor immigration problems.

"Ah, welcome to Scotland," Rev. Calder said. "Have you ever directed a choir before?"

"Indeed, I have," Amir replied. "Back home in Afghanistan, I sang in and directed the church choir. We were much smaller than this," he said, glancing around the room. "But music has always been my love, and I would be honored to share it with your congregation."

"Could you sing a hymn for us—give us an idea of your directing style?" Daniel asked, genuinely curious to hear Amir's voice.

"Of course." Amir nodded, standing up and taking a deep breath. He began to sing a hymn in his native language, Pashto. The hauntingly beautiful melody filled the room, and Daniel found himself mesmerized by the rich, resonant quality of Amir's voice. Once Amir finished the hymn in Pashto, he sang it again in English. Both renditions were equally moving.

"Thank you, Mr. Nazar," Rev. Calder said, clearly impressed. "Do you have time to answer a few more questions?" They discussed the position's pay and sometimes irregular schedule as well as the particular needs of the choir. Amir provided honest and thoughtful responses. By the time they were done talking, Daniel was ready to offer him the job on the spot.

"Thank you for seeing me," Amir replied graciously as he left the room.

Daniel and Rev. Calder sat in silence for a moment before Daniel finally broke the spell. "Well, I think we can both agree that there's really only one choice here."

"Indeed," Rev. Calder said. "Malcolm McDougal."

"Wait, seriously?"

"No," she replied with exaggerated disappointment. Then, she said with certainty, "It seems like the Lord has brought Amir Nazar to our kirk. I'll start on the paperwork if you want to call him with the good news."

"I'll call him right away," Daniel said excitedly.

"Oh, but before we make it official, might we call Mr. McDougal back in for a second interview—just for fun?"

Daniel laughed and rolled his eyes. "You're on your own there," he said as he left to call Amir.

Daniel stepped out of the church. He felt relieved to have finally found someone to take over his musical duties. Herding cats would be easier than directing that disorganized crew. About the only thing Daniel could ever get them all to agree on was their choir robes, and that was only because they'd had no other choice. They hadn't the budget for new ones. Poor Amir didn't know what he'd just signed up for.

As Daniel turned the corner, he nearly collided with Mr. Tweed, impeccably dressed as always, in a fashionable tweed suit and matching hat.

"Mr. Tw-um, Fraser," Daniel exclaimed. "Just the man I wanted to see!"

"Oh, aye?" George Fraser, aka Mr. Tweed, asked, surprised.

"Yes, I've been meaning to ask you how construction is going on the new wind farm in the Moray Firth. Any new updates?"

"I'm sorry, Reverend. I have an appointment down the road," Mr. Tweed said, glancing at his watch.

"So, you don't know anything about the body that washed ashore a couple of days ago?" Daniel asked. He knew that the only thing George Fraser valued more than punctuality was gossip. "I heard—"

Mr. Tweed stopped short and leaned on his cane so that he was at eye level with Daniel. "What did you hear?"

"I heard the guy might've worked on the construction crew," Daniel said.

"And?"

"And I thought you might know more since you're involved with the company."

"That's common knowledge," Mr. Tweed scoffed, clearly disappointed that Daniel had nothing juicier to share. "I really must be going," he said with a sly smile as he tapped on his watch.

"Wait, you know something. I can tell," Daniel said.

"I really can't say."

Daniel could see Mr. Tweed was taking great pleasure in having some secret knowledge. But Daniel also noticed that despite what Mr. Tweed said about being in a hurry, the man hadn't moved an inch since they'd started talking. Mr. Tweed wanted to spill, but he also wanted Daniel to earn it. *Fine, I can play games too*, Daniel thought.

"I understand if you don't know more. The wind company wouldn't likely share that kind of information with a mere investor. It's probably just for the top brass. I was talking with the hosts of The Highlands Bulletin the other day. They questioned whether it might've been a suicide and not related to the wind farm at all. I should go see if they've found anything more," Daniel said. He pulled out his cell phone and scrolled through his contacts list, pretending to look for their names. "I'm sorry to keep you from your meeting," Daniel said and turned to walk away.

But before he could take two steps, Mr. Tweed slid his cane in front of Daniel's foot. "I'm more than just an investor, you know. I'm on the board. Your wee podcaster mates don't know a fraction of what goes on in this city."

He swallowed the bait; now time to reel him in. "So, you don't think it was a suicide?" Daniel asked, putting his phone away.

Mr. Tweed hesitated and then spoke, "I don't know how the man died, but he *did* work on the construction crew for the wind turbines, poor chap."

"Really?" Daniel furrowed his brow, intrigued. *That was almost too easy*, he thought.

"Indeed!" Mr. Tweed continued, lowering his voice conspiratorially. "They're being very cagey about it, but I think he might have been in the country illegally. Immigration Enforcement has been crawling all over the site since the body was found. Tragic business, really. I'm worried it's going to hold up construction even more. This entire project has been one expensive delay after another."

"A tragic loss of life," Daniel chided gently, but the older gentleman merely waved a dismissive hand.

"Of course, of course. That goes without saying," Mr. Tweed said. "Well, I really must be off. Got an early tee time in the morning, you know."

"I thought you said you had an important meeting?"

"Aye, that's what we're meeting about," Mr. Tweed said. "Oh, and you didn't hear any of that immigration stuff from me."

Daniel moved his finger across his lips as if he were closing a zipper.

* * *

Before Amir's first meeting with the choir, Daniel gave him a proper tour of Church Street Kirk. They admired the stained-glass windows and high arches, exchanging stories about their respective experiences with choirs and churches. Daniel tried to drop hints of what to expect from the Church Street choir without scaring Amir away before his first day.

As they walked through the kirk hall, the sound of a radio someone had left on caught their attention. A news reporter's voice filled the room: "…the unknown body that washed up on the shore by the Kessock Bridge has been identified as Sayyid Ghulam. Police are still investigating whether it was a suicide or not, but we have been able to confirm that he was in the country illegally, working on construction of the new offshore wind energy project near Inverness. We've reached out to GlenBreeze Dynamics for comment. They claim that construction on the turbines was contracted out, and they are cooperating with local police and Immigration Enforcement's investigation. For more…"

So, Mr. Tweed was right, Daniel thought.

Amir's face turned pale, and he gripped the back of a nearby chair for support. "I… I know him," he stammered, looking at Daniel with wide, shocked eyes.

"Who?" Daniel asked.

"Sayyid. You met him that day at the bus stop. He stopped that boy who stole your bag," Amir said, swallowing hard.

"The same man who…?" Daniel asked.

Amir nodded. "Sayyid and his family are from Afghanistan, like me. He translated for UN peacekeepers before the Taliban took over. The last time we talked, he told me about the refugee aid worker he was in contact with. We are a close community, and I thought I could help them. He was so close to getting his legal status to live and work here in Scotland. I know Sayyid, he…he wouldn't have committed suicide."

Daniel placed a reassuring hand on Amir's shoulder. "We'll do everything we can to help his family and find out what happened. I promise you that."

Chapter Twelve

Coinneach Odhar kneeled at the edge of his mother's grave. A chilly wind whipped through his unkempt hair, and he pulled a tartan shawl around his shoulders. It had been his mother's, and he wanted to keep some part of her close to him. The sky above was a steel gray, as if even the heavens mourned with him. Tears streamed down his cheeks, blurring the already limited vision from his one seeing eye.

"Och, Mum," Coinneach whispered into the brisk air, "I'll miss ye. Ye were too good for this world, ye were."

He stood and shoveled on the last mound of dirt, then tamped it down with the flat blade of his shovel. The sound echoed through the church cemetery like a sorrowful drumbeat.

"Rest well," he said, wiping his wet cheeks with the back of his hand.

As he turned to leave, something caught his eye. He stumbled over to a warped and weathered grave marker, carved from a scrap of wood long ago. The once sharp letters were now worn down, but he could still make out the inscription, or most of it: "Fryja, daughter of K—"

"I remember the day she asked me to make this for ye. It must've been at least twenty years past—the same day I found the Seeing Stone," he mused, running his fingers along the cracks in the wood. "I wonder who ye were, Ms. Fryja."

In another twenty years, he imagined, the name might be completely erased, leaving the mysterious Fryja forgotten and lost to time once more. Coinneach slung his shovel over his shoulder and walked up the hill leading away from the cemetery, eager to warm himself by a fire. He'd spent too much of his young life living so close to the spirits of the dead. He was ready to leave that place and live amongst the living for a change.

The next morning, Coinneach stood at the edge of his family's croft, a rucksack on his back and the Seeing Stone clutched tightly in his hand. The cool breeze carried the scent of damp heather and peat smoke as he looked out over the wide, rolling hills.

"Goodbye, Mum," Coinneach whispered, straightening his shoulders. "It's time I made my own path in this world."

His visions had grown more intense the last few years, making his spirit restless. Now, with his mother gone, he had no more reason to stay put. So, with a resolute nod, he turned his back on their small cottage and set off to wander the countryside.

After several days of walking, he came across a farmer. "Och, there's a man with an eye for trouble if ever I saw one," grumbled the farmer as Coinneach approached. "What do ye want, lad?"

Ye've no idea, Coinneach thought as he ran a hand over his tangled hair. He had to admit that between his worn shoes, dusty coat, and unwashed face, he wasn't looking his best.

"I've come tae offer my services as a seer. I've the gift of second sight," Coinneach replied, trying his best to sound confident. "For a few coins or a hot meal, I can tell yer fortune."

"Is that so?" The farmer eyed him suspiciously. "All right then, let's hear it."

Coinneach held his Seeing Stone up to his blind eye and peered through the hole in the center. He hesitated before speaking. "I see three ravens, black as night, perched on a dying alder tree, struck thrice by lightning. Beware the day you see this tree, for tis an omen yer crops will fail that year," he said finally. When he pulled the stone away and looked at the farmer with his seeing eye, he wincing at the man's obvious displeasure.

"Fail?" the farmer sputtered, turning red in the face. "Do ye think I'd pay money for such a grim prediction? Tis more like a curse. Away with ye!"

"I can only tell what I see," Coinneach protested, but the farmer had already stormed off, muttering and cursing under his breath.

Undeterred, Coinneach continued on until he came to a village. Tired and hungry, he hoped he'd have better luck there. At the very least, he might find a barn to sleep in and beg or steal a few scraps of food. He approached a woman hanging laundry on a line outside her stacked stone cottage. "Excuse me, ma'am," he called out with a slight bow. "Might I interest ye in a glimpse of the future?"

"And what'll it cost me?" she asked warily, eyeing him up and down.

"Just a few pence or a hot meal, ma'am," he replied. "I promise, my visions are true." Coinneach held out his hand, having learned the hard way to get paid upfront.

"Fine," the woman agreed, handing over a couple of coins. "Whit do ye see for me?"

Coinneach peered into his Seeing Stone once more, swallowing hard as the vision unfolded before him. "In one month's time, when a strong gale topples the kirk's steeple, yer husband will return from the sea," he said. Coinneach smiled, watching her face light up with joy.

"And my boy?" the woman asked. "He took our son with him. They'll return together, no?"

Coinneach frowned and shook his head. "Your husband was alone."

"No!" The woman's smile vanished. "Ye must be mistaken!"

"I wish I were, ma'am," Coinneach said softly. "But the future isn't always what folk might wish."

"Then take yer cursed stone and be off! Yer no welcome here," she snapped as tears filled her eyes. Coinneach turned around and prepared himself for another cold night with an empty belly.

As he wandered from village to village, he tried his best to stay optimistic, but the weight of his unwanted gift began to wear on him. Folk whispered behind his back, calling him names like "doom-sayer" and "witch." He longed to share happier tidings, and he did so on occasion, but he had to be true to his visions. And the truth was that life was often harsh and capricious. People envied his gift until he foresaw a future they didn't want.

"I dinnae ken I can go on like this," he whispered to himself one night while he lay on his tattered blanket beneath a cloudless sky. "What's ahead for me?" he asked as he held the Seeing Stone to his unseeing eye. As usual, he saw nothing but darkness. It revealed the futures of everyone but himself.

The next morning, Coinneach decided to travel south in hopes of a change in fortune. Soon he found himself in Ross-shire, standing before the high stone walls of Brahan Castle, just north of the small shipping village of Inverness.

Chapter Thirteen

Sunlight streamed through the stained-glass windows, casting vibrant colors onto the wooden pews and their finely dressed occupants. Amir Nazar, the newly hired choir director at Church Street Kirk, raised his hands to direct for the first time. The choir began singing a traditional hymn, their voices harmonizing beautifully under Amir's guidance. Though they'd only had a couple of rehearsals with their new director, Daniel could already hear an improvement in how they sounded with someone other than himself at the podium.

The song ended, and pleased murmurs spread like static through the building. Rev. Calder nodded at Daniel, reassured in their recent hire. Then he noticed a strange energy coming from the choir, like they had a secret that they couldn't bear to hold in for even one more minute. One of the choir members caught his eye and gave him a mischievous wink. *Oh no, what are they up to now?* he worried.

Daniel recalled one of the initiation pranks they'd pulled when he'd reluctantly stepped into the choir director role. It was his first Sunday directing, and someone had replaced all the sheet music with copies of "Old MacDonald" just before the service. He kicked himself now, wishing he'd thought to warn Amir of the choir's mischievous nature.

As if reading his mind, the tempo of the music suddenly changed. It was upbeat and almost danceable as the choir began singing a new song. *Oh, here we go,* Daniel thought. But Amir appeared to be in on this stunt. He tapped his foot to the beat and guided them with his hands like he knew exactly what they were doing. Daniel glanced around the pews in surprise, shocked to see several people's toes tapping along with them. Even the reserved and very proper feet of Hugh and Margory Macpherson twitched up and down to the beat. Daniel overheard Hugh whisper to Marjory, "Well, I never thought I'd see the day where we'd be tappin' our feet in the kirk!"

But not everyone shared their enthusiasm. Daniel noticed that a few members of the kirk clearly were unhappy with the change of pace, sitting with their arms crossed and toes firmly planted on the ground. Mrs. Abernathy, a long-time member and stickler for tradition, muttered under her breath, "Lord, lord, lord, this is not what I signed up for."

Despite the mixed reactions from the congregation, Daniel couldn't deny the infectious spirit that Amir had brought to the choir. If Amir could channel their capricious energy for good, Daniel knew he could handle the naysayers amongst the crowd. Change, while sometimes difficult to accept, was a part of life and could be a beautiful thing.

As the service concluded, a hum of chatter filled the kirk like bees buzzing around a hive. Daniel stood at the back, pretending to rearrange hymnals, while he eavesdropped on various conversations.

"Amir's got a lovely voice, dinnae ye kin?" enthused one partitioner, her cheeks flushed from all the foot-tapping.

"Och, aye. A breath of fresh air, that's what this kirk's needed!" another agreed.

Then there was the grumbling. Mr. McKenzie rubbed his bald head. "Even if ol' Fisher was a murderer, at least he knew how to sing a proper hymn. None of this new millennial pop drivel."

"Ye're just stuck in the past, McKenzie," chided Mrs. Campbell, adjusting her hat. "A wee touch of youth and vigor never hurt anyone."

"Youth or no, I'm simply glad Reverend Darrow's back just to sermons now," whispered Mrs. Anderson to Mrs. Campbell, casting a sideways glance at Daniel.

And on that note, Daniel decided it was time to escape the cacophony of opinions. He spotted Amir outside in the kirk garden, looking thoughtful as he gazed at a cluster of vibrant thistles. Daniel approached him slowly, not wanting to startle the pensive choir director.

"Hey there, Amir," Daniel said, announcing his presence. "How are you feeling after your first Sunday service?"

Amir looked up and gave a small smile. "It went better than I expected, but I could sense some resistance from certain members of the congregation."

"Don't worry about them," Daniel reassured him. "Listen, when I first started here, I made my fair share of mistakes too, and people eventually accepted me."

"Introducing people to new styles of music and worship is not a mistake," Amir replied, his eyes filled with determination. "It's not the music I'm concerned about. Unlike you, I don't exactly blend in. People only notice you're a foreigner when you open your mouth. I am lucky if they do not turn away before they even have a chance to hear my accent. I'm used to people prejudging me, but most of them hold their comments at least until I'm out of the room."

Daniel's face softened, understanding the weight of Amir's words. "I heard plenty of positive comments today, too," Daniel said, trying to reassure him. "Trust me, they outnumbered the negatives. Give the others some time; they may take a while to warm up to change, but I'm sure they'll come around."

As if on cue, the kirk's resident cat, Sir Walter Scott, sauntered by, his orange tail high in the air like a flag announcing the presence of royalty. The cat bypassed Daniel without a glance, which was no surprise. Sir Walter held a long-standing grudge against Daniel for taking him to his yearly veterinary checkups. But to Daniel's astonishment, the usually cavalier feline leaped gracefully onto Amir's lap and began to purr.

"Looks like you've already won over our most discerning critic," Daniel said with a chuckle.

Amir laughed and scratched the cat behind its ears. Sir Walter purred even louder and turned in two small circles before settling in on Amir's lap like it was his new cat bed. Daniel shook his head, marveling at the unlikely friendship.

A high-pitched, metallic creak turned their attention. It was Ellie at the garden gate. They had planned to meet for lunch, but Daniel hadn't expected her to arrive so soon. Her eyes widened with surprise as she spotted Amir.

"Amir! Is that you?" Ellie exclaimed.

"Ms. Ellie Gray, how nice to see you," Amir grinned, rising to greet her. Sir Walter leaped from his lap with a scowl.

"Wait, you two know each other?" Daniel asked.

"Of course!" Amir answered warmly. "Ellie has been incredibly kind to the refugee community, treating our pets for free. She's an angel, this one."

"It's nothing," Ellie said, rolling her eyes. Her cheeks reddened slightly. "And how is the Hashi's cat?"

"He's much better now, thank you," Amir said.

"I told you about my pro bono work at the clinic, didn't I, Daniel?" Ellie asked.

"Yes, you did," Daniel said, recalling her mentioning something about volunteer work a while back. He felt a twinge of guilt for not asking more about it then.

"How do you two know one another?" Ellie asked.

"Amir's our new choir director," Daniel said proudly. Then he had another thought: If Ellie knew Amir, maybe she also knew the family of Sayyid Ghulam—the man whose body washed ashore near the Kessock Bridge.

Chapter Fourteen

A faint scent of antiseptic and overcooked vegetables lingered in the air as Daniel Darrow pushed open the door to Eliza MacGillivray's hospital room. Ellie Gray was right behind him. As they approached Eliza's bed, Daniel spotted a small, wilting bouquet perched on the windowsill—a meager attempt to brighten the sterile environment.

"Eliza, how are you feeling today?" Ellie asked, her warm voice providing a stark contrast to the cold, beeping machines surrounding the old woman.

"I'm no worse for wear," Eliza replied. Her voice betrayed a slight tremble. "I dinnae ken why these daft doctors won't let me go home." She forced a smile, but Daniel couldn't help noticing that despite her confident words, she looked frailer than ever. Her once rosy cheeks were now sallow, and her piercing blue eyes seemed clouded with worry.

"Perhaps they want to keep you around for the cheery company," Daniel said.

"Then they picked the wrong woman to imprison, didn't they?" Eliza scoffed.

"Are you eating enough?" Ellie asked. "You look too thin."

"'Tis these horrid fluorescent lights, that's all," Eliza said.

"I brought you a wee treat that might help," Ellie said with a sly smile. She retrieved a tin of buttery shortbread biscuits.

Eliza's eyes lit up as she reached for it. "Open it for me, will you, dear?" Eliza asked. Ellie smiled and cracked the lid. "Ta," Eliza thanked her. She took out a piece and then hid the tin under her covers. "Those nurses don't like me to have anything that tastes good!"

As she bit into the soft, sweet treat, Daniel thought he saw some color return to her cheeks.

"These remind me of the ones your mother used to make," Eliza said.

"Mum gave me the idea to bring them. She told me to tell you she's thinking about you and praying for a swift recovery," Ellie said.

"I wish you hadn't told her I was in here. She has worries of her own without adding me to the list. Besides, I'm fit as a fiddle," Eliza protested. "Now, enough fussing over my health. Have you two discovered anything more about my last vision?"

Daniel hesitated, exchanging a glance with Ellie, before nodding slowly. "I think so. A body washed ashore near the Kessock Bridge the day after you fell ill. Sayyid Ghulam. He was a construction worker on the new wind farm they're building in the Moray Firth. Police are saying he must have fallen or jumped from one of the unfinished turbines," Daniel said.

Eliza frowned, taking in this new information. "Jumped, you say? No, that doesn't fit. In my vision, I got the distinct feeling that the fall was *not* voluntary. This man may have fallen or been pushed, but he didn't jump."

Eliza's expression darkened as she reached for the two broken halves of the Seeing Stone on the tray table beside her bed. "My vision was cut short."

Ellie glanced at Daniel with concern etched across her face. She knew all too well how seriously Eliza took her visions, and the idea of an unfinished prophecy clearly troubled her. "You're worried something more might be waiting?"

"Aye," Eliza rasped, "prophesies are a tricky business. When they're interrupted, it's like leaving a book with the last chapters torn out. You never know how the story's meant to end."

"We'll do everything we can to figure this out. I promise," Daniel said firmly. He watched her clutching the pieces of the Seeing Stone in her slim hand. Daniel had a sinking suspicion that, whether logical or not, Eliza's health and her mysterious vision were now inextricably linked.

"Eliza, the Brahan Seer spoke to you during your vision?" Ellie asked.

"Aye," Eliza replied, casting her gaze downwards as if in deep thought. "It was a strange voice, like nothing I've heard before, and yet familiar. '*My lord seems to have little thought of you, or of his children, or of his Highland home,'* he said."

"Those are words from one of his prophecies?" Daniel asked.

Eliza nodded gravely. "Aye, his last. And tis what followed after that worries me. That prophecy led to the Seer's death."

Daniel leaned forward, intrigued. "His death? What was the prophecy about?"

"After wandering the Highlands sharing his gift of second sight, Coinneach Odhar eventually traveled to the Brahan Estate. There he began work as a laborer, for as our Lord himself says, 'A prophet is not without honor except in his own country and amongst his own kin.' Later, Coinneach gained notoriety as a Seer and eventually the protection of the Earl of Seaforth. The Earl treated him well, and all was well in the land."

"Until?" Daniel prompted.

"Until the day the Earl went away to France on business," Eliza continued, her voice grave with foreboding. "His wife, the Lady Seaforth, well known to be the ugliest woman in all of Scotland, became fearful for her husband's long absence. She sought the counsel of the Brahan Seer. Coinneach warned her that she would receive no comfort from his vision, but she insisted."

"My lord seems to have little thought of you, or of his children, or of his Highland home," Daniel mumbled to himself. "Oh, he cheated on her!"

Eliza nodded. "And so, in her anger and despair, Lady Seaforth betrayed her Seer. Coinneach Odhar was killed for daring to speak the truth to she who held power over him, his onetime protector," Eliza said with a trembling voice.

Ellie and Daniel exchanged somber glances. "That's terrible. But you can't possibly think you're bound for a similar fate, can you, Eliza?" Ellie asked.

Eliza shrugged. "Who can say? A seer can rarely see their own fate."

"Is this about Sayyid's death then?" Daniel asked.

Eliza's eyes narrowed. "When a prophet is silenced, tis not just their voice that's extinguished, but the truth they held within. And truth, spoken to those that dinnae want to hear it, can be a dangerous thing."

Daniel felt a chill run down his spine, both intrigued and troubled by

Eliza's implication. Ellie must have been thinking the same thing. "Are you saying Sayyid knew or said something that got him killed?" she asked.

"All I'm certain of is that it wasn't suicide that took him from this world. You must ask yourself, 'Who would not want to hear what he had to say?'" Eliza said.

"Or who would benefit from keeping him silent?" Daniel added.

Eliza nodded and then took Ellie's hand. "The truth is often hidden," Eliza said as she placed the two broken pieces of the Seeing Stone in Ellie's palm. "Take this. If you can find a way to mend it, perhaps you may see through the veil."

As Daniel and Ellie stood to leave, a gust of wind rattled the hospital window, sending shivers through the room. Outside, the Scottish landscape was ablaze with the green warmth of summer—a warmth Daniel was eager to return to after Eliza's chilling tale. "Get some rest, Ms. MacGillivray. We'll get to the bottom of this."

Chapter Fifteen

Daniel Darrow stood outside the entrance of Church Street Kirk. He held the door as Amir carried out the last of the donations. Daniel moved a large bag to the side so that Amir's box would fit in the boot, or trunk, of Rev. Calder's car.

"It's just you and me today?" Amir asked.

Daniel shut the boot. "Yes. Reverend Calder wanted to come too, but she got tied up. She did loan us her car, though. Sure beats carrying all this on the bus!"

"I thought your fiancé might be joining us. She's familiar with the community."

"Fiancé—that still sounds strange to say out loud," Daniel mused. "But no, Ellie's got surgeries all afternoon."

Amir nodded and got into the passenger side. Daniel got behind the driver's seat and started the car. With a nervous glance over his shoulder and a quick check of his surroundings, he hesitantly pulled onto Church Street. Before he made it even half a block, another vehicle was on his tail, honking its horn. Daniel's pulse quickened and his knuckles grew white as he gripped the steering wheel and checked his mirrors and turn signals.

"I think they want you to go faster," Amir said, nodding toward the speedometer.

"Oh, sorry. I haven't driven very much since I moved here, and Reverend Calder would kill me if I scratched her car," Daniel said. He had lived in Inverness for just over two years, but he hadn't had much practice driving there. To be fair, he hadn't been given many opportunities. All the people he knew that had cars preferred to drive themselves with him sitting in the passenger seat. Though now that he was causing a minor traffic jam, Daniel wondered if the lack of opportunity was purposeful. He cautiously pressed on the gas pedal, bringing them up to the speed limit.

"The refugee community will appreciate these donations. Food and clothing are always helpful, but even more, it helps people to feel welcome in a new home," Amir said, graciously changing the subject from Daniel's bad driving.

"I'm glad. And speaking of feeling welcome, I think these donations are a sign that some of the more reluctant members of the kirk are warming to you, too," Daniel said. "They've been collecting donations to repair the roof since before my time, but these items were gathered in less than a week!"

"That's wonderful news," Amir said. But his voice did not match his words in enthusiasm.

"Is everything all right, Amir?" Daniel asked.

Amir hesitated, his gaze focused on nothing in particular outside his window. "Yes…well, it's just—Sayyid's family will be there when we drop off the donations. After his body was identified, I went to see them and promised Samira, his wife, that I'd find out what happened, but…" Amir sighed. "I haven't found out anything helpful, and I've been too ashamed to face her."

Daniel frowned, feeling his new friend's pain. He thought of Eliza MacGillivray growing ever frailer each day in the hospital. He, too, had made promises that he had yet to make good on.

"What do you know about Sayyid's death? If you don't mind me asking?" Daniel said.

Amir rubbed his forehead. "Not much, I'm afraid. All I know is that it wasn't suicide, and it wasn't an accident."

"How do you know that?"

"I…I can't explain. It's a feeling I have. Something bad happened to Sayyid. I just don't know what," Amir said.

They drove on in silence for several minutes. Daniel thought again of his last conversation with Eliza. She, too, had been certain that Sayyid's death was no accident.

"You don't believe me," Amir said despondently.

"No, that's not it. I think I do believe you," Daniel said. "It's just that…" Daniel hesitated, not wanting to say the words out loud.

"If it wasn't an accident, then Sayyid was murdered," Amir said, completing Daniel's thought.

Daniel nodded. "Did he have any enemies? Anyone who would want to hurt him?"

"Many people here have been good to us and made us feel welcome. But not everyone. We have gotten dirty looks while walking on the street or riding on the buses. Some people feel that immigrants, refugees especially, are a burden on the city. We take jobs that belong to Scots, they say. But we just want to provide a better life for our families, like everyone else. Most of the crew building those wind turbines are immigrants. The work is hard and dangerous, and the company can pay my people less because many are scared of being deported. What happened to Sayyid—I fear that could just as easily have been my body that washed ashore. If I hadn't gotten this job at Church Street, I would be on that construction crew."

Daniel didn't know what to say. He'd felt out of place at times and experienced a fair share of cultural missteps, but nothing like what Amir was describing.

"Sayyid was also Muslim, and that didn't help—being Muslim and dark-skinned," Amir continued. "With the all the fighting and terrorists you see on the news every day, it's easy for us all to be seen as the same—as alien and enemy."

"So, you think someone killed him because of his religion or race?" Daniel asked.

Amir shook his head. "I don't know. It's possible. People have been killing one another for religion for centuries and longer."

"That's true, though I pray it's not the case here," Daniel said. He thought of Eliza's vision and how she said she'd seen him standing on the Kessock Bridge wearing priest's robes, shouting something while she fell from the sky. He'd assumed that meant that he was supposed to have some role in solving Sayyid's murder, but perhaps it meant something else. Her vision had been interrupted. Perhaps the robes were symbolic of a larger conflict to come?

Daniel clenched the steering wheel tighter. The police seemed all but certain that Sayyid's death was an accident or suicide. But if it was something more sinister, like Amir and Eliza believed, then, for their sakes and for the whole Inverness community, he had to get to the bottom of it before this one death boiled over into more.

"Have you or anyone else received threats?" Daniel asked.

"There are always little things," Amir replied, evident frustration in his voice. "The refugee community has gotten a lot of attention in the press since Sayyid's death—most of it negative. Samira is worried that now her family may be deported."

"We'll figure this out, Amir. I promise," Daniel said.

Amir looked at Daniel and nodded. He then gazed back out his window. "I only hope we can before anyone else gets hurt."

Me too, thought Daniel. *Me too.*

Chapter Sixteen

Daniel broke down cardboard boxes for recycling after they had finished distributing the kirk's donations. He loaded the trash back into the car while Amir talked with a family he knew. When he opened the boot for the larger, flattened boxes, he noticed one donation bag remained. He took it out and glanced at Amir, who was still busy in conversation. Daniel placed the bag in the passenger seat and finished loading the car.

He knew who the bag was meant for. One family hadn't shown up that afternoon—the one family Amir had dreaded seeing. But if they were going to uncover what happened to Sayyid, they would have to face his family eventually. And Daniel knew that in this case, sooner was preferable to later.

"What a success!" Amir said as he approached the car. His eyes sparkled with satisfaction. "After everything that's happened, they needed to know that people still care. I think those gifts helped the soul as much as the body."

"I'm glad. And I hope it won't be a one-time thing, either. Next time we'll get more of the kirk involved. I can see real friendships developing if we can get people visiting together face-to-face," Daniel said.

Amir smiled and opened the passenger door. His expression turned somber when he saw what was occupying his seat.

"We've got one last stop before we head back to the kirk," Daniel said. Amir didn't say anything. "You know we have to."

Finally, Amir took a deep breath and picked up the bag. "They live over here," he said solemnly, and led Daniel to a small flat on the second floor of the building.

As they approached the door, Daniel felt a knot forming in his stomach. He knew that this would be a difficult visit. Comforting grieving families was never easy, but this one would be made all the more difficult because the wound was still so fresh. And until the cause of Sayyid's death was known, the emotional wound would be much slower, if not impossible, to heal. Daniel could see the trepidation in Amir's eyes as well.

"I promised Samira I would find out what happened to her husband. I hoped I would have good news or any news for her the next time I saw her again," Amir said.

"I know. She needs more than this bag of food and socks, but maybe it'll help a little until we can find out more. Maybe she can help with that?" Daniel suggested.

Amir nodded and handed the bag to Daniel before knocking on the door. "Samira? It's Amir. Are you home?"

No answer.

"I've a friend with me. We brought some food and clothes for you and the children," Amir said.

The door creaked open, and Samira emerged. She wore a light-colored hijab, or headscarf, and her eyes were red from crying. Her two young children clung to her legs, sensing their mother's sadness. Despite her obvious grief, she managed a weak smile.

"Thank you," she muttered, "Please, come in." The two young boys hid behind their mother when Amir and Daniel stepped inside. Daniel estimated their ages at no more than four or five years old.

"Hi, I'm Daniel Darrow. I work with Amir at Church Street Kirk. We were passing out some donations this afternoon," Daniel said, holding up the bag awkwardly.

"Boys, don't be rude. Say hello to our guests," Samira said.

The two children peeked out from behind her. Daniel smiled and kneeled, offering them the bag. Their eyes lit up at the promise of a present. The taller one stepped forward and accepted the bag. Its weight was too much for him, though, and he nearly dropped it.

"Oops," Daniel chuckled, helping him place it safely on the floor. The boys eagerly dug inside, pulling out cans of food and bundles of socks. The littlest one stuck out his bottom lip and gave Daniel a betrayed look when he realized the bag contained nothing more—no toys or anything sweet to eat. Daniel quickly realized his mistake and searched in his jacket pockets for candies or anything else to offer them.

"I'm sorry. I should've brought chocolates. But some of those socks are pretty cool, right? Look at the fun tartan patterns," he said feebly.

The older boy picked up a pair of socks and shrugged, then handed it to his brother. The younger brother examined it incredulously. "I like Pokémon," he said.

"I'll remember that next time," Daniel said.

"I see they're still a handful," Amir laughed and ruffled the hair on the littlest one's head.

"Oh yes," Samira said with a slight chuckle. "Please, sit down."

Daniel and Amir sat on the couch while she pulled up a chair. A small framed photograph of the family stood on the end table beside the couch. The youngest boy sat atop his smiling father's shoulders. Samir noticed Daniel looking at the photo. "Sayyid was a great father," she said.

"Y'all look very happy together. I'm so sorry to hear of his passing," Daniel said.

"How are you and the boys doing?" Amir asked.

"We are coping. This food will help. Thank you," Samira said and then waved the two boys off to go play in their room. When they were gone, she turned to Amir. "Have you...Have you found out what happened to my Sayyid?"

Amir shook his head and looked away from her.

"You believe, like Amir, that your husband's death wasn't an accident?" Daniel asked.

"I know he did not jump like the police are saying," Samira said gravely.

"Did he ever mention any problems at work?" Daniel asked.

"Sayyid should have never been on that crew. He was a scholar. Before we fled Afghanistan, he worked at the university and then was a translator for the United Nations peacekeepers. What did he know about construction or wind turbines?" Samira said. Tears formed at the corners of her eyes, and she covered her face with her hands.

"I'm sorry. I shouldn't have asked," Daniel said. "I was just—"

"It's too soon," Amir said. He stood to leave, not wanting to cause her any more distress.

"Wait," Samira said with a sniffle. She wiped her eyes. "The foreman, Mr. Christie. Sayyid often complained about that man. He never told me exactly what they argued about, but he said that no one on the crew dared cross the man because Mr. Christie always threatened to call the police or immigration."

"I thought Sayyid was close to getting his legal status?" Daniel asked.

"He was, but it can be a tricky process," Samira said.

Daniel exchanged a glance with Amir. Finally, they had a lead. "Thank you for sharing that with us. I wonder if the police have questioned him?" he mused.

"Please, don't tell the police. I shouldn't have said anything. Sayyid kept quiet to protect us and the other men on his crew. He may now be free of Mr. Christie's threats, but we are not," Samira said, with fear in her voice.

"No, you were right to speak," Amir said, "and it will stay between us. But I will speak with this Mr. Christie. Tell the boys goodbye for us."

"Thank you for being a friend to Sayyid, even in death. Please be careful. I fear that whatever happened to him could happen to any one of us," Samira said.

As they left the flat, Daniel's mind reeled with the weight of this new information. "We need to talk to the other men on the construction crew and find out what Sayyid and the foreman were arguing about," he said to Amir on their walk back to the car.

"Yes," Amir agreed, "but we need to speak with the foreman too, and discreetly. We do not want to raise suspicions or draw extra attention to the families."

Daniel nodded and thought for a moment. "I might have an idea of how we can do that."

Chapter Seventeen

Daniel stood nervously at the arrivals gate. His eyes darting back and forth through the steady stream of passengers. They were coming—all the way from North Carolina to meet Ellie, his new fiancée. Daniel tugged at his collar, a bead of perspiration forming on his brow. Inverness did not usually feel this balmy. Could he truly be more nervous about his parents meeting her than when he'd actually proposed? If only they'd given him a bit more notice! The call he had received as they were boarding the plane was hardly enough time to prepare. He knew they would expect him to be their full-time tour guide, but with everything going on at the kirk and wind farm, he was pressed just to find time to pick them up at the airport.

"Daniel!"

His heart skipped a beat as he spotted his parents emerging from the crowd. His father, a bear of a man in his sixties with salt-and-pepper hair, wore a lopsided grin beneath his mustache. Daniel's mother, on the other hand, was petite and had a bob of curly hair that she refused to let succumb to the graying of age. It was the same shade of chestnut brown as it had been for the past twenty years. Both recently retired, they had an air of newfound freedom about them. Their matching Hawaiian shirts and oversized sunglasses were a testament to that.

"Mom, Dad!" Daniel greeted them warmly. He embraced them each and then simply had to ask, "What are y'all wearing?"

"We're on vacation, my boy!" Daniel's father answered, as if that was sufficient reason.

Daniel chuckled and focused on helping his mother wrestle with her luggage to hide his embarrassment. "I'm surprised he got you to wear one too," Daniel whispered to her.

"Don't worry, these awful shirts will get lost in transit before they get a second wear," his mother replied with a conspiratorial wink.

"What are you two whispering about?" Mr. Darrow asked.

"Nothing. I was just saying how I didn't expect you so soon. You're lucky I've got a spare room in my flat. Young Hugh, my sometimes-flatmate, is off gallivanting in South America, or so I last heard."

"Thanks, son," his father chuckled, "but we've already booked a hotel. No need to put us up when we can have a *wee* adventure of our own."

"All right, then," Daniel conceded, trying his best to mask his relief. "Let's get you settled in. You must be tired after the long flight." He loved his parents, but they could be a lot. He imagined his father in his small flat or being invited to high tea by his landlords, the extremely fastidious and proper Macphersons—talk about a bull in a china shop!

"I still can't believe you just decided to hop on a plane over here," Daniel said as they made their way through the airport. He couldn't help but feel a mix of excitement and anxiety. How would his parents react to Ellie? And what would they think of the life he'd built for himself in Scotland?

"You didn't think we'd pass up the chance to meet our future daughter-in-law, did you?" his mother asked. "Besides, your father's always wanted to visit Scotland. His ancestors are from here, you know."

"I know. I suppose I should be grateful he didn't show up in a kilt," Daniel said.

His father frowned. "I would have, but your mother thought airport security might get a little too frisky with me. She said that if anyone was going to get frisky with me in a kilt—"

"Oh, please stop talking!" Daniel interrupted him and winced. "The Hawaiian shirts look great, and I'm sorry I said anything."

His mother's face turned three shades redder, and she slapped her husband on the arm.

"It's what she said," his father said with a shrug. "Anyway, now that I'm retired, it seemed like the perfect time to check off a Scottish vacation from the ol' bucket list."

"Speaking of which," Daniel said, steering the conversation towards a less cringy topic, "Reverend Calder, my very generous boss, has invited us all to a traditional Scottish meal tomorrow night."

"That sounds great!" his father exclaimed, his stomach grumbling at the mere mention of food. "I can't wait to tear into a hearty meal after that awful airline food."

"Ah, but it gets better. You picked a good time to visit," Daniel said. He reached into his jacket pocket and pulled out three small pieces of paper. "Three tickets to this year's Highland Games! Reverend Calder gave me the day off tomorrow to take you. But I've got to warn you, after that I do have a lot of work to tend to."

Mr. Darrow snatched the tickets from Daniel's hand like a kid in a candy store. "I can't believe our luck! Do you think they'd let me compete? I'd love to try my hand at the caber toss."

"We know you're busy, busy. You've got a wedding to plan," Daniel's mother said, ignoring his father.

"Among other things," Daniel said. Church services, wedding planning, potential murder investigation—why not add parental tour guide to the list?

"I notice you said three tickets. Will Ellie not be joining us?" Mrs. Darrow inquired, her eyes full of anticipation.

"No, she has work, too. But she'll be there for dinner after. She's looking forward to meeting you both." Daniel tried to hide the worry that gnawed at him. If he felt overwhelmed by his parents' unexpected appearance, he could only imagine what Ellie must be feeling.

As their hotel taxi drove them through the winding streets of Inverness, he admired the picturesque place that had become his home. The River Ness flowed serenely through the heart of the city, flanked by rows of historic buildings that seemed plucked from a postcard. Daniel remembered the day two years ago when he had arrived in the city and experienced its charm for the first time. Reverend Calder had met him at the airport bus terminal and driven past the kirk and down these same streets. He watched his parents now, their faces glued to the car windows, and he felt a sense of pride similar to what he imagined she had felt.

It was easy to fall in love with such a beautiful city. If only it was all beauty. Daniel caught a fleeting glimpse of the Kessock Bridge in the rearview mirror. He thought of Samira and her two small boys in their small flat. He wondered if they'd had a similar experience of Inverness when they first arrived with Sayyid. What did they think of the city now that he was gone?

Chapter Eighteen

"Your old man's been practicing some Gaelic for the trip," Mr. Darrow announced proudly, waking Daniel out of his musing. "*Càit a bheil an taigh beag?*" he said. "That means 'Where's the bathroom', right?"

"I don't know, Dad," Daniel replied, stifling a chuckle. "But most people here speak English, so I think you'll be okay."

"Ah, but that's an important phrase to know, huh?" his father retorted with a wink.

"Yeah, I suppose so," Daniel said. He saw his mother shaking her head, as if to say, *Don't encourage him.*

When they reached their hotel, Daniel helped his parents carry their luggage inside.

"All right, I'll leave you both to settle in," Daniel said as he stood in the doorway of their room. "I'll pick you up in the morning for the games."

"You're not going to stay with us? We just got here," his mother said.

"I've got some phone calls to make," Daniel said.

"You can do that here. I'm sure there's a phone somewhere in this room."

"Honey, he said he'll be back in the morning. Besides, I could do with a good rest. I didn't sleep a wink on the plane—not enough room to stretch out my legs," Mr. Darrow said, and then fell backward onto the bed.

"We're so proud of you, and we can't wait to meet Ellie. She is going to be there tomorrow night?"

"Yes, Mom. See you later," Daniel said and hugged her goodbye. As he closed the door behind him, leaving his parents to unpack and unwind, he couldn't shake the butterflies that fluttered in his stomach. Tomorrow, his two worlds would finally meet, and he could only hope that they would all survive it.

* * *

Daniel arrived at his parents' hotel room early the next morning. "Are you ready to go?" he asked as his mother opened the door for him. "Have you had breakfast yet?"

"Your father insisted we eat at the hotel restaurant," his mother said.

"I needed to fuel up before the caber toss," Daniel's father hollered. He appeared from the bathroom wearing short pants that hadn't been in style since at least the 1980s and a too-tight-fitting muscle shirt.

"Dad, you can't honestly think they'll let you compete. Have you seen the guys that do that? They're huge. I've seen you struggle with the vacuum cleaner," Daniel said.

"That thing's possessed. I swear," his father countered.

"You are not going out in public wearing that," Mrs. Darrow said.

"But—" Mr. Darrow protested.

"We're leaving in fifteen minutes," Mrs. Darrow said in a tone that said his fashion choice was not open for discussion. She nodded toward his suitcase. Mr. Darrow frowned and sulked back to the bathroom.

"That's the last time I let him pack unsupervised," she said with an exasperated sigh.

Daniel laughed and waited for his father to return wearing slacks and a camp shirt more befitting a man who had recently retired. When they exited the hotel, Mr. Darrow raised his hand to hail a taxi.

"No need, Dad. Bught Park is a short walk from here," Daniel said. The largest public park in Inverness, Bught Park, was nestled between Tomnahurich Hill and the Ness River. On the other side of the river was Belfield Park, where Daniel rented a flat from the Macphersons, and to the south was the smaller Whin Park, the site of Inverness's famous Christmas Winter Wonderland. Crowds had already gathered outside the vendors' tents and track fields. The last time Daniel had seen the park so busy was at the annual Bonfire Night celebration.

Daniel led the way to a seating area where they could catch a good view of the first bagpipe marching band warming up. Mrs. Darrow cringed at the loud, discordant piping while Mr. Darrow's eyes lit up with excitement. "I could pull off the kilt look," he said to Daniel as he surveyed the band.

"It's not as easy as it looks," Daniel said, remembering the first time he'd worn a kilt to a kirk dance. It was a loaner from Young Hugh Macpherson, who was shorter than Daniel. Much to Daniel's embarrassment, the garment had ended up resembling more a miniskirt than a proper knee-length kilt.

After the pipe bands and a perusal of the craft tents, where Mr. Darrow couldn't help himself purchasing a block of local whisky-infused sheep's cheese, they returned to the stands to watch the track and field *heavies*: the shotput, hammer toss, and the highly anticipated caber toss. Three kilted men carried a thick wooden pole measuring six meters, or nearly twenty feet, to one end of the lawn. They maneuvered it so that it stood upright like a telephone pole. The first participant, a mountain of a man, walked up to the pole. He waved both arms to psych up both himself and the crowd for the forthcoming feat of strength.

The man squatted and lifted the heavy beam from the ground with both hands. His face turned as red as the plaid pattern on his kilt as he struggled to stand while balancing the caber against one shoulder. The audience sat silent as the man ran a few steps before tossing the pole into the air. The pole landed on its top. The crowd cheered, urging the pole to continue forward, but it wavered and fell over at an angle. The man who had thrown it walked away, crestfallen.

"What's the point of this game again?" Daniel's mother asked.

A man sitting next to her answered. "This is yer first caber toss, is it?" Mrs. Darrow nodded. "Well, the goal is to have a straight flip—tossing the caber end over end and with it landing at a straight twelve o'clock position from the thrower," the man said, demonstrating a flipping motion with his hands.

"How heavy is the caber?" Daniel asked.

"About thirteen stone," the man said. "Em, a hundred eighty pounds?" the man clarified upon seeing Daniel's bewildered expression.

"What if he can't lift it?" Daniel's father asked.

"Then he loses, doesn't he?" the man said with a shrug. "Ah, there was one time though, couple years back, a block tried to cheat. His team tried to sub in a rotted beam, they did. It looked polished and freshly cut on the outside, but inside it was all rotted, making it lighter. Twas quite the scandal. The whole team was thrown out in disgrace and banned from ever competing again."

Chapter Nineteen

After an afternoon in the sun, Daniel's parents had wanted to stop by their hotel before dinner—his mother to freshen up, his father to nap. Sparing his parents another walk through the city, Daniel hailed a cab to take them to the restaurant. His heart pounded in anticipation as he and his parents entered the warmly lit room. The rustic wooden beams and walls adorned with old photographs of moody, windswept Highlands landscapes made him feel like he'd stepped back in time. A large taxidermied ram's head met them just inside the entrance, along with the hum of lively conversation filling the air.

"Ah, Daniel! Over here!" Rev. Calder called out from a corner table, waving them over with a welcoming smile. She stood up to greet them, her plump, rosy cheeks the same color as the tartan scarf around her neck.

"Mom, Dad, this is Reverend Calder," Daniel said.

"Mr. and Mrs. Darrow, em, Aloha?" she said, extending a hand to each of them.

"I thought that shirt was going to get *lost?*" Daniel leaned over and whispered to his mother.

"You're welcome to have a go, but—" she offered a defeated shrug. Daniel knew the rest of that sentence: *but I've been trying changing that man for over thirty years.*

Before Daniel could respond, his mother's attention had already shifted.

"Ah, and this is Ellie," Daniel said. Ellie stood, adjusting her glasses nervously.

"Ellie!" Daniel's mother cried, ignoring Rev. Calder's hand and rushing toward Ellie with arms extended. The look of surprise and terror in Ellie's eyes reminded Daniel of a similar expression on the stuffed ram's head. "Oh, I can't believe Daniel made me fly halfway around the world to finally meet my future daughter-in-law!"

"It's a pleasure to finally meet you, too," Ellie managed to respond as she had the air squeezed out of her.

"Mom, here, have a seat," Daniel said. He pulled a chair out for her on the other side of the table, hoped to give Ellie some breathing room.

"Oh, but I want to sit next to Ellie," his mother said, finally releasing her. She scooted quickly into the adjacent seat.

"Thanks, son," Daniel's father said and sat in the chair that Daniel was holding.

Ellie shot a glance at Daniel. *What just happened?*

I don't know, Daniel said with an apologetic shrug. "Ellie, meet my mom and dad."

Once they were all seated, a server came and took their drink orders. Daniel's father excitedly ordered a round of Scotch for the table. When Ellie declined, Mrs. Darrow glanced at her with a raised eyebrow, then caught her breath and stared at Daniel.

"Is there some other news besides the wedding?" Mrs. Darrow asked with bated breath.

"Huh?" Daniel asked, oblivious to her meaning. "I don't think so."

"It's nothing like that," Ellie said. "I just have an early surgery tomorrow and don't want to wake up with a headache."

"Nothing like what?" Daniel asked. Reverend Calder leaned over and whispered into his ear. Daniel's eyes grew wide as saucers. "Mom!" he gasped and then covered his face with his hand.

"What? I'd like to see my grandbabies before I die. Your father and I are not getting any younger," Daniel's mother said. "You *are* planning on having babies, right?"

"Ellie, I am so sorry," Daniel said, too embarrassed to look up from his placemat.

"My mum's the same way. She's been talking about how she's looking forward to being a gran since I was a wean myself. I was like, 'Mum, you've got a kid right here.' She said she wanted one she could simply spoil and then send back to its parents," Ellie said.

"Exactly! She gets it," Daniel's mother said.

"Speaking of parents, will yours be joining us tonight?" Daniel's father asked.

The baby talk hadn't seemed to rattle Ellie, but Mr. Darrow's question struck a chord. Ellie bit her bottom lip and looked down at her glass of water. She took a nervous drink.

"Ellie's father passed away when she was a kid. I told you that," Daniel said.

"Right, I'm sorry. I'd forgotten. Long plane ride and all," Mr. Darrow said. "But your mother?"

Daniel could feel Ellie's unease from the other side of the table. He had to say something to get his parents off the subject. "Sarah, perhaps you could tell us about this traditional Scottish meal we're about to enjoy?"

"Ah, a fine question," Rev. Calder replied enthusiastically, happy to serve as a tension release valve. "When Daniel told me this was your first visit to Scotland, I knew I had to treat you to a few of the culinary treats of this great land."

"My family goes back to Scotland on my father's side," Mr. Darrow said proudly.

"I know," Rev. Calder said with a wink toward Daniel. "Tonight we will have braised lamb, haggis, and a side of neeps and tatties. Now, I know haggis has a bit of an infamous reputation, but trust me, if done right, it can be a delicacy with no equal! The chef here has a recipe that's been in her family for generations."

Daniel's mother gave him a suspicious look, but Mr. Darrow was completely taken in by the change of subject. His eyes lit up as he leaned in to hear more. Ellie exhaled a sigh of relief. When their food finally arrived, Mr. Darrow was practically salivating like a dog eager for his favorite bone. Several minutes of silence followed as they dug in.

"So, Mr. Darrow?" Reverend Calder eventually asked. "What is it that you do back in the States?"

"Mmm," he swallowed. "Been a mechanical engineer for a fabrication and construction company in Raleigh for years. Or was," he said, and took another large bite. "Just retired."

"Are you both retired?" Ellie asked.

Daniel's mother shook her head. "Only semi. I still adjunct a few pottery and sculpture classes at the community college. Honestly, I don't know how he does it. I'd be bored out of my mind without some kind of work."

"I find ways to occupy my time. In fact, just the other week, I—"

Daniel's cell phone rang, interrupting his father's story. He pulled it out of his pocket and glanced at the caller ID. "Excuse me, everyone," he said. "I need to take this."

"Daniel, your father's just in the middle—"

"I'm sorry," Daniel said as he held his phone to his ear and stood.

When he returned to the table, he was happy to see that everyone appeared in to be good spirits and at ease with one another. He'd hated leaving Ellie alone there, but hopefully, when she found out why, she'd understand. "So, what did I miss while I was gone?"

"Reverend Calder here has been telling us about a wonderful local tour guide by the name of Philip Morrison," his father said, his eyes shining with excitement. "Apparently, he's the man to see if you want a *proper* tour of Loch Ness!"

"And Ellie was telling us there's a beautiful old castle there where you proposed," his mother added.

"They're both right, but that might have to wait. Mom, would you mind if I stole Dad tomorrow?" Daniel asked.

"What did you have in mind, son?" Mr. Darrow asked.

"If you're up for it, I was just invited on a tour of the new wind farm being built in the Moray Firth. I know it's not quite the same as searching for Nessie, but I think you might like it. Besides, I don't know much about the mechanics, so I could use your engineer's eye."

Mr. Darrow's face lit up at the suggestion. "That sounds absolutely fascinating, son! I've always wanted to get up and poke around inside one of those towers."

"Perfect." Daniel grinned, knowing his dad would appreciate the opportunity to indulge his technical curiosity. Of course, he couldn't let on the true reason for the tour, at least not in front of his parents.

"That's all right," Rev. Calder chimed in. "We can always save the search for Nessie for another day. After all, she's been hiding in that loch for centuries—I doubt she'll be going anywhere anytime soon!"

Chapter Twenty

The damp sea breeze tugged at the tail of Daniel's jacket as he and his father stood in the bustling Port of Inverness. Gulls screeched overhead, their cries melding with the hum of ship engines. He stared down at the docks, searching for a familiar cargo ship. His mind flashed back to the night when he and his sometimes-flatmate, Young Hugh, had snuck aboard Carmen Oreiza's old container ship to search for smuggled goods.

He doubted the ship would be there; the captain was likely scared off of Inverness for good, but Daniel couldn't help looking. Though it had been less than a year, it felt like a lifetime ago since he'd last been here. The strangeness of returning sent shivers down his spine.

"Whatcha looking for, son?" his father asked, peering out into the expanse of water with a quizzical look.

"Oh, nothing," Daniel replied, attempting to sound nonchalant. That was not a story he wanted to recount right now. Hopefully, this trip would go more smoothly. At least he'd been invited to the dock this time. No cover of night and dark ski masks.

"There they are! Reverend Darrow!" a voice shouted, snapping Daniel from his thoughts.

George Fraser, dressed sharply as always in a matching tweed suit, waved at them from the edge of one of the docks, his white hair fluttering about like dandelion seeds caught in the wind.

"Dad, I'd like you to meet Mr. Tw—um, Mr. George Fraser," Daniel said, gesturing toward the impeccably dressed gentleman. "He's a member of the church and our ticket to tour the wind farm."

"Ah, pleasure to meet you, Mr. Fraser," Daniel's father said, extending a hand.

"Likewise," Mr. Tweed replied, shaking it firmly.

"I've done some work with clean energy projects myself, so I'm eager to get a closer look at this one," Mr. Darrow said with a grin.

"My dad was a mechanical engineer back home," Daniel explained.

Mr. Tweed looked Daniel's father up and down quickly and nodded. Daniel was thankful he'd convinced his father to forego the Hawaiian shirt for today's outing. "We could use a chap like you out there. Help put this blasted project back on schedule," Mr. Tweed said. "Now, if you'll follow me, I'll show you to the boat that will take us out to the turbines."

As they made their way to the small boat bobbing gently in the waves, Daniel couldn't shake the nagging feeling of uncertainty gnawing at his gut. He was glad to see his father and Mr. Tweed getting along so well, but memories of past misadventures at the Port weighed on him. And his conscience was uneasy with the fact that he hadn't been completely honest with either one of them about his own motives for the day. He glanced quickly at the palm of his hand where he'd written the number 4. That was the turbine that Amir had discovered Sayyid had been working on before his death.

The boat's engine roared to life, sending ripples across the water as it cut through the waves. The wind whipped at their faces, causing Daniel's eyes to water. His nylon jacket flapped loudly in his ears. He glanced over at Mr. Tweed, who seemed unfazed by the elements, his tweed suit miraculously appearing untouched by the sea spray. His cane was hooked loosely over his arm as he deftly steered the small boat over the choppy water. Daniel couldn't help but be impressed.

Daniel had ridden in both a car and golf cart with Mr. Tweed before, and the speed with which they now flew over the water was consistent with the older man's driving record. He steered the boat under the imposing steel structure of the Kessock Bridge. "We could really use some positive press for this project. After the, em, *accident*, it seems all anyone wants to talk about is health and safety regulations," Mr. Tweed shouted over the noise of the engine.

The accident? You mean a man's possible murder? Daniel thought. Mr. Tweed certainly had a flair for understatement.

"And now there's all these inspectors and insurance men. Delay after delay. This supposed investment has turned into a real money pit, as they say," Mr. Tweed continued. "Perhaps after our tour today, you can help get the public back on our side, Reverend?"

Understatement and misplaced concern. But Daniel couldn't let his disappointment in George Fraser show. After all, Mr. Tweed wasn't the only one with ulterior motives today.

"Of course," Daniel replied, fighting against the wind to be heard. "I'll do my best. Clean energy projects like this one are important, especially in these times."

As they passed under the bridge, the sea suddenly opened up before them, revealing the vast expanse of the Moray Firth. The choppy water caused the small boat to bounce and sway, forcing Daniel to grip the railing tightly. In the distance, dark clouds loomed on the horizon, a stark contrast to the clear sky above them. Daniel hoped it wasn't an omen of things to come.

"Ah, would you look at that?" Daniel's father chimed in, gazing in awe at the giant steel towers rising out of the water.

As they got closer to the wind turbines, the boat slowed down, and the waves and noise calmed. Daniel's father leaned over to him and asked, "Now, what's this about an *accident?*"

"Oh, um, about a week ago, a man, one of the construction crew, fell from the top of one of the towers," Daniel said.

Mr. Darrow's jaw dropped. "You didn't think that was information I would want to know before agreeing to this trip?"

"Sorry," Daniel said, sucking air through his teeth. "I wouldn't have invited you if I thought it was dangerous."

"Well, it's too late to turn back now, isn't it?" Mr. Darrow said with less gusto in his voice than usual.

In more ways than one, Daniel thought.

The small boat bumped against the windmill's dock with a gentle thud, signaling their arrival. Daniel felt a tingling sensation in his stomach as they disembarked, part excitement and part apprehension. The completed wind turbine towered above them, its enormous blades standing still like swords drawn and ready for battle. Daniel imagined himself as a tiny David standing hopelessly outmatched before Goliath. But Eliza and Sayyid's family were counting on him, and he knew couldn't let them down. So, he took a deep breath and stepped off the boat.

Chapter Twenty-One

"Ah, Mr. Fraser. Right on time as usual," called out a man in a hard hat and neon orange safety vest. He strode towards them with the swagger of someone used to ordering others around. The wind ruffled his thick, unkempt beard, but otherwise could not sway the man's stocky figure. He tied the boat to the small dock at the base of the windmill tower before extending a hand to help them off. "This is Keith Christie, construction foreman," Mr. Tweed explained.

"Daniel Darrow," replied Daniel, trying to match the firmness of the foreman's handshake. "And this is my father."

"Nice to meet you both," said Christie, nodding at Daniel's father. "Chelsea," he said after a moment.

"Huh?" Daniel asked. Christie held out his right forearm. A blue lion with a golden tongue stood menacingly from the length of his wrist to his elbow. Daniel quickly looked away, unaware he had been staring at the tattoo.

"The football club," Mr. Tweed said to Daniel. Then, to Keith Christie, he added. "You'll have to excuse my friend; he's American." The foreman nodded as if that explained everything.

Keith Christie. So, this was Sayyid's former boss. Samira had mentioned how the two did not get along, but she couldn't say why. *Perhaps now I can get some answers*, Daniel thought.

"How goes the construction?" Mr. Tweed asked.

"I've got crews working on towers three and five today. This one here's the first to be completed—structurally, that is," Christie said, giving the tower an affectionate pat. The clang of his hand reverberated through the massive structure like a steel drum. We're waiting on the computer techs to come set up all the techy things. Come along, I'll show you around."

They followed him to a heavy door that reminded Daniel of the lower-decks hatch of a cargo ship. "Is it safe to go in?" Daniel asked, eyeing a ring of rust surrounding the perimeter of the door.

"Just needs another coat of paint," Christie said dismissively. He opened the door with a loud creak and flipped on a light switch. The light flickered a few times before finally deciding to remain lit.

"Reminds me of the story that fellow told at the Highland Games—the team that tried to cheat with the rotted caber," Daniel's father whispered to him.

"I was just thinking that exact thing," Daniel said.

"Eh? What's that?" Keith Christie asked.

"Oh, nothing," Daniel said quickly, hoping the foreman hadn't overheard them.

Yellow-tinted safety lights lit the inside of the tower like a subway tunnel—only this tunnel went straight up. A narrow steel ladder followed the lights higher and higher until it grew so small it looked like a mere silver string stretching into infinity. Daniel felt lightheaded as he gazed up.

"Hope yer not afraid of heights or closed spaces," Keith Christie said, with a laugh that felt more taunting than humorous. Daniel could sense that he did not enjoy other people poking around in his domain.

"Bit of a climb, isn't it?" Daniel's father asked skeptically as he stared up at the ladder.

"Best get to it, then," Christie said and stepped up the first few rungs.

"I don't know if I can make it all that way," Daniel's father confessed, patting his well-padded midsection.

Even without his father's bulk, Daniel didn't imagine he had the endurance for such a climb either. He clearly hadn't thought this part through. "How tall is this thing?" he asked.

"Have you ever been to Big Ben in London?" Christie asked. "It's about that to the nacelle. Add another hundred meters to the tip of the blades."

Daniel's determined expression fell. He'd never visited it before, but he knew Big Ben was one tall clock tower.

"Well, come on, lads. I've not got all day," Christie called down.

Daniel sighed and then took a deep breath before reaching for the ladder. Then he glanced back at Mr. Tweed. Mr. Tweed was spritely for his age, but surely, he didn't expect to climb all the way to the top of that never-ending ladder. Tweed hadn't said a word or even moved during this entire exchange. He knew something.

Just as Daniel put his foot on the first rung, both Mr. Tweed and Christie burst into fits of laughter. Daniel jumped back in case the convulsive howls caused Mr. Christie to lose his grip and fall on top of him. Their laughter echoed up the length of the tower.

"He was actually going to do it!" Christie said, climbing off the ladder.

"You often make things more difficult than they need be, but I'll give you this, Reverend, you've got determination!" Mr. Tweed laughed. "Mr. Christie, would you kindly show our guests to the lift?"

Christie nodded and ushered them to the opposite side of the ladder, where a small elevator-sized box was attached to a thick wire that paralleled the ladder's upward path. "This'll get us up to the nacelle in about fifteen minutes."

When they reached the top, they stepped off the cramped lift into a slightly less cramped room filled with a web of cables and wires and all manner of machines that Daniel hadn't the slightest clue as to their functions.

"Welcome to the heart of the turbine. Follow me, I'll show you the gearbox and generator and various systems that keep everything running properly," Christie said.

Daniel's father's eyes lit up like a kid on Christmas morning at the sight of all the literal bells and whistles in the nacelle. "Spectacular, just spectacular."

"Indeed, quite the marvel of modern technology," agreed Mr. Tweed, although Daniel could tell he was far more interested in the project's speedy completion and financial success than its mechanics. They followed the foreman and Daniel's father around the space as they gleefully discussed far more technical issues than either Daniel or Mr. Tweed cared to understand.

As the tour wound down, Daniel felt no closer to understanding what had happened to Sayyid. He knew he'd never gain such close access to the wind farm again, so he decided to press his luck. "Could we visit one of the unfinished towers? It would be really interesting to see what these look like before they're all put together. Kind of a before and after. Say, tower Four?" Daniel asked.

Chapter Twenty-Two

M r. Christie frowned. "I'm afraid that particular tower is off-limits right now. I'm sure you've heard a man fell to his death there last week. The police have deemed it a crime scene."

"Really? A *crime scene?*" Daniel asked, raising an eyebrow. "But I thought their official position was that he either jumped or fell accidentally."

"Well, yes, but…" Christie hesitated, clearly not enjoying being questioned. "The fact remains, it's still under investigation and still off limits."

"Of course," Daniel replied, his thoughts racing. He wondered if the foreman's reluctance was because of respect for the police investigation or something else. He didn't seem like the type that held a great respect for authority—other than his own. Did he know more than he was letting on?

"I was simply thinking that if we could see that the site is actually safe and make people aware of that, they'd be more inclined to believe the police report. Getting the public back behind this project might speed it along," Daniel said. He directed the last sentence toward Mr. Tweed.

At the mention of speeding the project along, Mr. Tweed's ears perked up. He looked at Daniel shrewdly, then leaned in and whispered something into Keith Christie's ear. A moment later, they shook hands. Daniel noticed a colorful, folded slip of paper pass subtly between them in the exchange—a banknote. Mr. Christie's reluctance evaporated as quickly as the morning mist.

"All right, then," he grumbled, motioning for them to get back on the lift. "I'll show you around number four, but we must be quick, and you're only seeing what I'll allow."

Daniel smiled and nodded. He'd taken a chance, and it had paid off. Now, if he could just find something useful at that tower. He let Mr. Tweed and Christie get a few paces ahead before leaning toward his father and saying softly, "Let me know if you see anything off about this next one."

"Like what?" his father asked.

"I'm not sure. Just keep an eye out," Daniel replied. His father nodded conspiratorially.

They boarded Mr. Tweed's boat, and Mr. Christie directed them towards Tower Four. Inside, it appeared much the same as the turbine they had just toured. But unlike the first one, Number Four was headless, missing its nacelle and blades. Mr. Christie didn't bother with any ladder jokes this time. He simply ushered them into the lift and rode it to the top.

Instead of a cramped, enclosed room with generators and gears, they stepped out onto an empty metal floor fully exposed to the outside—no walls, no ceiling, only a short lip around the circumference. Daniel stepped carefully outside and took in the stunning view. From such great a height, he could almost see where the Moray Firth opened into the North Sea. Inverness looked like a distant miniature city with the Kessock Bridge made of toothpicks. A sudden gust of wind tugged at this jacket and he gripped the side of the lift to steady himself. If he'd gotten dizzy at the sight of the never-ending ladder earlier, he was downright nauseous now.

"Is this where he was working? The man who fell?" Daniel asked, pointing toward a section of flooring that was still unfinished. Daniel's father eyed it critically, nodding to himself but offering no further commentary.

"That's close enough," replied Mr. Christie, crossing his arms defensively. "You saw what you wanted to see. Without proper safety equipment and training, it can be quite dangerous up here."

"Are you saying he didn't have proper equipment or training?" Daniel asked.

"What? No. I'm saying *you* don't, so let's head back down, shall we?" Christie said, irritated.

"Was Sayyid a good worker? Did he have problems with anyone on his crew?" Daniel pressed, hoped for some insight into what might have led to

Sayyid's death.

"How did you…?" Christie shook his head. His patience with Daniel's prodding was running thin. "Doesn't matter. Look, I'm not here to discuss every foreign worker's life story," Christie snapped. "They do a job. They leave. And I'm stuck trying to find someone to fill in the gap. End of story."

Sayyid didn't simply leave his job, Daniel thought, frowning at Christie's dismissive attitude. It was clear Christie felt no sorrow over Sayyid's death. But Daniel already knew that the two men did not get along. What wasn't clear was whether Christie's disdain was limited to Sayyid or if it extended to the rest of his crew. But, as they were currently over one hundred meters in the air with no safety railing, Daniel decided not to press him any further for the moment.

Once they had left Keith Christie behind and were back on dry land, Daniel's father finally spoke up, addressing both Daniel and Mr. Tweed. "I think you ought to get an independent inspector out here," he said gravely. "None of that structure looked safe to me."

"Really?" Mr. Tweed asked, taken aback. "What makes you say that?"

"It was harder to tell in the completed turbine we saw first; they covered it over well. But in that second one—let's just say I noticed more than a few things that concerned me," Daniel's father replied, his voice heavy with the weight of years spent as a mechanical engineer. "Shoddy materials and workmanship. It looks to me like corners are being cut, and that can only mean two things—either that Christie fellow is incompetent or very shrewd."

"You mean he's cutting corners on purpose?" Daniel asked.

"Either way, I'd get a second opinion before letting workers back up there," Mr. Darrow said.

Daniel glanced at Mr. Tweed. He could guess what the man was thinking: More delays, more cost. But Daniel's mind was focused on another thought: motive.

Chapter Twenty-Three

aniel and Ellie stepped into Eliza MacGillivray's hospital room. Eliza's frail frame appeared ghostly, covered in thin white bedsheets—a once vibrant thistle now as wilted as the flowers that lined her hospital room windowsill.

"Ms. MacGillivray?" Daniel asked softly, taking care not to startle her.

"Perhaps she's asleep?" Ellie asked him.

"Pish," Eliza muttered and pulled herself up. "I always have time for wee Ellie Gray and the future Mr. Gray."

Ellie chuckled and turned to Daniel with a raised eyebrow. "Um, we haven't exactly talked about—" Daniel stammered.

"What have you brought me?" Eliza asked, cutting him off. "More shortbread biscuits?" she asked with hopeful eyes.

"Sorry, no. I have flowers and a card from the children's Sunday School class. All the kids signed it," Daniel said, handing her a colorful, oversized card. "Everyone at the kirk misses you dearly, and we're all praying for your swift recovery."

As Eliza read the card, Daniel replaced the older bouquet on her windowsill with a new one. "Those are lovely, dear. Thank you," Eliza said. "Wait, those flowers aren't leftovers from the Sunday service, are they?"

"Um, would you believe me if I said no?" Daniel asked.

"Beware a man with a shallow purse, for his heart might match," Eliza said to Ellie.

"Is that another of the Brahan Seer's prophecies?" Ellie asked.

"No, just generally good advice," Eliza replied with a wink.

"You know that doesn't work the other way round," Daniel said, pulling up a chair to join Ellie at Eliza's bedside. "Being rich doesn't make someone a good person. I seem to recall another saying—something about a camel fitting through the eye of a needle," he said with a critical eye toward Eliza.

"I see I needn't go to church to receive my sermon for the week," Eliza said sarcastically. "Thank the weans for the card and tell everyone else I miss them, too. I'd be back next Sunday if these nurses would let me leave this dreary place."

As Eliza spoke, Ellie surreptitiously reached for her bag. It was larger than the purse she normally carried. With a sly smile, she placed the bag on top of the bedside table and unlatched the top. "Well, I brought along someone who might lift your spirits," she announced. Two long, furry ears popped out of the bag's opening, followed by two black eyes and a twitching nose.

"Ah," Eliza gasped. Her face lit up with surprise and joy, and she stretched out her arms to her beloved rabbit. The rabbit hopped to her and nestled in her lap. "Oh, my sweet boy! How I've missed you!"

The bunny sniffed at Eliza's hands, then nuzzled against her affectionately. Ellie smiled and glanced at Daniel. "I told you this was a good idea," she said.

"I should know by now not to doubt you," he said and then looked back toward Eliza and her rabbit, cheered by their joyful reunion.

"Ellie, what are ye like?" Eliza chided gently, shaking her head in amusement. "Sneakin' him in like this."

"Oh, I just took a note out of the Eliza MacGillivray playbook," Ellie said with a wink. "I knew he'd bring a smile to your face, and I think the wee thing was getting lonely at my house and me at the clinic all day long."

As Eliza petted her rabbit, Daniel absently traced the outline of a handprint on Eliza's colorful card. His thoughts drifted to the wind farm he had recently visited with Mr. Tweed and his father. The image of the towering turbines against the cloudy sky was still fresh in his mind.

"Eliza, I wanted to talk with you about something," he began hesitantly, clearing his throat. "I think it might have something to do with your most recent vision."

Eliza looked up from her rabbit. "Go on," she urged.

"My father and I went to visit the wind farm where Sayyid Ghulam fell. Sayyid's death has been all over the news, of course. They're saying he jumped or caused the accident himself. But, after visiting the site, I can't help wondering if his death might have been due to scrimping on the construction. You see, Dad's a mechanical engineer, and he mentioned that the construction seemed…well, shoddy and cheap."

Ellie's eyebrows shot up in surprise. "Really?" she asked. "They shouldn't be hurting for funds. I once mentioned the project to my mum, and she had, em, mixed feelings about it, to say the least. She listens and hears things, you know. She told me that company, GlenBreeze, received loads of grants and tax breaks to build it. The Highland Council postponed their planned improvements to the prison in order to move funds around for the wind farm. Clean energy makes for better headlines during an election year than prison upgrades."

"Interesting," Daniel said, considering this new piece of the puzzle. "I wonder if George Fraser knows more than he's letting on about the finances. He did seem more concerned with losing money on the project than finding out what happened to Sayyid."

"He got you into the wind turbines. Perhaps he could get you a peek at their books?" Eliza suggested.

"If they don't want anyone knowing about misusing funds, what makes you think they'd write it down?" Daniel asked.

"Believe me, people like George Fraser know where every penny goes," Eliza said.

"Wait, Ellie, how did your mother find out about all that? I helped lobby for the wind farm, and I know they received some grants, but I never heard anything about taking funds from other projects," Daniel said.

"Gossip isn't confined to Church Street. People like to talk, especially if they haven't much else to do, so whether in a kirk or a prison, if you keep your ears open, you're bound to hear something juicy every once in a while," Ellie said.

Daniel considered her point. He'd learned over the past two years that the fastest way to keep apprised of the goings-on at Church Street was to eavesdrop on conversations in the kirk hall during the after-service tea and biscuits. He often found out more there in a few minutes than in several days of parishioner home visits.

"Did she hear anything else? A name? Where the money's being spent or not spent?" he asked. Ellie shook her head, *No*. "Then I guess I've got another date with Mr. Tweed."

Eliza erupted in laughter. "Mr. Tweed? Is that what you call him?"

Daniel's hands rushed to cover his mouth. He'd only ever told Ellie about his secret nickname for George Fraser, and now he'd let it slip to one of the biggest gossips in all of Church Street. "You can't tell him," Daniel pleaded.

"Mr. Tweed. Oh, I doubt he would like that name much at all," Eliza giggled to herself. "Don't you worry. Your secret's safe with me."

"Thanks," Daniel said, unconvinced.

"Without my Seeing Stone, no one is much interested in what I have to say anymore anyway," Eliza said sullenly. "Have you had any luck mending it?" she asked Ellie.

Ellie exchanged a glance with Daniel, then gently placed a worn velvet pouch containing the broken Seeing Stone in Eliza's hand. "I'm so sorry, but I'm still searching for a jeweler who can repair it. I did find someone who might be able to set the two pieces in a kind of locket for you, though. The pieces wouldn't be exactly back together, but at least they wouldn't be quite as separated."

Eliza frowned, studying the fragments. "No, my dear. That won't do. The Seeing Stone must be made whole for it to be of any use. And that can only happen with the same earth from which it was created."

Daniel and Ellie looked at each other, confused. Eliza sighed, her frail figure sinking slightly into the hospital bed. She handed the velvet pouch back to Ellie.

"You remember the tale of the Brahan Seer and where he discovered the Stone?" she asked, her gaze flickering between them.

"Loch Ussie, right?" Ellie asked.

"Aye," Eliza confirmed. She stared at them intently as if trying to convey the importance of her next words. "Only original clay from that loch can bind back what has been broken. The Stone must be brought back to its source."

"Or could we bring the source to the stone?" Ellie mused. "Daniel, your parents said they wanted to see the sights while they were here, no?"

"What are you thinking?" Daniel asked.

Chapter Twenty-Four

Daniel Darrow sat in his office, his thumb hovering over the screen of his cell phone. He checked the time again. "I hope you're awake, buddy," he said to himself as he pushed the call button. After a couple rings, Young Hugh Macpherson's face appeared on the screen.

"Sorry if I woke you. I'm not sure what time it is there," Daniel said.

"I was already up," Young Hugh shrugged and scratched his beard, which had grown at least an inch since the last time they'd talked. "These early morning shifts are killing me, though."

"Oh, you're on the clock. Should I call back later?"

"I can take a smoke break. What's up?"

"Thanks, I'll try to be brief," Daniel said. "When you were working on Carmen's crew last year, did she ever hire people that didn't have, um, entirely legal working status?"

Hugh thought for a moment and then shook his head. "Carmen may have shipped illegal goods, but I think all her hires were above board. I remember once Luka wanted her to take on his cousin, but she refused because he couldn't get a legal visa. She said she didn't want to give the Home Office or Immigration any reasons to come sniffing around. At the time, I figured she was simply looking out for the business, but now we both know she had other secrets to worry about. Why do you ask?"

Without revealing too many details, Daniel told him about Sayyid's death and his recent tour of the offshore wind turbines. "I think there might be a connection between Glenbreeze Dynamics' hiring and construction practices. The money doesn't seem to be adding up."

"Well, I don't know much about hiring or construction, but I have heard of your foreman with the blue lion tattoo."

"Really? You know him?" Daniel asked eagerly.

"I don't *know* him know him, but you don't work at the Port of Inverness for long without hearing tales the craggy fellow with the Chelsea Football tattoo on his forearm. He's a not a bloke you want to mess round with—short-tempered, mean, and a bit of a slave-driver, so I hear," Young Hugh said. "I know I can't talk you out of trying to help this family; just promise me you'll be careful around Lion Tattoo. This isn't like when we investigated Carmen. She could be cutthroat in business, but Lion Tattoo is *literally* cutthroat," Young Hugh warned.

"He's really that bad?" Daniel asked.

Young Hugh shrugged. "Like I said, I don't really know the man, but those were the rumors. Look, I've got to go. Say 'Hi' to my parents for me."

"You could call them yourself, you know," Daniel said. He never enjoyed being the intermediary between his former flatmate and his current landlords.

Young Hugh opened his mouth to speak, but then shook his head. "Well, at least give my love to Ellie then."

"Sure," Daniel said. "I'll talk to you later."

Young Hugh nodded and then ended the call.

Daniel scrolled the contacts list on his phone. After Young Hugh's warning, Daniel knew he needed more information before considering any kind of investigation of the foreman, Keith Christie. He needed to find out more about GlenBreeze Dynamics's financial records, and there was only one person who might get him that information. Just as he was about to click on the contact button for George Fraser, aka Mr. Tweed, the device buzzed in his hand. He blinked at the unexpected call. Mr. Tweed was calling him.

"What could he want?" Daniel wondered as he swiped to answer. "George Fraser, I was just about to call you."

"Ah, Reverend Darrow! Clearly, we're both men of impeccable timing." Mr. Tweed's voice boomed through the phone as if he were shouting into it. "I need to speak with you straightaway. It's urgent, lad."

"Of course. What's going on?" Daniel asked.

"Can't say over the phone," Mr. Tweed replied cryptically. "Meet me at the driving range of my golf club in an hour."

"Over by Tomnahurich Cemetery Hill?" Daniel asked. Mr. Tweed frequented many local golf courses, and Daniel didn't want to show up at the wrong one.

"Aye, that's the one. Half an hour. And don't be late."

"Understood. I'll be there," Daniel confirmed, but Mr. Tweed had already ended the call. As he put down his phone, Daniel felt a twinge of excitement, accompanied by a nagging sense of guilt. His parents' unexpected arrival had already taken up so much of his time, and he was way behind on his preparations for the upcoming Sunday service. He certainly didn't have time to run off to secret meetings at golf clubs.

But whatever Mr. Tweed wanted from him, it sounded urgent. And Mr. Tweed was a member of the kirk, so technically he could count this meeting as work. He closed the book and notes he had been taking and sent a quick text to Amir: *Something came up. Need to reschedule our meeting about Sunday's music.*

Daniel grabbed his jacket and slipped out of the kirk. His jacket flapped in the breeze as he hurried from the bus stop to the golf club. He made his way to the driving range and surveyed the line of golfers hitting practice balls onto the range. When he spotted a man with white hair and a tan tweed suit, he waved and headed over.

"Ah, there you are," Mr. Tweed said when he arrived.

"Sorry, I'm a bit late. I had to catch two buses," Daniel said.

"Never mind that now," Mr. Tweed said, impatiently gesturing for Daniel to join him on the tee.

Mr. Tweed overlooking tardiness? This must be serious, Daniel thought.

"You didn't bring any clubs?" Mr. Tweed asked, looking Daniel over.

"I don't own any. Was I supposed to?"

Mr. Tweed huffed and motioned to his golf bag. "Here, take one of mine."

"I thought you had something important you needed to talk to me about?" Daniel asked, confused.

"I do," Mr. Tweed said and then looked suspiciously from side to side. "But we must appear casual." He teed up a ball and took a swing, sending a golf ball flying through the air with a satisfying thwack.

"Right," Mr. Tweed began, reaching for another ball. "After your father suggested hiring an independent inspector for the wind farm project, I put the idea to the foreman, Mr. Christie."

Daniel raised an eyebrow. "And how did he take it?"

"About as well as the kirk cat takes to holy water," Mr. Tweed grumbled. He placed the ball on another tee and indicated that Daniel should take a swing. As Daniel got into position, Mr. Tweed continued. "Christie was vehemently against the idea—practically foaming at the mouth, if you can believe it."

Daniel nodded and swung, missing the ball entirely.

"Eyes on the ball," Mr. Tweed chided him.

"Sorry. We'll just call that a practice swing," Daniel said, repositioning himself. He tried again, and the ball went flying. It didn't soar half as far as Mr. Tweed's, but Daniel was happy to simply have made contact.

"Why would he object to an independent inspection?" Daniel asked as he watched the ball land and roll a few more yards.

"Ah, that's the million-pound question, isn't it?" Mr. Tweed said, leaning in closer with a conspiratorial gleam in his eye. "You see, when I invest in a company, especially one as vital to our community as GlenBreeze Dynamics, I like to know all the ins and outs of it. I don't take kindly to feeling like someone's keeping something from me."

"Understandable," Daniel agreed, watching as Mr. Tweed teed up another ball. "So, what did you do?"

"Being the resourceful man that I am," Mr. Tweed replied, just before launching the golf ball into the air, "I decided to dig a little deeper into Mr. Christie's past. And what I found was…intriguing, to say the least."

"What did you find out?" Daniel asked. "Have similar *accidents* happened on his previous job sites?"

Mr. Tweed held up a finger as he reached for another golf ball. He handed the ball to Daniel. "You're up."

Chapter Twenty-Five

aniel took the ball from Mr. Tweed and placed it on a tee. He was growing tired of this ruse, but if he wanted more information, he'd have to play along. He hit the ball on the first swing this time, and Mr. Tweed appeared slightly less embarrassed to be standing next to him. "All right, now tell me what you found out."

"Keith Christie," Mr. Tweed said, his voice dropping to a mere whisper, "used to work for the Philarguria Energy Corporation."

"Philarguria?" Daniel gasped, feeling as though he'd been punched in the gut. The name conjured up memories of the charred bodies of Tom Shaw and Broonburn House and of Ellie's mother being led away in handcuffs.

"Shh," Mr. Tweed admonished. "Here, try this driver," he said. He handed Daniel another club from his bag as he glanced around to see if Daniel's reaction had aroused any unwanted attention.

"You think they could be behind all this?" Daniel whispered.

Mr. Tweed narrowed his eyes and tapped his nose knowingly.

"I thought Alec Harrow, their old CEO, was in prison," Daniel said.

"That doesn't mean the end of the company. Philarguria is like a hydra—cut off the head and two more sprout," Mr. Tweed said.

"After the Broonburn mess, I'm surprised they'd even want to return to Inverness," Daniel said.

"The potential for a big payday attracts all manner of unscrupulous characters."

"Unlike the good folks at GlenBreeze Dynamics?" Daniel asked as he tried out the new driver. The ball flew much farther than his earlier attempts.

When he looked to Mr. Tweed for affirmation, the older gentleman returned an insulted glare, as if Daniel had just taken a swing at him rather than the golf ball.

"What exactly are you implying?" Mr. Tweed asked.

"Nothing," Daniel replied quickly, not wanting to offend his best source. "Other than the foreman connection, what makes you think Philarguria has anything to do with Sayyid's death?"

"They've covered up a murder once before, you remember," Mr. Tweed replied, his voice low and serious. "I doubt whoever is in charge now would hesitate to do it again if it meant getting what they want." He teed up a ball for himself.

Daniel was growing tired of drawing out tiny pieces of information like a dripping faucet. He put his hand on Mr. Tweed's shoulder before he could swing. "What do they want? They already lost the fight over mineral rights here."

"Isn't it obvious?" Mr. Tweed responded, leaning on his club. "They want to sabotage the wind farm and bankrupt GlenBreeze Dynamics. Whether it's to snuff out the competition so they can swoop in and take over or simply out of revenge, that's what they're after."

"Revenge?"

"You're the one who put ol' Harrow behind bars, and my connections with the local MPs helped sound the death knell to their schemes here, so to speak," Mr. Tweed said as he brushed Daniel's hand off his shoulder.

"Okay," Daniel said, pushing aside his apprehension. "What do we do now? How do we prove it?"

Mr. Tweed swung. "Ah, now that's where things get interesting," Mr. Tweed answered as he watched his ball soar far off into the field. After it landed, he turned to Daniel. "A little bird informed me that Philarguria is having a company retreat up at a lodge on Loch Ussie in just a few days. Some kind of wilderness, team building, and strategizing nonsense. Corporate hippies," he said sarcastically. "Anyway, all the big players will be there. It's the perfect opportunity to eavesdrop on their plans."

"Are you suggesting we crash their retreat?" Daniel asked hesitantly.

"Exactly!" Mr. Tweed whispered with a quick raise of his bushy white eyebrows. "But *crash* is a bit too...loud. We must be subtle and smart about this. To gather the evidence we need, we'll have to *infiltrate*."

"I don't know. That sounds like an invitation-only kind of event," Daniel objected.

"I can get us in; leave that to me. But if you have a better idea, I'm open to suggestions," Mr. Tweed said.

"We could question Keith Christie directly?"

"If he's working for them, do you really think he'd answer our questions?"

Daniel could think of a million excuses not to go along with Mr. Tweed's plan. He was be too busy with his church duties to go gallivanting off to a wilderness retreat. Eliza was still in the hospital, and he had a sermon to write. Not to mention that his parents were in town; they would expect him to spend time with them. Then there was a wedding to plan. Finally, Daniel shook his head. If there was a better way, he couldn't think of it.

"You've gotten awfully quiet, Reverend. Are you in?" Mr. Tweed asked.

"I'm just trying to imagine how this crazy plan of yours can work." Daniel thought for a moment more. If he could manage it right, this might present an opportunity to solve several of his problems at once. "You said it was a wilderness retreat at Loch Ussie?"

"Aye, Ben Harta Lodge. But think more luxury hotel than tents or caravans," Mr. Tweed replied.

"All right, I'm in."

Chapter Twenty-Six

Coinneach Odhar stood at the edge of a freshly tilled field and watched the setting sun cast its deep pinks and purples across the landscape. His muscles were tired from the day's labor, and his stomach growled.

"A fine job today, lad," said auld Tam, another farmhand who had taken Coinneach under his wing. "But remember, we're up before dawn to do it all again tomorrow."

"Aye, Tam," Coinneach replied with a weary smile. The work was hard, but steady and satisfying. There was no one to deny him his coin or run him out of town for receiving a grim fortune. He might go to bed exhausted, but at least he had a bed to go to. And sore muscles were a small price to pay for a full belly.

"Are you ever going to tell me the tale of what happened to yer eye?" Tam asked.

"'Tis nothing to tell. Just a childhood accident," Coinneach said.

"I'll get it out of you one of these days."

"I'm not for dwelling on the past nor the future. I'm interested in the present. And right now, I'm awfully hungry," Coinneach said, hoped to change the subject.

"Then let's get home and get some food in you," Tam said with a laugh.

As they trudged back toward the cottage that he shared with Tam and his family, Coinneach was tormented by old memories their conversation had dredged up. He was so young when his father had died, Coinneach had trouble conjuring his image. He saw the vague outline of a man looking after cattle on their small croft. Coinneach and his mother had managed to keep their small croft going, but it had been a constant struggle.

He winced as he remembered the day he'd stumbled upon the smooth, ring-shaped Seeing Stone along the banks of Loch Ussie. It cost him the use of one eye, but gave him the gift of second sight. It was a gift he never asked for, but one he accepted. After his mother's death, he had left the farm to seek his fortune as a seer. But life as a wandering prophet left him lonely and penniless. He had come to view the Seeing Stone as more of a curse than a gift. So, he'd given it up and moved south. He'd stuffed the stone deep in his pocket to be forgotten and never used again. He wondered what his parents would think of him now, having abandoned one croft only to work another. His life, it seemed, had come full circle.

Several days later, Coinneach was in the middle of bundling hay when he heard the swish of delicate fabrics behind him. He turned to see a noblewoman, her face flushed from the effort of walking through the soggy fields in her impractical shoes. Other than his employer, the laird himself, Coinneach had never met anyone else from the grand house. But where else could this finely dressed woman have come from? And what was she doing out here in the field?

"Can I help you, mum?" he asked.

"I'm looking for a seer, a man named Coinneach Odhar. He recently began working the estate," the woman said.

Why would a lady dirty the hem of her dress to converse with him? Coinneach wondered. "I'm sorry, I dinna ken the man," he said and returned to his work.

"Turn back round and let me see your face," she demanded. Coinneach obeyed. She examined him with her icy blue eyes, and a chill ran down his spine. "I think you do. I'm told he has long black hair and a glassy eye."

Coinneach brushed his hair forward to cover his blind eye and stared at the ground. "I'm just a simple laborer, Mum. I don't want any trouble."

"Please," she pleaded, "I need to know my family's future. There are rumors spreading amongst the neighboring lairds. I fear they're plotting against us."

"You'll have to seek answers somewhere else. I'm no seer, not anymore,"

Coinneach protested.

"My husband took you in, gave you food and lodging. You owe us this," the woman insisted.

"And I serve the laird with my daily labor. I earn my keep, mum."

"Please, you must help me," she pleaded. Her eyes softened, and her tone was no longer that of a demanding noblewoman. "I fear what might happen to us, to all of us, if we fail to act."

Coinneach hesitated, torn between his desire to live a normal life and the guilt of leaving the woman who employed him in distress. Finally, he sighed and reached into his pocket, pulling out the smooth Seeing Stone. "I cannae guarantee you will like what I see," he cautioned her.

"Tell me."

He held the stone up to his blind eye as he focused his other on the laird's wife. A vision began to form, hazy at first, then clearer.

"I see…a terrible misfortune befalling your family," Coinneach murmured, his voice straining under the weight of the vision. "'Tis not your neighbors that betray you, but your land. I see crops withered, your animals fallen ill and dying, and your children destitute, roaming the country as beggars."

The laird's wife gasped, her hands flying to her mouth in shock. "What? That can't be! You must have seen it incorrectly."

"My vision is clear. I'm sorry. I did warn that you may not like it."

"You're no prophet! You're a liar and a witch," she shouted, anger and repulsion filling her words. She spun around and stormed back to the main house.

That evening, the laird's wife told her husband everything that Coinneach had foreseen. The laird, a practical man who believed in hard work and little else, scoffed at the idea.

"The man works for us," he said, waving away his wife's concerns. "He would never let something bad happen to his benefactors."

"Please, my love," the laird's wife begged, tears filling her eyes. "We must act before it's too late. You must send him away. Perhaps his curse will go with him."

"This so-called prophecy is merely the overactive imagination of an insignificant man seeking attention—nothing more. Let us go to bed and speak of it no more," the laird said. But his wife persisted, insisting that he send Coinneach away.

"Fine," he conceded, "I won't dismiss a good laborer, but for your peace of mind, wife, I will send him out to cut peat. He'll be far from the house then. So far, you'll have to send a runner out daily with his meals."

Chapter Twenty-Seven

The next morning, Coinneach received his new assignment and began the long journey to the peat bog. Along the way, he came across a stray dog. Normally, he wouldn't welcome the company of such a mangy, flea-bitten companion, but this was lonely work, so Coinneach allowed the dog to accompany him. He reached the bog just before sunset and set up camp for the night. He shared some of the supper he had brought along with the dog. A bitter mix of sorrow and nostalgia for his wandering prophet days filled his heart as he gazed up at the stars before he fell asleep.

Coinneach awoke to the mangy dog licking his face. "Ah, you'll have to wait for your breakfast until the laird sends us food," he said. "If you're that hungry, go find a rabbit or something." He shooed the dog away and picked up his peat spade.

As the day progressed, Coinneach's stomach growled angrily, protesting the long hours of labor that had gone by unaccompanied by food. With a sigh, he decided to take a break and rest on the soft grass that surrounded him. "Where's my dinner?" he muttered to himself. "The lady must want me to starve out here—punishment for my prophecy." Exhaustion overcame him, and he fell into a deep sleep.

"Oi, Coinneach!" a voice called, waking him. Coinneach blinked groggily up at the young boy who'd been sent to deliver his meal.

"What took you so long? A man needs sustenance for such a hard job as this," Coinneach said, indicating the peat bricks he had piled beside him.

"I would've come sooner, but this is a special meal for you, prepared by the laird's wife herself," the boy said with pride as he handed Coinneach a basket of bread and cold broth. When the boy noticed his skepticism, he added sheepishly, "Twas hot when I started out," before scampering back home.

Coinneach took a greedy bite from the bread and was about to wash it down with a spoonful of broth before something stopped him. Despite his great hunger, he had a feeling that something was off. Why would she send him way out into the peat bog and then take special care to prepare his meal herself?

He reached deep into his pocket and pulled out the Seeing Stone. "Let's have a wee peek then," he said as he held the stone to his eye. He saw a pack of thirsty wolves lapping at the shore of a pond. But it was an unusual pond, perfectly round like a wooden bowl. One by one the wolves keeled over, dead. Deep blue poison dripped from their open mouths.

"By the saints, she means to kill me!" Coinneach gasped, dropping the Seeing Stone in horror. He reached to dump out the bowl of broth, but the stray dog was eagerly lapping it up. "No! Get away!" he shouted at the dog and snatched the bowl away. Within moments, the dog's excited wagging turned to panicked yips. It lay on the ground whining uncomfortably.

"What were you thinking, you greedy thing?" Coinneach asked, petting the dog's head. "Wait here. I'll see what I can find to mend you." He stood and set about searching for herbs to counter the poison. His wandering days had taught him much about medicinal plants, some through kindly farmers, some through trial and error. He had to hurry because he didn't know how much broth the dog had swallowed or how potent the laird's wife had made her poison. When he returned, he made a fire and boiled down the thistle and other herbs he'd found into a strong, healing brew. He gave most of it to the dog and drank a little himself for good measure. Only time would tell if his potion was effective.

In the morning, Coinneach awoke and blinked in surprise as he noticed that the dog, who had been lying nearby, was missing. For a moment, he felt a pang of worry—had the animal wandered off during the night to perish alone? He called out for it and, to his great relief, a scruffy head popped out of the nearby heather a few minutes later. "I'm glad to see you're feeling better. But if we're to survive another night, we should leave this place."

As he made his way down the road, the dog marched happily along at his heels. Coinneach was lost in thought, reflecting on his recent brush with death, so he didn't notice the sound of horse hooves cantering toward him.

"Pardon me, sir," a man on horseback called out. He wore a fine cloak with the crest of a noble family emblazoned on it. "Are you by any chance Coinneach Odhar? The famous Seer of Brahan?"

Coinneach hesitated for a moment, unsure how he should answer. But the man's crest wasn't that of the estate he was fleeing, and something about this man's demeanor seemed sincere, so he nodded cautiously.

The man smiled and dismounted from his horse. "My master, the Earl of Seaforth, has been searching for you. He wishes to speak with you about matters of great importance."

"I'm sorry to disappoint your master, but I am no prophet for hire, and my visions do not always please those that hear them," Coinneach said. Everyone knew of the Earl of Seaforth's reputation as a man of great wealth and generosity, but after his latest experience, Coinneach was hesitant to trust this messenger. He had narrowly escaped the whims of a minor laird. If he should anger a man as powerful as the Earl, he might not be so lucky.

Sensing Coinneach's hesitation, the messenger quickly added, "My master values your abilities and has heard many tales of your foresight. He offers you his patronage and protection while you are in his service."

Coinneach considered the messenger's proposal. The Earl would be honor-bound to uphold his promise. And the prospect of steady meals and a roof over his head was appealing. Coinneach turned to the dog at his heel. "Well, boy, you ken we should trust him?"

The dog sat, wagging his tail excitedly, and gazed up at the messenger. Coinneach shrugged. He didn't have a better plan. "Show me to your master," he said.

Chapter Twenty-Eight

Indistinct conversations and the sounds of shuffling feet and swishing coats filled the nave as people filtered out after the Sunday morning service. Daniel Darrow stood amid the bustle, chatting with Amir Nazar, the choir director. "How are Samira and her boys doing? Have you seen them again since we dropped off those donations?" he asked.

"They're…adjusting. Samira is strong and hides her sadness well for her sons. And children are resilient," Amir said. "You visited the offshore turbines? Have you learned anything new?"

"Listen," Daniel said, before lowering his voice and leaning close. "We know Sayyid had trouble with the foreman." Amir nodded. "Well," Daniel continued, "I found out some interesting background on the guy, and I might have a lead on the people responsible for Sayyid's death."

Amir's expression turned serious. "Really? Who is it? What can I do to help?"

Daniel hesitated as he weighed the consequences of divulging too much information. If Mr. Tweed was correct and the Philaguria Company was behind it, then Daniel knew he'd have to share his part in why they were out for revenge. He hated keeping Amir in the dark, but he also didn't want to jeopardize their budding trust and friendship. "I'll know more in a day or two," he said, hoping to buy himself enough time to find out for sure.

Just then, Daniel spotted his parents weaving their way through the crowd toward him. Grateful for the timely interruption, he quickly changed the subject. "Amir, I don't think you've met my parents," he said, gesturing to the approaching couple.

"Nice to meet you both," Amir said politely, extending his hand.

"Likewise," Daniel's father replied, shaking Amir's hand firmly. "You made some of those old hymns into real toe-tappers. From what our son has told us, that choir can be quite the handful."

"Thank you. They can be," Amir laughed and glanced over at the mostly empty choir chairs. Several empty robes were strewn over seats by singers eager to get out of the stuffy robes and beat the crowd to tea and biscuits in the kirk hall. A few choir members lingered, chatting and putting their own uniquely rhythmed spins on the morning's hymns. Two of them had somehow managed to fit into one large robe, creating a two-headed singer to the delight of several small children gathered nearby.

After a few more minutes of small talk, Amir excused himself. Daniel turned to his parents. "So, are you two ready for our wee adventure today?"

"Absolutely!" Daniel's father exclaimed, unbuttoning his blazer to reveal an outlandish outdoorsy shirt adorned with cartoonish camping motifs. The sight of it made Daniel chuckle. Despite his mother's flustered eye roll, he couldn't help but admire his father's enthusiasm.

"Let me introduce you to the guys who will be joining us," Daniel said, gesturing toward the trio of men who had just approached, each sporting their own unique sense of fashion: Mr. Tweed in his customary tweed suit, Philip Morrison wearing waterproof trousers and jacket over a light fleece top, and William MacCrivag in a mismatched getup of plaid trousers, a polo shirt, and jacket that appeared to be a few inches too narrow around the waist to fully button.

"Right then, let's be off," Mr. Tweed declared, eager to begin their journey after introductions had been exchanged. The group made their way outside toward two cars parked on the curb near the kirk.

"Dad, you and Mr. Morrison can ride with Mr. Fraser. You remember Philip owns a Highlands touring company? He'll be able to answer all your questions on everything Scotland a lot better than me," Daniel said. Mr. Darrow's eyes lit up at the prospect while Mr. Morrison cringed with an expression that said, *Why did I agree to this?*

But it was too late to back out now. Daniel's father was already opening the passenger door to Mr. Tweed's gleaming luxury sedan and ushering him inside. "What can you tell me about the Darrow clan of Dingwall?"

"Mom, we'll ride with Mr. MacCrivag. His little green car's not quite as—Wait," Daniel said as Mr. MacCrivag pushed a button on his key fob, flashing the lights of a shiny new electric car parked behind Mr. Tweed's. "Is this yours?"

"Indeed, she is," Mr. MacCrivag said, running a hand affectionately over the smooth hood.

"What happened to ol' Greenie?"

"Traded her in," Mr. MacCrivag said. "I must admit, I miss the ol' lass sometimes, but when she left Philly and me stranded the last time, I knew it was time to move on. All this renewable energy talk around town got me thinking, so I traded her in for this electric beauty."

Daniel opened the passenger door for his mother, but she simply stood there, scanning the surrounding area. "Won't Ellie be joining us?"

"Not today. She's the on-call vet this weekend at her clinic," Daniel said.

"I was hoping we could talk about wedding plans," his mother said with a frown as she got inside.

They drove north, crossing over the Kessock Bridge, its tall towers and suspension cables glistening in the late morning sun like a spider's web. As they drove over it, Daniel was reminded of Eliza MacGillivray's ominous vision. He peered out his window, searching for the offshore wind turbines. From this distance, they looked like shining chopsticks rising from the blue-green sea.

"Do you know if Ellie wants white or red roses for the wedding?" his mother asked, interrupting Daniel's musing. "Red is a more traditional choice, but I've always liked white better."

"I don't know what kind of flowers she wants," Daniel said.

"You have to make these decisions soon. Florists and venues get booked up. You don't want to settle because you procrastinated," his mother said.

Daniel nodded absentmindedly, only half-listening as his mother delved into the minutiae of floral arrangements, caterers, and color schemes. He glanced over at Mr. MacCrivag, who seemed to be doing his best to feign interest in the conversation while trying to keep up with Mr. Tweed on the winding road that led to Loch Ussie.

"Ah, here we are!" Mr. MacCrivag announced after half an hour. He pulled his car into a small parking area near the loch. Daniel breathed a sigh of relief, grateful for the reprieve from wedding talk. He was excited to marry Ellie, but right now, he needed to focus. And, unless Mr. Tweed's plan to infiltrate the Philaguria company retreat involved masquerading as florists, his current mission had nothing to do with flower arrangements.

Chapter Twenty-Nine

"Mom, don't forget to change into your shoes," Daniel said as they got out of the car.

"What about you?" she asked, pulling her walking shoes out of a large bag.

"Mr. Morrison is taking you and Dad on a hike around the loch. I have to help Mr. Fraser and MacCrivag with a business thing. We already talked about this," Daniel said.

"You ready, honey?" Daniel's father asked, kitted out in his loud camping shirt, khaki shorts, knee-high socks, and hiking boots. "It's just beautiful out here, isn't it?" He inhaled deeply and gazed at the water and green hills around him with delight. "You wouldn't believe the knowledge this man has! We're in for quite a treat today."

Philip Morrison chuckled. "Your husband had very, em, extensive questions on the ride up."

As his parents prepared to join Philip Morrison for their nature tour, Daniel reached into his satchel bag and pulled out a small glass jar. "Dad, could you get me some clay from the shore while you're down there?"

"Clay?" His father asked, eyeing the jar suspiciously

"It's a long story," Daniel said. He handed over the jar before his father could respond further. "Thanks. Y'all have fun!"

Once they were out of sight, Daniel, Mr. MacCrivag, and Mr. Tweed climbed back into Mr. Tweed's car and set off for Ben Harta Lodge, the picturesque setting of the Philaguria company retreat.

"I owe Philip one for taking care of my folks this afternoon. I hope they're not too exhausting," Daniel said to Mr. MacCrivag.

"Ah, he's in his element. He acts put upon, but truly, he loves that sort of thing. The more questions, the more chances for him to show off!" Mr. MacCrivag said with a chuckle. "Now, I'm truly the one you'll owe after today."

"I hear there's an open bar," Mr. Tweed chimed in.

"That's a start," Mr. MacCrivag said with a wink.

The car bounced along the winding road, trees and water blending into a blur of green and blue as they sped toward Ben Harta Lodge. Expecting some kind of fancy log cabin, Daniel was surprised when the lodge's towering structure came into view. Mr. Tweed's description of a "posh outdoors retreat" was an understatement. The many arched windows sparkled in the sunlight. Turrets adorned its tall stone walls and a massive balcony overlooked the loch. A wide circular driveway surrounding an elaborate stone fountain stood in front. It was as if the lodge had been plucked straight out of a children's fairytale book and planted amongst the tall scotch pines. Mr. Tweed parked at the very back of the long driveway.

"Why'd you stop? Do you expect us to walk the rest of the way?" Mr. MacCrivag asked skeptically.

"Of course. We can't risk someone recognizing me or my car," Mr. Tweed explained. "Now listen. William, I've managed to get you on the guest list as a local IT consultant."

"Me?" MacCrivag exclaimed, his eyes widening in surprise. "But I don't know anything about IT, do I! What if someone asks me to look at their computer or fix the…what's it called? The internet wireless thing?"

"The router?" Daniel suggested.

"How should I know?" Mr. MacCrivag asked, throwing up his hands. "The Reverend should do it. He knows about computers and posting clouds and all that nonsense."

"No, it has to be someone no one would recognize," Mr. Tweed insisted.

"But—"

"Ah, but that's the beauty of it!" Mr. Tweed replied with a confident twinkle in his eyes. "You see, no one truly knows anything about IT. Just make up some techy-sounding words. These bigwigs pride themselves on being smarter than anyone else, so when they don't understand what you're saying, they'll act like they do because they're too proud to admit they don't."

"He's not wrong," Daniel said with a chuckle. "And when in doubt, just turn whatever it is off and then back on again—that usually solves the problem."

Mr. MacCrivag shook his head and sighed. "There'd better be some top-shelf Scotch at that open bar. I'm going to need a stiff drink to get through this!"

Mr. Tweed handed Daniel a black shirt and tie. "On to you. Your job is to sneak in through the back entrance and act like the help."

"Wait a minute," Daniel protested. He checked the tag on the shirt and wondered how Mr. Tweed knew his size. "What if someone recognizes me? You just said—"

"Trust me, lad," Mr. Tweed reassured him. "No one in there will pay any attention to the help."

"Right," Daniel muttered under his breath. "So, we just eavesdrop on conversations for any mention of GlenBreeze's finances or the Moray Firth wind farm?"

"Exactly," Mr. Tweed confirmed.

"So, where's your costume, then?" Mr. MacCrivag asked.

"Ah, well, I shall be monitoring things from the car," Mr. Tweed replied. "Someone has to keep an eye out for any unexpected surprises, after all."

Daniel rolled his eyes as he put on the shirt and tie. Before exiting the car, Mr. Tweed gave them one last word of advice. "Keep your ears open, but don't trust anyone. The people in there, they're like a den of vipers."

"More like a den of lions, as rich and powerful as they are," Mr. MacCrivag scoffed. "Ha, did you see what I did there, Reverend? Den of lions? And your name's Daniel."

"Yeah, I get it. Like the biblical story. Very clever," Daniel said, holding his forehead in his hand. They would need more than a stiff drink to get through this—more like a miracle. "Let's get this over with."

They walked halfway up the driveway together before pausing to part ways. "Should've known ol' Fraser would sit this one out. Men like him aren't used to getting their hands dirty," Mr. MacCrivag grumbled.

"We're not doing this for him. We're doing it for Sayyid and his family and all the other construction workers who could be in danger out there," Daniel said.

"Tell yourself what you want, lad. George Fraser's in this for the money, that's all. Me? I'm doing it for the open bar," Mr. MacCrivag said. He gave Daniel a parting salute and headed for the main entrance.

"Good luck," Daniel said as he turned to make his way toward the back of the towering building. There had to be a servant's entrance somewhere back there. He spotted a catering van and made a beeline for it. Sure enough, the people carting in food all wore black shirts and ties just like his. *How did Mr. Tweed know?* Daniel adjusted his tie and took a deep breath, steeling himself for the mission ahead. *No one notices the help,* he told himself. He slipped in around the back of the van, grabbed a tray, and followed the others inside.

Chapter Thirty

The clatter of plates and the hum of hasty instructions flew around Daniel as he slipped through the back servant's entrance, which led to the large prep kitchen at Ben Harta Lodge. He quickly surveyed the busy scene. Workers in matching black shirts and ties buzzed around him, moving with purpose and efficiency.

Standing still and clutching a tray of small sweet breads, Daniel stood out like a wrench in the gears of a finely tuned machine. A flush of panic started in his stomach and quickly spread through his extremities, rendering him immobile. He had worked in a fast-food restaurant in high school, but nothing about that experience had prepared him for this. The multiple ovens and stovetops, scents of baking bread and roasting meats and vegetables, cooling tables, and the sounds of chopping and clanking and boiling—this was a far cry from the deep fryer and burger grill he had known so many years ago.

"Oi, you!" shouted a stout woman with short, slicked-back hair and a no-nonsense expression. "Get those buns on the tables, pronto!"

Daniel looked at her with wide, confused deer eyes. *Me? What?*

"Pronto means now!" the woman barked and pointed toward the pâtissier station.

Daniel glanced down at the tray he was holding. *Oh, the bread!* He hurried over to deposit the tray on the table while narrowly avoiding bumping into the other caterers. Relieved the woman shouting orders hadn't seemed to detect that he was an outsider, Daniel tried to slip into the background. If someone noticed that he wasn't supposed to be there, their plan would be ruined.

"Watch it!" snapped an older man with a bushy mustache, as Daniel nearly collided with him.

"Sorry," Daniel mumbled and then ducked under two men carrying a large cake. If he stayed in this kitchen much longer, he was bound to be found out. Daniel snatched a tray with champagne flutes on it and made for the closest exit. "Phew," he muttered under his breath as he moved further from the chaos of the kitchen. Now he had to discover where the Philarguria elites were congregated.

He walked down the grand wood-paneled halls, following the faint sounds of conversation and laughter. That had to be them. It certainly wasn't coming from the staff. All the staff he'd encountered so far were too busy or stressed to even think about laughing. Finally, he came to a large, open room filled with people who were not wearing matching black shirts and ties. The room smelled of polished leather and taxidermied animal heads. Men and women in suit jackets or chic jumpers and pullovers lounged in plush, high-backed leather chairs and sofas. Beyond them, large floor-to-ceiling windows offered breathtaking views of Loch Ussie and the green hills beyond.

In the center of everything, he spied William MacCrivag holding a laptop computer with a flustered expression on his face. Daniel couldn't help but think back to his terrible pun in the car—the den of lions. He tried to recall the details of the biblical story of the prophet Daniel, favored advisor to the king of Babylon, who had been thrown into a den of lions after being set up by jealous rivals. Looking back over the occupants of this room, Daniel felt a kinship with his biblical namesake. They were both pawns caught in the games of the rich and powerful—elites who could toss people like him aside without a second thought.

Well, Daniel thought, *I have one thing the biblical Daniel didn't—alcohol.* With his tray full of champagne flutes leading the way, he stepped into the room. "Excuse me, sir," he said, sidling up to a group of executives with his most charming smile. "Care for a drink?"

"Ah, just what I needed!" one of them exclaimed, plucking a flute from the tray. The man wore a light wool pullover that perfectly matched the scene—luxury with a pretense of a nature enthusiast. This grand room was clearly the closest that sweater or its wearer would ever get to the actual wilderness.

Daniel offered the others in the group drinks and then lingered a few steps away in hopes of overhearing something good.

"Did you hear about Thompson?" one of them asked with a chuckle. "He went for a wee hill walk yesterday and wandered onto some sheep farmer's property. Got chased by an angry ram and fell right into an enormous pile of manure!"

"Thompson's an idiot. He wouldn't even be here if he hadn't brought in the Glencova account. How he managed that I'll never know," another remarked.

"Probably got chased into it by another angry ram," one of the others laughed. "Let's just hope Glencova doesn't end up a stinker like him!"

"Oi, you there, waiter. Are you going to just stand there or are you going to give us more drinks?" the man in the sweater called out.

Daniel nodded and held out his tray. "What's Glencova?" he asked as they switched out their empty glasses for full ones.

"Possible new fracking site," one of the group explained.

"Right, a real ground-breaking discovery!" one of the more inebriated of them laughed. "Get it? Groundbreaking!"

"Aye, we get it," the first said and then took his glass. "And I'll take this too. You need to sober up before dinner."

"So what? Y'all work in energy production?" Daniel asked, trying to appear naïve. He didn't have time to stand around and listen to drunken jokes all day. They needed a little prodding. "Like that new wind farm down near Inverness?"

"Y'all?" the man in the wool sweater said. "Seems our waiter's a cowboy!"

Oops! So much for keeping a low profile. Daniel slowly stepped away from them.

"Hey, cowboy, if you're leaving, why don't you go rustle us up some more drinks!" wool sweater said.

Daniel nodded and continued his retreat.

"Can you believe that guy? *Like the wind farm down near Inverness?*" one of the others mocked, imitating Daniel's accent. "As if we'd get anywhere near something like that."

"Wind farm—more like money pit," another cracked.

If Philarguria was trying to sabotage the wind farm, those people certainly didn't know about it, Daniel thought. He moved on to another group. He took their empty glasses and listened carefully before moving on again. He continued around the room until his tray was full of empty glasses. As he debated whether to brave the kitchen again to swap out the tray with full glasses, he realized that no one had mentioned anything even remotely related to the wind farm or the company's finances. It was all trivial banter, ego-stroking anecdotes, or insults directed towards people who were out of earshot. *I hope MacCrivag's had better luck than me*, he thought.

Like Mr. Tweed had said, none of the wealthy guests seemed to notice Daniel, but a couple of the other waitstaff were beginning to give him dirty looks as he just stood there with a tray of empty glasses. It looked like he'd have to return to the kitchen after all. When he arrived, the place was even busier than before. Dinner preparations were fully underway; pots and trays and plates and people were flying all around.

Daniel hesitated in the doorway, trying to envisage an unobstructed path to the drinks table. He twisted and twirled, dodged and sidestepped his way through the room. With just a few feet to go, he could taste success when—BAM! He collided with a prep chef carrying a plate of freshly sliced potatoes. Empty champagne glasses and potato slices flew into the air and landed with a crash, scattering across the floor. For several seconds, the entire kitchen was dead silent.

"What's wrong with you? Look what you've done!" the prep chef shouted at Daniel.

"I'm sorry, I didn't see you, I—" Daniel stammered.

"That's why I said 'corner,' isn't it! Keep your ears open. Now look at this mess!"

Daniel bent down to start cleaning up. "Not with your hands! There's broken glass. Is this your first time in a kitchen? Let me get a broom," the chef said and stormed off.

Before he could move, Daniel heard another voice boom from across the room. "What is going on? Everyone back to work!"

It was the woman with the short, slicked-back hair who had been barking orders when he'd first arrived. Cooks and servers parted like the Red Sea before Moses, creating a path as the kitchen manager marched straight toward him.

Chapter Thirty-One

"What are you doing here?" the kitchen manager demanded.

"Um," Daniel stammered.

"Let's try an easier question. What's your name, lad?"

Daniel didn't answer. Even if he hadn't been undercover, this woman was intimidating enough to render anyone speechless.

"You don't know what you're doing here, and now it seems you've forgotten your name?" she said.

"I, um, I was returning the empty glasses," Daniel finally muttered.

The woman eyed him suspiciously. "You're serving drinks?"

Daniel nodded.

"Where's your gold pin?"

Daniel stared at her, confused.

"All drinks servers wear a gold pin on their shirt pocket."

"It must've fallen off," Daniel said. *Why hadn't Mr. Tweed told me about the gold pins?*

"That's an interesting accent you have. I don't remember hiring anyone with that accent," the manager said, her eyes narrowing.

Daniel took a step back. His shoes crunched on broken glass. "Let me go see if I can find that pin. It's probably out in the hallway," he said, backing up toward the door.

"You don't look familiar at all, come to think of it," she said. But Daniel was already out the door. "Hey, come back!" she shouted.

Daniel sprinted away down the hall. When he reached the main room, he wiped the perspiration from his brow and steadied his breathing. He needed to find Mr. MacCrivag and get out of there without drawing any more attention to himself.

He scanned the room, but didn't see Mr. MacCrivag. *Where was he?* Then, near a tall, large leafed plant in the corner of the room, Daniel spotted a pair of plaid trousers. Their wearer's face was hidden behind a book, but that had to be him. No one else here would be caught dead in an outfit like that.

Daniel had found him and just in time too; the sound of heavy footsteps echoed down the hallway, growing louder with every second. Daniel sent a quick SOS text to Mr. Tweed and headed inside. He slipped past groups of executives talking shop and cracking jokes. He was careful not to make eye contact with any in case they asked him to refill their drinks.

"Psst, MacCrivag is that you?" Daniel whispered urgently.

"No, ye've got the wrong—" Mr. MacCrivag pulled the open book down just low enough for him to peek over the top of it. "Oh, it's you," he said, relieved.

"What are you doing back here?"

"Things were going to plan at first. I said things like a Wi-Fi router, and it's in the cloud, and RAM, data, ROM disks. I listened for juicy corporate gossip. Then I ran into someone who actually knew a thing or two about computers, didn't I? She started talking way over my head and then gave me a real suspicious eye when I couldn't keep up. So, I said I needed to go find another drink, and I've been hiding back here ever since. That's her there blocking the exit," Mr. MacCrivag said, nodding to a tall woman in a dark suede jacket standing near the main entrance.

"I've had some trouble of my own," Daniel said.

"The hall?"

Daniel glanced back to see the kitchen manager standing in the doorway, hands on her hips, eyes scanning the room like a hawk searching for its prey. He quickly ducked and turned back toward Mr. MacCrivag. "Yup. We need to get out of here. Now!"

"How? They appear to have both our exits covered," Mr. MacCrivag said.

Daniel's mind raced. They had each blown their covers, and Mr. Tweed wouldn't be able to wait at the front of the driveway for long. He had to think of something quick. "They know our faces, but they don't know *our* faces," Daniel said, a plan germinating in his head.

"What?"

"Your tech woman knows you, but she doesn't know me. You distract the kitchen manager while I get her out of the way. Then we'll meet outside. Hopefully, George will be waiting with the car," Daniel said.

"How do I distract her? She looks—" Mr. MacCrivag grimaced.

"Scary? I know," Daniel said. "Just act mad and complain about the champagne. Tell her it was flat or made someone sick. Or tell her you saw a server without a gold pin running in the opposite direction."

"Gold pin?" Mr. MacCrivag asked. "What about you? How are you going to get techy out of the way?

"Just go. I'll think of something. I've got a little experience making a scene," Daniel said. He sidestepped away, careful to keep his back toward the hallway door. He nearly ran into a server with a full tray.

"Ah, there you are," Daniel said, acting like he knew him. "They need you back in the kitchen."

"What? Why?" the server asked.

"Someone complained. It sounded like an emergency," Daniel said, nodding toward the hall where the kitchen manager was trying to desperately to see around an agitated-looking Mr. MacCrivag.

The server's eyes grew twice as large when he saw her. "She never leaves the kitchen!" he said, his face as white as a ghost.

"Hurry, I'll take your tray," Daniel said. He grabbed the drinks tray from him and held it up to shield his own face from the manager.

"I'm fired for sure," the server said as he walked nervously away.

Daniel felt bad about scaring the poor guy, but not as bad as he knew he was about to feel when he met MacCrivag's tech woman. He weaved his way through the crowded room toward the main entrance. "Excuse me, ma'am, would you like a drink?"

"I suppose one more wouldn't—"

Before she could reach for a glass, Daniel tilted the tray toward her. Four full glasses of champagne tumbled off and spilled all over her dark suede jacket.

"You stupid boy! Look what you've done!" she shrieked, throwing up her hands.

"I'm so sorry. My hand slipped. Let me find you a napkin or—" Daniel said.

"You've done enough. Get out of my way," she shouted, shoulder-checking him as she marched angrily away.

Daniel glanced back to see if Mr. MacCrivag had extricated himself from the kitchen manager. He had, but was now having a difficult time making his way across the room. It seemed that Daniel's distraction had cleared the exit of one obstacle just to create another. The clattering glass and screaming had brought a crowd of curious guests to form between them. Mr. MacCrivag toddled at the edge of the crowd, trying without success to pick a way through to the exit.

Time for some more quick thinking, Daniel thought. But this time, he was all out of champagne glasses to spill on people. And everyone was staring at him. *Well, as long as I have everyone's attention, I'd might as well use it to my advantage.*

"Dinner is served! Everyone to the dining hall, please," Daniel said in his most authoritative voice. He pointed vaguely across the room, not knowing exactly where the dining hall was located.

The guests exchanged confused glances. It was still a bit early for dinner, but most of them were already quite tipsy, so they didn't question Daniel's order. He motioned again, this time like he was shooing away a herd of sheep. "Go on, before the food gets cold."

The crown turned around and began to amble off, also unsure of the dining hall's exact location. But it was enough of a dissemination for Mr. MacCrivag to squeeze through. Daniel threw open the large doors and grabbed MacCrivag's arm, pulling him out into the crisp early evening air. They ran down the gravel circle driveway where Mr. Tweed's sedan was already accelerating toward them.

"About time, lads!" Mr. Tweed called out.

Daniel and Mr. MacCrivag tumbled into the backseat, slamming the door shut just as the kitchen manager and a confused drinks server appeared at the lodge's entrance.

"This is the third time I had to circle round. They wouldn't let me park in front and were beginning to get suspicious," Mr. Tweed said.

"Just drive!" Daniel shouted.

"Oh, now you're in a hurry," Mr. Tweed said sarcastically as he pulled away from the building, leaving a cloud of dust behind as they sped away.

"A close shave, that," Mr. MacCrivag muttered, out of breath.

"Indeed," Daniel agreed. "I hope it was worth it."

Chapter Thirty-Two

Coinneach Odhar stood on the crest of a hill, gazing out over a small corner of the Earl of Seaforth's vast estate. He took a deep breath, savoring the fresh air and his sudden change in fortune. From being cheated and cast out of villages and then nearly poisoned by those who didn't appreciate his visions to now having the patronage and protection of one of the most powerful men in Scotland, Coinneach's life had taken quite a turn.

"Seer!" a voice called from below. A crowd from the nearby village had gathered at the base of the hill. "We heard you were here. Come down and share your gift of prophecy with us."

Yes, gone were the days of being derided or feared. With the Earl's blessing, people now treated him with deference. He finally felt valued in a way he hadn't since before his mother had passed away. Perhaps his gift was just that—a gift, not a curse. He raised his hand in greeting and began to make his way down the slope.

"Look with favor on your servants, and share your wisdom with us," an elderly woman said when he reached the crowd.

"Of course, though you may not like what I see," he warned them.

"Good or ill, we must know so we can prepare. Tell us the truth, that's all we ask," another villager said.

So Coinneach advised them on matters great and small—the best times to plant and harvest, which fields might turn barren and which to leave fallow. He warned them of dangerous portents that would spell doom for one clan or another. Some visions were inexplicable even to him—streams of fire and water running through the streets and lanes of Inverness, or fully rigged ships sailing past Tomnahurich Hill where no waterway existed, much less one that could convey large ships.

He spent most of his days walking the countryside and towns, prophesying and advising any who sought his counsel. As word of his talents spread, folk traveled near and far to seek his advice. Before long, his days of solitary wandering became fewer and fewer.

One day, a messenger wearing the seal of the Earl of Seaforth arrived while Coinneach was staying in Inverness. "Great Seer of Brahan," the messenger said, dismounting his horse, "you've been summoned to the castle."

"Ah, the Earl seeks another prophecy regarding one of his rivals?" Coinneach asked.

"I was only told to bring you there with the utmost urgency," the messenger said and handed him a letter bearing the Seaforth seal.

"Read it aloud," Coinneach told him.

"The letter is for you," the messenger protested. But Coinneach, being illiterate, assured him it was okay. Coinneach broke the seal and handed the letter back to him. He opened it and read:

"Coinneach Odhar, the Seer of Brahan, is sought for an audience at Brahan Castle, wherein his wisdom may be shared. Make haste and journey swiftly. I await thee with earnest anticipation.

Signed, The Lady Seaforth, Countess Isabella."

"Is there no signature from the Earl?" Coinneach asked, surprised.

The messenger shook his head. "'Tis only the Countess's."

A few eavesdropping townsfolk began snickering. "Oh, a private audience with the Countess," one said provocatively.

"When the cat's away, the mice will play," another laughed.

"Our Coinneach has enough foresight not to be tempted so."

"Least not by the Countess. She's a face only a mother could love."

"Would take a better mother than I to love that face!"

With each insult, the messenger grew more frustrated until finally he rebuked the crowd. "Enough, all of you. The Countess is a powerful woman. Should she hear tell of your mockery, you'll lose more than your loose tongues!" The crowd fell silent and quickly dispersed. Satisfied, the messenger mounted his horse and offered a hand to Coinneach. "Shall we away?"

Coinneach had never met with the Countess alone, but if this man was any indication of her current disposition, he knew he had no choice but to obey. So, he simply nodded and got up behind the man on his horse.

As they approached the castle, the grandeur and scale of the fortress left Coinneach momentarily breathless. High stone walls loomed overhead, topped with towering spires and battlements. Guards, clad in shining armor and bearing the same Seaforth crest as the messenger, watched their approach with steely gazes.

"Coinneach Odhar, the Brahan Seer, here to see the Countess Isabella by her summons," the messenger shouted. The heavy wooden gate lowered, and they entered the courtyard. A servant took their horse, and two guards escorted Coinneach to the castle's great hall.

Although he had been there before, the hall's grandeur and opulence always astounded Coinneach. Large tapestries depicting scenes from ancient battles and legends adorned the walls. In between the tapestries hung coats of arms and the heads of great boars and stags. The scent of beeswax from the many candelabras filled the air.

At the far end of the hall, the Countess Isabella stood with her back toward them. The giant fireplace framed her figure, and its flames cast her long shadow across the stone floor. She turned and, with the light exaggerating the severity of her features, her reputation for homeliness became vividly clear. With a flick of her wrist, she beckoned him forward. Coinneach willed himself to keep a neutral composure as he approached.

"You summoned me, your Ladyship?" Coinneach said.

"Tell me," she demanded, "what news of my husband?"

"Is your husband not here with you?"

"My Lord is away in Paris. I have not heard from him in many days," she answered.

Coinneach felt a sudden unease at this news. While the Earl was in residence, Coinneach enjoyed his favor and protection. But would that protection be honored with the Earl away? Coinneach knew he had to tread carefully. "I can assure ye that the Earl is in good health. He is well and safe."

"I did not summon you all this way to waste my time with platitudes and generalities."

"I am sorry, my Lady, but I dare not say more."

"Unacceptable!" the Countess snapped. Her expression became fierce and impatient. "You will use your Seeing Stone and tell me everything!"

Coinneach's courage wavered. He felt his heart pounding in his chest. He felt for the reassuring weight of the smooth stone resting at the bottom of his pocket. "I must warn you, you might not like what I see. 'Tis best to be content knowing your husband is safe."

"And I must warn you, my patience wears thin. You will do as you are told, or you'll regret it!" she said. Her voice was cool and cruel.

A shiver shot down Coinneach's spine. He glanced behind him and saw that the two guards remained steadfast at the door. She had given him no choice and no escape.

"Very well," Coinneach said. Trembling, he raised the Seeing Stone to his blind eye. The room seemed to grow darker as Coinneach peered into the depths of the Seeing Stone. *Please let this vision not be my undoing*, he thought, desperately. The air grew thick with tension, and even the Countess seemed to hold her breath in anticipation. Images swirled before him, slowly taking shape. His heart raced as the vision became clearer.

"Well?" the Countess demanded.

"I see the Earl," Coinneach began hesitantly, his voice barely louder than a whisper. "He is…"

"Speak up!" The Countess's patience had reached its limit.

"The Earl is indeed well, but I…" he said, taking a deep breath. "Forgive me, but what has been seen must be spoken. The Earl, he is…" Coinneach paused, bracing himself for the storm that was sure to follow.

Chapter Thirty-Three

As the sun dipped low in the sky, casting a warm golden glow over the bustling streets of Inverness, Mr. MacCrivag pulled up to the hotel. Daniel Darrow and his parents climbed out of the crowded back seat, practically tumbling over one another onto the sidewalk. Daniel thanked Philip Morrison and MacCrivag for their help that day. He complimented Mr. MacCrivag again on his new electric car. There was no way they would have all been able to fit in his old little green car, much less make it all the way to Loch Ussie and back in a day.

"Boy, am I glad to stand and stretch my legs," Daniel's father said as he watched Mr. MacCrivag's car roll down the road.

"I bet Philip's glad to have some peace and quiet," Daniel's mother said.

"Ah, Philly's a good guy. He doesn't mind. Can I help it if I'm a curious man and he happens to be a wealth of knowledge?" Mr. Darrow said. "It was rude of that Fraser fellow to drive back on his own, though. That fancy car of his had more leg room."

"Well, the project we were helping him with didn't go quite as expected," Daniel said.

"No one enjoys receiving bad news, but that's no excuse to abandon us and drive away sulking," Mr. Darrow said.

"More like inconclusive news. Anyway, I think he needed to be alone with his thoughts," Daniel said. "Shall I walk you inside?"

They entered the hotel and went up to his parents' room. "Daniel, you really should have joined us on our hike," his mother said. "Philip Morrison was such a captivating guide."

"Next time, for sure," Daniel replied.

"Next time, it should be you *and* Ellie," his mother said.

Daniel laughed and rolled his eyes. But the mention of Ellie did remind him of a fleeting glimpse he'd caught of a text message from her earlier in the day. He'd been too busy sending Mr. Tweed a hurried message for a quick getaway to look at it, and then, in all the excitement, he'd forgotten about it.

"Speaking of Ellie, I think she texted me earlier," Daniel said, retrieving his phone from his pocket. "I was too distracted to look at it."

"Too distracted for a message from your future wife?" His mother teased, raising an eyebrow.

"The project I was helping Mr. Fraser with was very, um, tense," Daniel said. When he saw the notifications screen, his heart skipped a beat. Ellie had texted him—more than once.

Hope you're having a good day. Tell your parents Hi for me. Love.

Off so see Mum. Miss you.

Call me when you can. Urgent.

Where are you?

"Excuse me," Daniel muttered to his parents. He stepped outside and dialed Ellie's number in a hurry. Her voice came through the line, shaky and fraught with tension. "Where have you been? I texted."

"I saw. What's up?"

"There's been another death, Daniel. Eliza's simply beside herself about it."

"What? Who?" Daniel asked. "Is she okay?"

"I tried checking on her this afternoon, but she wasn't taking visitors. Perhaps she would see you, though? She seems to trust you, and you are her minister," Ellie suggested.

"I can try. How late are visiting hours?" Daniel asked. He'd been looking forward to a relaxing evening with his parents after such a long day— ordering takeout and watching a movie, but Ellie's voice sounded urgent.

"I think we have time. Where are you? I'll come pick you up."

Daniel told her the name of the hotel and then stepped back inside his parents' room to apologize once again for leaving them alone. Before he left, his father handed him the glass jar with clay from Loch Ussie.

"Here's that mud you wanted, son," he said with a bemused expression on his face, clearly hoping for an explanation. But Daniel simply thanked him and left without further comment.

Daniel only had to wait a couple of minutes outside before Ellie's car arrived. He got in, and she pulled away before he even had time to buckle his seatbelt. Her speedy arrival told him he might need it tonight.

"So, what's going on? Who died?" Daniel asked.

Ellie stared at him for a moment in disbelief. Her cinnamon-colored hair was pulled back into a tight ponytail that emphasized the worry lines creasing her forehead. "You haven't heard? It was Lexi Campbell. She... she was in a car crash last night."

"Lexi Campbell?" Daniel asked. That name sounded so familiar. But where did he know her from? Then it hit him like a load of bricks. Lexi Campbell, co-host of The Highlands Bulletin podcast. Only two weeks ago, he had been sitting across from her as she interviewed him about the wind farm. He remembered liking her much better than her co-host. Her questions were more thoughtful than his clickbait style of interrogation. Daniel had listened to the latest episode of the Bulletin just that morning when he'd been getting ready for the Sunday service. That seemed like a lifetime ago now.

"Eliza is absolutely devastated," Ellie continued, bringing Daniel back to the present. "I know that podcast was popular, but I can't understand why she's taking it so hard."

"You said you haven't been able to talk to her?" Daniel asked. None of this made any sense.

"Mum told me," Ellie said, swerving around a car that was going too slowly, which, as far as Daniel could tell, meant a crawling pace of ten over the speed limit.

"I went to visit her before lunch," Ellie continued, "and she told me that Eliza had called her that morning, simply hysterical. Eliza didn't go into details except to say that Lexi's crash wasn't an accident and that she feared she would be next."

"Next? Like *murdered* next? That's sound pretty paranoid," Daniel said.

"Mum was really worried about her. Eliza's older and with her history of seeing visions, Mum wondered if she was finally losing her mind. So, I tried to check in on her later, but the nurse said she'd practically barricaded herself in her room. She's known me my whole life and she refused to let me in."

"And you think I can get through to her?" Daniel asked, doubtfully.

"We have to try. She's not taking her medicine. The nurse said if she keeps this up, they'll have to move her to a different facility."

"Like a psychiatric ward?"

"That's what she implied."

Ellie raced down the road, accelerating around the bends and curves and other drivers. Her driving mirrored Daniel's thoughts. Eliza MacGillivray had always been eccentric, but he never thought it would come to this—a paranoid mental breakdown. Perhaps she'd had a premonition of Lexi's death? Could she even see into the future without her Seeing Stone? And why did she fear for her own life? After he and Mr. MacCrivag failed to uncover anything at the Philaguria company retreat, this never-ending day felt like a puzzle without corner pieces. He had no fixed marks to build upon, only a pile of seemingly random pieces that didn't want to fit together.

Chapter Thirty-Four

Daniel and Ellie navigated the empty hospital corridors. Visiting hours were nearly over and, other than the hospital staff, the place was deserted. When they reached Eliza's room, Daniel looked at Ellie, unsure of how to proceed. She knocked on the door and motioned for him to speak.

"Um, Ms. MacGillivray? This is Daniel Darrow. Can I come in?"

No answer.

Daniel lifted his palms and looked at Ellie. *What now?*

She motioned toward the door, *Try again.*

"Eliza, I've got Ellie Gray with me. We'd love to visit with you a bit, if that's alright."

Still no answer.

Daniel looked back at Ellie. "She yelled at me to go away, so I guess this is progress?" Ellie whispered with a shrug.

"I've brought a little present for you. Some clay from Loch Ussie, like you wanted. Remember?" Daniel said. He heard a faint shuffling around inside. Daniel held the jar of clay in one hand and slowly turned the door handle with the other. "Okay, we're going to go ahead and come in. Shout if you're not decent."

Ellie chuckled and rolled her eyes—*Seriously?* Daniel offered an uncertain smile and gently opened the door. Eliza was sitting up in her bed, staring out the window. When they stepped inside, she turned toward them. Her eyes, usually bright with life and mischief, now held a haunted look that sent shivers down Daniel's spine.

"Quickly, come in and shut the door!" She gestured nervously, her eyes darting to the hallway behind them.

Daniel shut the door and then held out the jar. "I'm sorry it's so late, but I just got back and I thought this might cheer you up."

Eliza peered at the jar and then at Daniel suspiciously.

"It's from Loch Ussie. My parents wanted to see the countryside. My dad especially, he's a real history nut. Philip Morrison gave them a tour of the loch. You know Mr. Morrison? He moved here from Stornoway to take over Archie Caird's tour company. Of course, you know him. MacCrivag's been a member of Church Street nearly as long as you have," Daniel rambled on. Eliza's disposition unnerved him, and he needed to fill the silence.

"Is that…mud?" Eliza squinted at the jar, her paranoia momentarily forgotten. "Why on earth would I want mud at a time like this?"

"For your, um, never mind," Daniel mumbled and placed the jar on the windowsill.

"Were you followed?" Eliza asked, her eyes searching their faces for signs of danger.

"No, it's just us," Ellie reassured her, placing her hand on the older woman's arm. Eliza flinched at her touch. "Mum's worried about you. What's going on?"

"You're not recording this?" Eliza asked. Daniel and Ellie exchanged baffled glances and then shook their heads, *No*. "Let me see your mobiles," Eliza demanded. They handed over their phones, and Eliza examined the devices before placing them under her pillow. She eyed them suspiciously before deciding she could trust them. She gestured for them to come closer.

"You've heard about Lexi Campbell's death?" Eliza asked, her voice barely above a whisper.

They both nodded solemnly. "Car accident. It's just…tragic," Daniel said.

"Accident? I assure you, Reverend, Lexi Campbell's death was no accident!" Eliza's eyes widened as she spoke, and for a moment, Daniel saw the flicker of something else beneath her fear—determination, perhaps, or even anger?

"That's what they do," Eliza continued. "They make it look like an accident, so no one asks questions. Like the man who *accidentally* fell from the wind turbine, Sayyid Ghulam."

"Who's *they*? Who would do that?" Daniel asked. Eliza stared at him like he'd just asked a question with the most obvious of answers. "Philaguria Energy?" Daniel suggested. "George Fraser thinks they're trying to sabotage the wind farm. It makes sense—get rid of the competition. In fact, he recently found out that the construction foreman who gave us a tour of the turbines is a former Philaguria employee."

"George Fraser?" Eliza asked, alarmed. "He's the last person you should be with up there. It's a wonder you didn't meet the same fate as Mr. Ghulam."

"You can't be serious. George wouldn't kill someone. It's not in his nature. But even if he could, he wouldn't have killed Sayyid. He's heavily invested in GlenBreeze Dynamics. And he's told me that ever since the investigation into Sayyid's death halted construction, the company's been bleeding cash," Daniel said.

"Exactly," Eliza said, as if Daniel had just answered his own question.

"I don't follow," Daniel said.

"It always comes down to money, doesn't it? An accidental death would naturally prompt an investigation, but once GlenBreeze Dynamics passes a safety review, which they will likely conduct internally, they can resume business as usual. But a murder investigation..." Eliza said, her voice trailed off, leaving the unsaid conclusion hanging in the air like a dark cloud.

"Would take much longer," Ellie jumped in, completing her thought. "So, while they may be losing money now in the short term, a murder investigation would cost them a lot more longer term."

"Wait, let me get this straight," Daniel said. He stood and scratched his head. "You're saying that the very company losing money because of Sayyid's death actually killed him and covered it up in order to *save* money?"

Chapter Thirty-Five

Daniel paced to the door and back. He could accept the supposition that Sayyid's death was no accident. But could he really believe someone at GlenBreeze Dynamics was behind it? For the last several days, Mr. Tweed had convinced him that Philaguria Energy had killed Sayyid as a form of corporate revenge or sabotage. And Tweed's theory had made sense. Philaguria had covered up a murder once before, after all. But they had found no evidence at the company retreat that Philaguria had any interest in the wind farm at all.

So, was Mr. Tweed simply trying to throw him off the trail? It seemed like an overelaborate ruse. Still, as Eliza had pointed out, money is a powerful motivator. And the more money that's on the line, the greater the lengths people are willing to go to keep it.

"Okay, let's put aside the possibility that George Fraser could be involved in this—" Daniel said, returning to his seat at Eliza's bedside.

"Why?" Eliza asked, interrupting him. "If you're so keen on underestimating people, might I remind you of a certain ex-choir director sitting in a prison cell right now?"

"Fair point," Daniel conceded. "But what does any of this have to do with Lexi Campbell's fatal car crash?"

"Ah, poor Ms. Campbell," Eliza sighed. She gazed out the window for a moment before returning her attention to Daniel and Ellie. "I'd been talking with her about my vision and theories, hadn't I. She was working on a follow-up story for her computer radio program."

"The Highlands Bulletin podcast?" Daniel asked.

"Aye, that's it. She didn't take as much convincing as you two. She was ready to publish the story when, well…" Eliza's voice trailed off.

"Eliza, are you saying that someone killed Lexi to silence her?" Ellie asked, her eyes widening with realization.

"We need to find out what Sayyid and Lexi knew that would make killing them less expensive than keeping them alive," Daniel said.

"Exactly," Eliza said. "And since Lexi got her story from me, it's my fault she was killed."

"You can't blame yourself; you couldn't have known that would happen," Daniel said.

"But I should have seen it coming. I've always seen things coming. Or I used to," Eliza said as she touched the place on her neck where her Seeing Stone once hung. She glanced over at the jar of clay Daniel had placed on the windowsill. "That's from Loch Ussie?"

Daniel nodded.

"Thank you for bringing it. But I fear that even if the Seeing Stone can be mended, it might be too late."

"Too late for what?" Daniel asked.

"Too late for me," Eliza said grimly. "If they're willing to kill a reporter, what's keeping them from coming after her source next?"

"That's why you're not allowing visitors," Ellie said.

"Don't take it personally, luv. I don't know who I can trust, and I didn't want to put anyone else in danger."

Ellie took Eliza's hand in hers. "You're in a hospital. You're safe here. You have doctors and nurses caring for you."

"You have a good heart, Ellie. Too good. You lack your mother's sense of skepticism and suspicion," Eliza said. Ellie pulled back her hand. "It's a blessing, dear. You see the good in people. But such rosy vision can also keep you from seeing the danger that's right in front of you."

"Eliza, Ellie's right. You're safe here," Daniel said. He wasn't sure if Eliza's words were a compliment or an insult, but he could tell that Ellie was uncomfortable with the comparison. "But if you feel you're truly in danger, we should go to the police. Maybe they can do something."

"You don't think I've tried that already?" Eliza asked. "The police don't believe me! They think I'm a feeble old woman who's lost her mind. No, the police wrote me and my prophesies off long ago."

"Okay, then we…" Daniel sighed, trying to think of what might calm or reassure her. After seeing Ms. MacGillivray in this state, he couldn't leave her alone. But neither could he stay with her; he had his parents and his church duties to attend to, not to mention trying to uncover Sayyid and Lexi's true killer. "We could talk to the nurses—let them know that you're concerned and—"

"You're not getting it, Reverend," Eliza interrupted him again. "Oh, I wish Elspeth were here. She would understand. She doesn't deserve to be locked away in the dreadful place."

Ellie's mom is a sweet woman, but she did burn down that historic manor, Daniel thought, knowing better than to speak his objection in present company. Instead, he asked, "Why would Mrs. Gray understand?"

"Because Elspeth saw the connection between the Broonburn estate and Philaguria's scheming. She knew their offer to renovate the place and provide local jobs was too good to be true—and it was. Why would an energy company want to get into the less lucrative tourism industry? Well, I got suspicious after I learned of Lexi's death, and I took a page out of her book, so to speak. I followed the money to discover that GlenBreeze Dynamics, the company behind your precious wind farm, recently made a large donation to this very hospital," Eliza said.

Just then, a knock sounded from the door. A nurse peeked her head in. "I'm sorry, but visiting hours are just about over. Unless you are family, you'll have to leave."

"Sure," Daniel said. "Just let us say goodbye, and we'll be out in a couple of minutes."

"Five minutes," the nurse said sternly and shut the door.

"We have to say something," Daniel said, turning back to Eliza and Ellie. "Even if GlenBreeze has some influence here, they can't have gotten to everyone in the hospital."

"Daniel's right," Ellie agreed. "There's got to be plenty of good people here.

I have an old friend from uni that works in the morgue, perhaps he—"

"No," Eliza interrupted. "There's something more I haven't told you. My last vision—the one that cracked the Seeing Stone and put me in this dreadful hospital—I finally remembered the rest of it."

Daniel and Ellie leaned in closer, anxious to hear her words. They dared not speak or even breathe, worried the slightest noise might scare Eliza back into silence. Eliza closed her eyes and rubbed her finger and thumb together as if the Seeing Stone was still whole and in her grasp. When she opened her mouth, her words came out no louder than a whisper:

"Beware the hand that offers gold, lest it unsheathe its claws. When raven caws, the trusted heart shall pierce as thistle under foot."

Daniel and Ellie leaned back and glanced at one another nervously. "What does it mean?" Daniel asked.

"Betrayal," Eliza said, opening her eyes. "The Brahan Seer was betrayed by his benefactor, the one he'd trusted for protection. So was Sayyid."

"And you think you'll be next. That's the real reason you wouldn't let anyone in to see you, isn't it," Ellie said.

Eliza nodded. "That's the thing about betrayal—you never see it coming. The best thing for me now is to keep my mouth shut. If they believe they've scared me into silence, they may leave it at that. I am a batty old woman, after all," she said with a chuckle. "So, we'll let them think they've won, and I'll focus my energy on healing and getting out of here as quickly as possible."

"Are you sure?" Ellie asked. Eliza nodded. "You're not alone in this. Call me or Daniel anytime, and we'll be here. Well, call *me* first—he tends to be slow to pick up his phone," she said with a critical eye toward Daniel.

Daniel grimaced and shrugged apologetically. "We'll get to the bottom of this, I promise."

Eliza smiled. "Tell that nurse when you leave that I wouldn't say why I'm so bothered. Tell her I didn't say a thing to you. Be careful out there and be wary of who you trust."

Chapter Thirty-Six

A cheerful melody echoed through the empty nave of Church Street Kirk, bouncing off its stone walls and reverberating through its high wooden beams. Amir Nazar sat behind the piano with his eyes closed while his fingers danced across the keys. Daniel paused for a moment to listen before approaching. Despite his best attempt at stealth, Amir soon became aware of his presence.

"Ah, Daniel," Amir said, opening his eyes.

"Please, don't let me stop you. That's beautiful," Daniel said.

Amir grinned and continued playing for another couple of minutes. "Are we meeting in here?" he asked once the song had finished.

"I thought so," Daniel said. He pulled up the calendar on his phone. "Yeah, that's what I have. So, where's the boss?" he asked, glancing around the cavernous space.

"Sorry, sorry," Reverend Sarah Calder said as she hurried in and took a seat on one of the choir chairs near the piano. "I forgot we were meeting here. My office is such a mess right now. Let's see, we were going to discuss this Sunday's service, yes? It's Trinity Sunday, so we've got readings from, let's see..." She opened a large binder and flipped through its pages. "Ah, the first chapter of Genesis, Psalm 8, and the 28th chapter of the book of Matthew. Amir, what were you thinking about hymns?"

"Here's what the choir has been working on this week," Amir said, handing her a notepad. Rev. Calder looked it over and nodded approvingly.

"I haven't heard this one in a long time. That should be fun," she said. "I can work it into my sermon."

"World Environment Day is this week too. Should we emphasize that? We do have the Genesis passage," Daniel suggested. "And I think the children's Sunday School has been making a big Noah's Ark banner about endangered species to hang in the kirk hall."

"We should mention it," Rev. Calder said after considering for a moment. "And have the weans put up their poster. But let's not emphasize the day quite like we did last year."

"No? I thought folks really enjoyed that service," Daniel said.

"Aye, but that was a year ago, before…well…the kirk and city are in a different place now," Rev. Calder said, trying her best to be diplomatic.

"You mean before the wind farm," Daniel said. Rev. Calder nodded. "Last year, it was just a nice idea. People were still reeling from Philaguria's fracking scheme and Broonburn. But now the wind farm's a reality. Some people don't like the way it looks and…" he glanced at Amir, his words failing.

"And now there's been another death," Amir said, finishing Daniel's thought. "I hear people talk. They are wondering if there is a true difference between Philaguria and GlenBreeze Dynamics. It seems whenever there is a new energy project in this city, people end up dead."

"I'm beginning to wonder if there's a difference, too," Daniel said. "I mean, obviously, the type of energy is different. I helped campaign for renewable energy, but—"

"Exactly," Rev. Calder interjected. "I know your friend's death was deemed an accident," she said to Amir, before returning her focus to Daniel, "but it's still got the town shaken up. People are questioning more than simply the aesthetics of the wind farm. They're doubting its overall safety and whether it's truly beneficial for the community. And since you campaigned for the project, Daniel, I'm afraid some of that doubt is being directed at you."

"Me?" he asked, incredulous. "But I did my research. Unlike Philaguria, this project is actually going to create long-term jobs and help the environment."

"Sometimes people just need someone to blame, and since you were the face of the campaign, at least for the kirk, you're an easy target.

Regardless," Reverend Calder said, refocusing the conversation, "we must remain sensitive to the congregation's feelings during this time. And on that note, Amir, let's strike *The Bright Wind of Heaven is Blowing*. No wind-related hymns. How about something a bit more, em, grounded, like *Rock of Ages*?"

Amir nodded. After a little more back and forth, they eventually finalized the plan for the service. Before they dispersed, Amir had one last item for the agenda. "I'm sorry if this sounds silly, I don't want to waste your time, but I've been having trouble with the kirk cat."

"Sir Walter Scott? I thought he liked you," Daniel said.

"What mischief has he gotten into now?" Rev. Calder asked.

"It might be easier if I showed you," Amir said.

"Reverend Darrow?" Rev. Calder said. Daniel raised his eyebrows in protest. "You're our resident cat keeper."

"Yeah, I'm not sure how that happened," Daniel protested.

"Cats, like our Lord, work in mysterious ways. Ta," Rev. Calder said and waved them goodbye.

"Alright, show me," Daniel said, admitting defeat. He followed Amir to his office—the room that had once belonged to Mr. Fisher.

The ex-choir director had never invited Daniel into his office before. Once Amir opened the door, Daniel knew why. The room was far larger than he expected—prime real estate within the small kirk building. Especially considering his own workspace had once been a storage closet. He still occasionally found a can of donated food stuffed in some forgotten corner. Daniel wished he'd thought to explore the room when he was serving as the interim choir director, but memories of Fisher had hung around the place like a spider's web that Daniel hadn't wanted to disturb.

"Here's the latest," Amir announced, gesturing toward a pile of shredded sheet music in the corner. It appeared as though the cat had taken it upon himself to construct a cozy bed from the remnants.

"Well," Daniel mused, stifling a chuckle. "Sir Walter's always had a critical ear for music."

"Very funny," Amir replied, rolling his eyes. "Luckily, those are just copies. I have to keep the original scores locked up."

"Sorry," Daniel said. "Let's see if we can cat-proof this room. Do you know how he's getting in?"

"I always close the door when I leave," Amir said.

As they searched the room and tightened all the vent covers to deter any future feline intrusions, Amir asked Daniel about his recent trip with George Fraser to the Philaguria retreat at Loch Ussie. "Did you learn anything useful about Sayyid's death?"

"Unfortunately, no," Daniel admitted. "It was a wild goose chase, really. I think we should focus our efforts a little closer to home—GlenBreeze Dynamics."

Amir raised a skeptical eyebrow. He hadn't gotten a chance to meet Eliza MacGillivray, so Daniel wasn't sure whether Amir would believe her unique insight. Even after two years and twice as many prophecies, Daniel found her visions eerily discerning. "Let's just say I have a hunch," Daniel said.

"So, what does your hunch say we should do next?" Amir asked.

"Do you remember the last time we talked to Samira?" Daniel asked as he tightened a screw on the cover of an old floor vent. "She mentioned Sayyid having some trouble at work."

"Yes, an argument with the foreman," Amir said.

"Having now met the man, I wouldn't be surprised if more of his employees had complaints about him. He didn't seem to think very highly of, well, immigrants. But I'm also wondering if the problem might have gone deeper than that. We need to find out what he and Sayyid were arguing about."

"I suppose you could not just ask the foreman?"

"And risk ending up like Sayyid? No, there's only one other person still alive that might've been privy to that conversation."

Chapter Thirty-Seven

The sound of children's laughter filled the air—a stark contrast to the gray clouds that hung low over Whin Park. Daniel, Amir, and Samira sat on a cold metal bench, watching her two boys chase each other around the playground. The weather that afternoon mirrored their somber mood.

"It's good to see them playing and laughing like this," Amir said.

"I try to get them out of the flat as much as I can. It's not good for boys to be inside all day. I don't want them to forget their father, but some days Sayyid's presence in those small rooms can be…" Samira paused for a moment, thinking of the right words. "It is hard to breathe."

"I know it's difficult to talk about," Daniel said gently, leaning forward to address her more directly, "but is there anything you can remember about Sayyid's job or his relationship with his boss that might help us understand what happened?"

Samira sat in silence for several moments. Her eyes darted back and forth between Daniel and Amir before settling back on her children at play. "Sayyid did not want me to worry, but I know they did not get on well."

"I met him, the foreman. And he didn't strike me as an easy man to get along with. My friend George Fraser set it up. He had a theory about the foreman, but it didn't really pan out. Is there anything else you can remember about the disagreements between him and your husband?"

"I…I don't know. I can't think of anything."

Daniel studied her body language, noting the way she tugged nervously at her headscarf while avoiding direct eye contact. This was more than mere modesty or shyness. It was clear she was holding something back, but he couldn't pinpoint exactly what. As if reading his mind, Amir placed a hand on his shoulder.

"Daniel, why don't you go give the boys a push on the swings?" Amir said. "I'll stay here with Samira for a moment."

"Sure." Daniel rose from the bench. Perhaps a one-on-one conversation with someone she was more familiar with would yield better results.

As Daniel reached the swings, he found himself lost in thought—picking apart every word of their brief exchange and searching for any hidden meanings behind Samira's hesitance. He gave each boy a gentle push, their giggles cutting through the day's dreary pall. He glanced back at Amir and Samira, noticing the intensity of their quiet conversation.

"Higher, higher!" the older boy shouted. Daniel complied, pushing him high into the air.

"All right, kids," Daniel said when he noticed Amir finally standing up from the bench. "Looks like it's time for us to go."

Samira walked over to them and helped the youngest out of his swing. "But I want more!" the older boy shouted, kicking his feet to restart the swing. Samira gave him a look that only a mother could give. "Fine," the boy said and hopped down.

"Thank you for your time, Samira," Amir said kindly, his tone conveying a mixture of gratitude and concern. "Boys, mind your mother. I'll see you again soon."

"Bring Rev Darrow. He's better at swings," the oldest boy said.

"Okay," Daniel laughed. He nodded to Samira. "Take care."

She nodded back and took her boys each by the hand. As they walked away, Daniel turned to Amir. "Well?"

Amir shook his head and started walking in the opposite direction. Daniel followed. They strolled to the shore where couples paddled small boats around a calm section of the river.

"All right," Daniel said, unable to wait any longer. He glanced back and could no longer see Samira or her children. They were clearly out of earshot now. "What did she tell you? It's obvious she was holding something back."

Amir sighed. He stared out across the water. "She's afraid, Daniel. She's holding back because she's terrified."

"Of what?" Daniel furrowed his brow. "Christie, the foreman?"

Amir shook his head and then turned to face Daniel with a serious look in his eyes. "You."

"Me?" Daniel asked, baffled. "She's afraid of me? Is it the religious difference? Or my history with the police?"

Amir shook his head and turned back to gaze at the small boats floating calmly down the river. "It's your connection to George Fraser. She knows he's an important person at the wind farm, and she's afraid of what might happen to her or her boys if she talks."

"Fraser?" Daniel asked. That was the second time in as many days he'd heard George Fraser, Mr. Tweed, spoken of with such fearful suspicion.

"How well do you know this George Fraser?" Amir asked.

"Enough to consider him a friend. He may be a bit stuffy and condescending, but I don't think he could murder someone. His business and political connections were instrumental in getting the wind farm here."

Amir raised a suspicious eyebrow.

"So, of course, he would have a lot to lose if there were problems with the project," Daniel admitted.

"Enough to silence someone who found out about those problems?" Amir asked.

Daniel thought of Lexi Campbell and Eliza MacGillivray. If Mr. Tweed or someone else was trying to keep people silent, it was working.

Chapter Thirty-Eight

Daniel pushed open the door to the bakery and was immediately struck by the aroma of freshly baked breads and desserts. He breathed in the sweet, buttery air and smiled. Now this was one aspect of wedding planning that he could get behind!

Vintage floral wallpaper covered the walls of the small shop. Below the long front counter were display cases filled with all manner of sweet treats: biscuits, short breads, jelly tarts, eclairs. The scents and warmth of the shop wrapped around him like a plush blanket, inviting him to slip into a delicious sugar coma and forget the troubles of the outside world.

"Ah, there you are!" Ellie greeted him, her cheeks flushed with excitement as she waved from a small round table near the window. "I thought your mother was joining us for the cake tasting?"

"I thought I might be late, so I texted her to meet us here. My last meeting was…a lot," Daniel said and sat down next to her.

"Oh?"

"We don't have to get into it now. This is supposed to be fun," Daniel said. He stared out a nearby window as rain began to patter against the glass.

"We have to wait for your mum, anyway. Here, have a macaron and tell me about it—if it's not, like, confidential or something," Ellie said. She pushed a small plate with two little pink sandwich cookies toward him.

"Won't this ruin my appetite for cake later?"

"I won't tell if you won't," Ellie said with a wink and picked up one of the macarons for herself.

Daniel laughed and bit into the crunchy shell of the cookie, which gave way to a sweet, soft interior. If the cakes here were anything like this, they were in for a real treat. He glanced up at Ellie, hating to rain on her good mood. "I met with Samira earlier this afternoon."

"How is she? I can't imagine what she must be going through. And her boys? Oh, and Gula, this must be hard on her, too," Ellie said.

"Gula?" Daniel asked.

"Gula," Ellie repeated, as if he should know. "Their pet partridge. I treated it for mites once. Never mind, that's not important. You said you met with Samira?"

"Yes, and her boys were there. They seemed okay. I don't know how much they truly understand about what happened to their dad. But Samira, she's scared."

"Why?"

Daniel glanced around the small shop and then leaned in closer. "She's terrified of George Fraser. I don't know exactly why, but she thinks he had something to do with Sayyid's death," he whispered.

"Really?" Ellie asked, surprise and concern etched across her face. She leaned close and lowered her voice as well. "You remember, Eliza warned us about Mr. Fraser, too. I don't think it's a coincidence."

"I've been thinking the same thing. On the bus ride over here, I kept going over her last prophecy from the Brahan Seer," Daniel said. He pulled a pocket notebook from his jacket and flipped through the pages. "Here: 'As you will know that which will make you unhappy, I must tell you the truth. My lord seems to have little thought of you, or of his children, or of his Highland home.'" Daniel closed the notebook. "Eerie, isn't it?"

Ellie's expression changed to puzzlement.

"Maybe I'm reading too much into it, but it does seem to fit," Daniel admitted. "George Fraser is a wealthy, powerful man. If he is involved in this, he clearly has little regard for others or this city."

Ellie nodded solemnly. "So, you're finally a believer in the Seer and Eliza's visions?"

"I don't know. I guess so? Either way, I have to know if he had anything to do with Sayyid's death. No matter how unhappy such knowledge would make me. It wouldn't be the first time I trusted someone who didn't deserve it." Daniel said, thinking of Amir's predecessor at Church Street. He put his half-eaten macaron down. The sense of betrayal had put a sour taste in his mouth.

"There's one thing I don't understand," Ellie said. "Why would Fraser want you to go with him to spy on that Philaguria company retreat? If he knew he or GlenBreeze was the real villain here, why the ruse? Why take that trip and risk getting caught?"

"To throw me off? Cast the blame somewhere else? Given my history with that company, he must have known I'd be more than willing to believe that Philaguria was behind another murder. And they're still full of greedy, ruthless people. Perhaps Fraser hoped I'd overhear what I wanted to hear and corroborate his story? Me pointing a finger away from his company would be more convincing than him doing it."

"So, what are you going to do? How do you go after someone like George Fraser, with all his family's money and connections? Church Street Kirk isn't the only organization he donates to. The cardiac ward of the hospital isn't called Fraser Tower for nothing."

"Now I can understand Eliza's paranoia," Daniel sighed. "Well, we've taken down one powerful businessman before; we can do it again. But first, we have to find out what Sayyid knew that could've gotten him killed. And the only person who might know that won't talk to me. The second I mentioned that I was friends with Fraser, she clammed up."

Ellie pursed her lips thoughtfully before responding. "Well, maybe she just needs someone she trusts a bit more to help her open up."

"Amir was with me. He tried but—"

"Someone prettier than Amir," Ellie retorted.

"Wait," Daniel said, confused, "*you?*"

Just then, the tinkling of the bell above the door announced the arrival of Mrs. Darrow. "Hello, you two!" she exclaimed, pulling up a chair and joining them. "This place is just precious! Sorry I'm late. I had the worst taxi ever. I couldn't understand the driver; he couldn't understand me. I thought folks in this country spoke English?"

"That's what I thought about Americans," Ellie quipped under her breath. Daniel chuckled.

"What's that, hon? You'll have to speak up," Mrs. Darrow said.

"Nothing. I'm glad you could make it," Ellie said.

"And then it started to rain. Ugh, I'm soaked. Anyway, tell me all about these cakes! Have you found any favorites yet?" Mrs. Darrow asked. She glanced around the bakery, eyes beaming. "Just so precious."

"Actually, Mom, we were waiting for you," Daniel said as he stood. "And now that you're here, I'll go tell them to bring on the samples!"

"Perfect. While you're doing that. Ellie and I can talk color schemes! I was thinking pink and white, or perhaps cream. Classic," Mrs. Darrow said. She quietly clapped her hands. "Oh, this is going to be such fun."

"See if they serve wine too!" Ellie said with a desperate quiver in her voice as she watched Daniel walk away.

Chapter Thirty-Nine

The sun had barely crept below the horizon when Daniel and Ellie arrived at Samira's apartment. Daniel held a small paper bag from the bakery in one hand and a closed, dripping umbrella in the other. Ellie held a box of birdseed treats for Gula.

"Ready?" Daniel asked.

Ellie replied with a determined nod, her eyes partially covered by the fog on her glasses lenses. She wiped them clean and then knocked on the door. They waited in tense silence. After what felt like an eternity, the door finally creaked open just enough for Samira to peer out. Her eyes darted between the two visitors.

"Ellie, Reverend Darrow?" she asked uncertainly.

"Good evening, Mrs. Ghulam," Ellie said warmly, holding up the box of birdseed treats. "I brought a wee treat for your feathered friend."

"And I've brought something too," Daniel said, holding the bakery bag in front of him like an offering.

With a cautious smile, Samira opened the door wider, allowing them to enter. The room was dimly lit, casting shadows across the humble furnishings. "Thank you," she murmured, carefully taking the box from Ellie and setting it aside.

"How is Gula? I trust the medication I gave you took care of her mites?" Ellie asked.

Samira nodded. "The mites are gone, but she's been less active, less vocal since Sayyid..."

"That makes sense," Ellie said. "Animals form emotional bonds like people.

Gula's probably missing him, too. Hopefully, these treats will cheer her up a bit."

"These are for you and the boys," Daniel said, handing her the bakery bag. "Shortbread."

"They're in their room now. I'll save this for after dinner," Samira said, a subtle hint that she did not anticipate this unexpected visit to last very long.

"I know that we don't know each other very well, but I hope that you can trust me," Daniel said. "I really do want justice for your husband. If you could just give me a minute to explain."

Samira motioned for them to sit down in the living room. "Can I offer you a drink?" She didn't want them to stay, but she shared her adopted country's etiquette regarding visitors and tea.

"Thank you, yes," Ellie said. She continued while Samira put on a kettle. "Mrs. Ghulam, I know you're scared about what happened and about the future, but we've always gotten on well," Ellie said, trying to reassure her. "You trust Amir. You trust me. You can trust Daniel. He has his flaws, sure," she said as she took his hand and looked into his eyes, "but I trust him enough to want to spend the rest of my life with him. He has a good heart and a stubbornness for not giving up on people or causes that others have long written off."

"You are a lucky man, Reverend. Ms. Gray is a good and kind woman. Thank you both for the treats, but I've already told you all I know," Samira said.

She was clearly still hesitant to open up. *Well,* Daniel thought, *Ellie did the best she could. She got us in the door. The only card I have left to play is the truth—full disclosure.*

"Mrs. Ghulam, can I tell you a story? It's kind of long, but I hope it will prove what Ellie's said about me and why it's so important that we talk to you," Daniel said. Samira nodded. "Okay, have you ever heard of Broonburn House?"

Daniel proceeded to tell her about his history with Philaguria Energy and Ellie's mother. He told the story of his old flatmate and of Amir's predecessor at the kirk. He told her of Eliza MacGillivray's prophecies and their suspicions about Mr. Tweed. When he was finally finished, their cups of tea were dry. Samira leaned back in her chair to process everything he had said.

"I know that you're scared," Daniel said. "But we want to help you and make sure that what happened to Sayyid doesn't happen to anyone else. And we can't do that unless you talk to us."

"Please, Mrs. Ghulam," Ellie added.

Samira bit her lip, torn between her fear and their pleas. Finally, she let out a trembling breath and whispered, "There is one thing I have not told you. Sayyid…he was worried about something at work."

"Right, the foreman. They had arguments," Daniel said.

"It was more than arguments. Sayyid did not tell me. He did not want to worry me. We had already been through so much, and he was only trying to provide for his family," Samira said. She started to tear up and reached for a tissue. She wiped her eyes and then stood.

Wondering if that meant the end of the meeting, Daniel began to stand. Perhaps they had pushed too hard.

"Please, sit. I must show you something," Samira said.

Daniel watched her leave the room and then looked at Ellie. Ellie shrugged and shook her head. Neither one of them dared speak. They simply waited in anxious anticipation for Samira's return. Daniel could hear the faint voices of Samira's two boys talking and laughing in another room. The wind howled outside the window. The storm outside was intensifying. Daniel dreaded going back out into it. He heard thunder and then a strange tapping coming from the window. He turned to see what it was, but it was too dark to see anything. Lightning struck, and in that brief moment of illumination, Daniel saw a large black bird flutter away. Its caw echoed through the night.

"Was that a crow?" he asked.

"Raven," Ellie said. The apprehension in her eyes told him that she was thinking the same thing he was—Eliza's final prophecy. "Beware the hand that offers gold, lest it unsheathe its claws," she whispered.

"When raven caws, the trusted heart shall pierce as thistle under foot," Daniel answered.

They heard footsteps approaching and turned to see Samira returning with something in her hands.

"I found this among his things after…after he died," Samira said as she returned. She handed Ellie an unsealed envelope. "He never sent it."

Ellie carefully unfolded the letter inside and began to read out loud. "Dear Mr. Gilbert Ross at GlenBreeze Dynamics." Ellie paused and glanced up. "Gilbert Ross?"

"Never heard of him," Daniel said. Samira shook her head.

"I write to you again about my worries over the safety of workers and the construction of the wind turbines at the Moray Firth site. I confess I am not an expert in construction, but I have been chosen as spokesman for my crew. They tell me the building materials are weak and insufficient. We do not have proper safety equipment or supplies. I have brought this concern to our foreman, Mr. Christie, but he does nothing. A friend, I will not say his name, saw Mr. Christie pass several pound notes to a building inspector last week. It may be nothing, but it is not a thing I can simply ask Mr. Christie. I fear that if something is not done soon, someone will get hurt. This is the third official complaint I have made. Please respond, or I will seek help outside the company. Signed, Sayyid Ghulam."

Ellie took a long breath and handed the letter to Daniel. He scanned it, unable to believe what he had just heard.

"This is…" Daniel said, folding the letter and slipping it back inside the envelope. "Mrs. Ghulam, thank you for sharing this with us. This goes much farther than a mere complaint. I toured one of the towers with my father, who's a mechanical engineer, just retired. Anyway, this reminded me; he actually said something very similar about shoddy materials."

He handed the envelope back to Samira. She was about to put it away when he had a second thought. "Wait, you never shared this with the police?"

"I did not want them to think we were troublemakers. And I do not want anyone else to get hurt. There must be a good reason Sayyid never sent it," Samira said.

"Or he never got the chance," Daniel said. "Could I take a picture of the letter? Don't worry, I won't show it to anyone else without your permission.

But it could be important."

She hesitantly handed it back to Daniel, who spread the letter out on the arm of the couch and snapped a picture of it with his phone. He thanked her again and told her to tell her boys 'Hi' for him.

As they left Samira's apartment, Daniel turned to Ellie. "I have to confront George Fraser about this. I won't tell him about the letter, but I've got to know if he knew anything about Sayyid's complaints."

"Or if he knows who Gilbert Ross is," Ellie added.

Daniel nodded and picked up his umbrella. They could hear the rain and the wind battering against the building even before they reached the exit. "Are you ready for this?" Daniel asked, opening the umbrella. Ellie wrapped her arm around his, and they stepped together out into the storm.

Chapter Forty

"Ah, ma chérie," the Earl of Seaforth murmured in his thick Scottish accent, sensing the young woman's hesitation. She turned her head coyly and ran a finger down the gilded wood bedpost, which shimmered in the soft candlelight. Mirrors framed in gold hung from the walls, reflecting the tiny dancing flames of the crystal candelabra and sconces. Fine purple velvet window drapes muffled the sounds of the bustling Parisian streets outside.

"I am a wealthy and respected man back in my homeland," the Earl said. His voice oozed with arrogance as he caressed the lace collar of her blouse.

"My lord, n'avez-vous pas une femme, a wife, et des enfants?" she asked, tilting her head to meet his gaze. Her eyes searched his for any indication that he might change his mind and withhold payment.

"Right now, my family is but a distant memory," Lord Seaforth replied, not missing a beat. "From the moment I laid eyes upon you, you have consumed my thoughts entirely. You are my world."

The young woman smiled, flattered by his words, and leaned in to kiss him. "Then let me consume more than your thoughts, mon seigneur," she whispered, as they fell back onto the bed.

* * *

Coinneach Odhar stood in the great hall of Brahan Castle before the Countess, the Lady Seaforth. He held his breath as he removed the Seeing Stone from his eye, releasing the image of her husband's affair.

"As you would know that which would make you unhappy, I must tell you the truth. My lord seems to have little thought of you, or of his children, or of his Highland home," Coinneach said. "I'm sorry, my lady."

The Countess's face flushed crimson as she listened. Rage and embarrassment contorted her features into a truly terrifying visage. She clenched her fists, barely able to contain herself. She glanced at the guards standing at the door on the other side of the room and then back at Coinneach.

He could see the storm brewing behind her eyes, and he stepped back, bracing himself for the outburst. The Countess's eyes narrowed as she stared at him, but instead of shouting, she beckoned him forward with her finger. Coinneach approached her cautiously. Her icy silence frightened him more than any shouting. When he was so close to her face that he could smell her wine-soured breath, she spoke, her voice barely a whisper.

"How dare you utter such vile lies about my husband and in my home?"

"Please, my lady, you insisted," Coinneach stammered, trying to apologize once more. But the Countess cut him off with an impatient wave of her hand.

"Twas bad enough that you would accuse my lord in private, but to do so within earshot of the guards and servants? This will be a scandal for the whole of the Highlands!" Her lips trembled as she whispered. "I'll never be able to face my ladies or the wives of other lairds if this gets out—to think that I have less charm than some common French maid..."

Coinneach opened his mouth to speak, but she continued, her voice cold and hard.

"Perhaps you should have lied, Seer. For the truth cannot save you now. The only way to save face is to make everyone believe that you are nothing but a liar and a slanderer."

Before he could react, the Countess's hand flew through the air, hitting his face with a resounding crack. The sharp sting brought tears to his eyes, and he blinked furiously, trying to maintain what composure he had left.

"Guards!" she bellowed, her voice echoing through the cavernous hall. "I know you've been listening to that false prophecy. So, hear me now. Seize him!"

The men who had been pretending not to listen immediately sprang into action, rushing to her side. They grabbed Coinneach roughly by the arms, forcing him to his knees.

"Coinneach Odhar, the so-called Seer of Brahan, you have spoken evil and vilified the mighty of the land," the Countess declared, her voice booming through the hall. "You have defamed a mighty chief in the midst of his vassals, abused my hospitality, outraged my feelings, and sullied the good name of my lord in the halls of his ancestors!"

Coinneach struggled to stand, but the guards held him fast. He tried to find words, but his mind was a whirlwind of fear and surprise.

"Silence!" the Countess snapped. "There is but one punishment befitting these crimes and one satisfaction for my vengeance—death."

"Please, m'lady! Grant me mercy, or at least wait for the Earl to return and confirm my vision!" Coinneach begged.

She was unmoved. Her expression remained cold and resolute as she raised her hand to silence him. "Enough! We will lead a procession from the castle to Loch Ussie, so that all may bear witness to your betrayal and my lord's strength. There, you will be executed immediately." She turned to one of the guards. "Send out messengers, spread the word," she said and then stormed out of the hall.

Her pronouncement hung heavily in the air. Coinneach's heart sank as the guards began to drag him away. He couldn't help but wonder how his fate had turned so quickly. Had he not been warned of the Countess's fickle temper? He silently cursed the Seeing Stone for showing him everyone's fate but his own.

On the shores of Loch Ussie, a crowd had gathered. Their murmurs filled the air with an uneasy anticipation. The Countess stood before them, proud and authoritative. Her steely gaze never wavered from the detested figure of the once respected and sought-after Seer, now condemned and shamed.

"Bring forth the barrel of tar!" she commanded. As servants hurried to obey, she raised her voice once more to address the masses. "Hear me, people of Brahan and of the Highlands! Many amongst you have suffered under the evil visions of this man, this false prophet. Now he has dared to blaspheme our noble house with vile lies!"

Murmurs of discontent rippled through the crowd. Coinneach looked out at the eyes of those who once revered him—eyes now turned cold with hate and bloodlust. He knew there was no way out for him now. Still, he struggled against the hands that held him, his heart pounding desperately for life.

"Any last words, oh great Seer?" the Countess asked with a mocking sneer.

Coinneach wrenched his arm free and reached into his pocket, drawing out his Seeing Stone. He put it to his blind eye for what he knew would be the last time. "Upon my death, a raven and a dove shall meet. If the dove be foremost and the first to take flight, you shall know my soul is free from its earthly trials and ascends to Heaven."

"Surely you—" the Countess started, but Coinneach interrupted her.

"Wait!" he said in a commanding voice. "Now I see far into the future, and I read the doom of the clan of my oppressor. The line of Seaforth will, ere many generations have passed, end in extinction and in sorrow. I see a chief, the last of his house. He will be the father of four fair-haired sons, all of whom he will follow to the tomb."

"More lies and slander!" the Countess shouted, her fury reaching a boiling point. She knew she shouldn't have allowed him any final words and now she meant to silence him forever. "Coinneach Odhar has insulted your lord and thus insulted you, Lord Seaforth's faithful servants. He has enjoyed such unhallowed communion with the unseen world. Can any of us truly believe he shall enter the blessed and holy gates of Heaven?"

"No!" cried a villager.

"Judas!" howled another

"Send the false prophet to his fate!" another shouted.

"Throw him headfirst into the boiling tar!" the Countess ordered, her eyes dark with triumph.

The guards moved him into position, preparing to carry out their grim task. Realizing this was his final moment, Coinneach hurled the Seeing Stone as far as he could into the loch's deep, blue waters. "Whosoever should find that stone shall be gifted—or cursed—just as I have been!" he declared, his voice trembling, yet defiant.

* * *

"What should we do with him?" one of the Countess's guards asked her, pointing to the barrel. Splashes of tar trailed out its overfull top and down the sides, becoming less viscous as it cooled.

"Nail on its lid and leave it for three days. Let it be a reminder to all of the power of the house of Seaforth and the terrible fate of any who dare reproach it," the Countess said.

As the crowd began to disperse, a young girl pulled on her father's coat and pointed down the shoreline. "Da, look!"

Her father gasped when he saw. "A raven and a dove together. Tis just as the Seer foretold!" He nudged those around him, who then shared his stunned silence.

After several minutes, their quiet was broken by the hammering of the lid onto the top of the tar barrel. The noise frightened the dove, which immediately took flight, circling above the crowd before flying away over the loch. The raven, however, simply cawed its displeasure and stubbornly stood its ground.

As if with one mind, the crowd slowly turned their heads toward the Countess. Fuming, she stared at the dove until it disappeared into the sky. "Lies," she mumbled to herself. Then she spun around on her heel and marched away toward the safety of her castle.

Chapter Forty-One

Daniel Darrow sat behind the desk in his cramped closet of an office at the kirk. He gripped a phone receiver in one hand and held the other hesitantly over the dial pad. He thought back to the final part of Eliza MacGillivray's vision: Beware the hand that offers gold, lest it unsheathe its claws. When raven caws, the trusted heart shall pierce as thistle under foot. Eliza believed that Sayyid and Lexi had died because someone had betrayed them, and she feared she would be next.

But Daniel had been in her vision too, standing on the Kessock Bridge, watching the deadly scene unfold. He couldn't shake the nagging feeling that her warning might be meant for him as well. If Keith Christie was Sayyid's betrayer, then who was Daniel's? Only one person seemed to fit the bill; only one man who kept popping up at every stage of his investigation—Daniel's friend and benefactor of sorts, George Fraser, aka Mr. Tweed. Was he really ready to confront his friend? And what if he was wrong? An accusation of murder was not something one could easily take back without serious consequences for the relationship. Daniel sighed and dialed the number. His call went straight to voicemail.

How was he supposed to find out if Mr. Tweed was involved in Sayyid's death if the man was screening his calls? Daniel knew he couldn't wait until next Sunday morning to see him. Someone else might get hurt or worse by then. And there was no guarantee Mr. Tweed would even show up for the Sunday morning church service.

Daniel scrolled through the kirk's mailing list to find his home contact information. Perhaps Mrs. Fraser would know where he was, if she was home. The phone rang twice before someone picked up. "Hello, Mrs. Fraser? This is Reverend Darrow from Church Street."

"Oh, hello, Reverend. You're lucky you caught me. I was just walking out the door," Mrs. Fraser said.

"I'll be quick then," Daniel said. "I was actually hoping to talk to your husband. Is he around?"

"No, have you tried his mobile?"

"I have, but I think it might be off."

"Hmm, that's right. He had that board meeting this morning, didn't he," she said.

"GlenBreeze?" Daniel asked.

"Aye, that sounds right. The wind farm one. He's had so many investments over the years, I can't keep track. But he doesn't like to be interrupted during things like that. You might try the office if it's urgent. I'll warn you, though, George won't even take my calls during business meetings," Mrs. Fraser said with a half-hearted laugh. This was clearly an unresolved sore point in their many years of marriage.

Daniel thanked her and then hung up. He looked up the number for the GlenBreeze Dynamics Inverness office, but then changed his mind. If Mr. Tweed wouldn't pick up for his own wife, he certainly wouldn't interrupt his business for him. *Well,* Daniel thought, *if he won't come to me, I'll just have to go to him.*

He looked up the office address instead. *A board meeting, huh? All the company bigwigs will be there.* One of them would have to know something about the turbines' shady construction and safety practices. Maybe he could even meet the mysterious Gilbert Ross, the addressee of Sayyid's unsent letter. Daniel grabbed his jacket and bus schedule. *Back into the lions' den,* he thought as he headed out the door.

Daniel pushed through the heavy glass doors into the lobby of the GlenBreeze Dynamics Inverness headquarters. His shoes squeaked on the gleaming marble floor as he approached the reception desk. Behind the desk, which appeared to be carved from a single polished slab of wood, stood a young woman wearing a smart, expensive-looking blouse. Behind her was a massive screen displaying a digital map of the company's regional and global operations.

"Excuse me, I was hoping to speak to George Fraser. Do you know if he's in today?" Daniel asked.

"Do you have a meeting?" she asked.

"No, I'm a friend. If you could just tell him I'm here, Daniel Darrow. I'm sure he'll want to see me," Daniel said.

"Just a moment," the receptionist said. She picked up the phone on her desk and punched a button. "Hi Orla, I have a Daniel Darrow here for Mr. Fraser. Mm-hmm. Mm-hmm. Cheers, ta."

She put down the phone and turned back to Daniel. "He's in a meeting right now. If you'd like, you can wait there, and I'll call you when he's available," she said, pointing to a seating area consisting of two leather sofas and another polished wood slab coffee table. It was hard to miss. The accent wall behind one sofa was painted in a vibrant, stylized tartan pattern.

To pass the time, Daniel caught up on several emails on his phone. He inspected a nearby display showcasing miniature models of wind turbines, each intricately crafted with tiny plaques detailing the turbines' date and height. Finally, he resorted to leaning back into the plush leather sofa and counting the ceiling tiles.

The sound of voices and footsteps interrupted his daydreaming. Two large doors flung open from the back of the room, releasing a flurry of activity into the lobby. Daniel glanced at the digital clock on the big screen behind the reception desk. It was noon, and a meeting had clearly just ended. The receptionist was preoccupied with her phone. If Daniel was going to catch Mr. Tweed, now would be the time. He stood and scanned the crowd of suits and polished shoes, searching for a familiar face.

Then he spotted him—a head of white hair bobbing above the others, George Fraser, dressed in one of his signature tweed suits. Daniel hurried forward, eager to catch his attention before he disappeared behind another set of closed doors. "Mr. Fraser!" Daniel called out and waved, hoping to be heard over the din of conversation.

Mr. Tweed turned with a look of surprise on his face. "Reverend Darrow?

What are you…We don't have a meeting scheduled, do we? Not here."

"No, but I was hoping to catch you. We need to talk about new developments concerning that little trip up to Loch Ussie the other day," Daniel said.

"Well, catch me you did," Mr. Tweed said. He whispered something to a colleague and then faced Daniel. "Come, let's talk in a more, em, private place."

He ushered Daniel down a hallway and into an empty room. It was a simple office with a desk, a couple of chairs, and pictures of someone else's family adorning the wall behind the computer monitor. Mr. Tweed shut the door and double-checked the handle before speaking. "Now, what's this about?"

"We haven't really had a chance to talk about the Philaguria company retreat that you had William MacCrivag and I crash," Daniel said.

Mr. Tweed motioned with his hand for Daniel to keep his voice down. "You didn't find anything. What more is there to discuss?" He pulled out a chair and offered it to Daniel.

"I want to know if you truly believed Philaguria was behind the troubles at the wind farm and Sayyid's death, or if it was all an elaborate play to throw me off the scent," Daniel said, remaining standing. He knew that if he sat down or got too comfortable, he would lose his nerve.

Mr. Tweed did not have the same worry. He took the chair he had offered Daniel and leaned against its back. He rubbed wrinkles into his forehead with one hand. "Perhaps I was too eager to suspect them. I was nursing old grievances rather than trying to see with clear eyes."

"What grievances?" Daniel asked.

"Years ago, when they bought the auld Broonburn Estate out from under me. I was all set to transform the place into a truly world-class golf resort. I had my investors in a row. Our offer was accepted. Then," he clapped his hands once, "just like that, they swooped in and outbid us," he said with a sigh, shaking his head. Then he glanced up at Daniel. "I'm not the only one to be blinded by past prejudice, though. If I recall, you were also quite eager to accuse them."

Daniel sucked in a breath through his teeth and sat down in the other chair. He couldn't argue with Tweed about that. "You really believed we would uncover something at that retreat, didn't you?"

Mr. Tweed nodded. "Aye, though after we came up empty, I had to rethink things. I still don't trust that foreman, Christie, but his past with Philaguria might simply be a coincidence. Actually," Mr. Tweed leaned in close and lowered his voice. "I'm beginning to suspect we should be looking closer to home, much closer."

Daniel raised a suspicious eyebrow and leaned forward in his chair, despite there being no one else in the small office to overhear them.

"I suspect someone within this very company is behind our troubles and poor Sayyid's so-called accident."

"Really?" Daniel asked. "Because I've been thinking the same thing." Mr. Tweed's words had completely thrown him. If Tweed was behind Sayyid and Lexi's deaths, he sure was good at hiding it. Daniel leaned back in his seat and stared at the tile ceiling.

Chapter Forty-Two

"So, you suspect someone higher up in the company, too?" Mr. Tweed asked Daniel. "Wait, is that what this surprise visit is about? You didn't want to simply catch up with me. You wanted to *catch* me!" Mr. Tweed sat up straight in his chair. His bushy, white eyebrows narrowed on Daniel, and he struck the floor with the butt of his cane.

"I can't believe you would come here and accuse me. Me, of all people. After everything I've done for you, all we've been through," Mr. Tweed said.

"It's not like you were at the top of my list or anything, it's just—" Daniel stammered.

"But there *is* a list, isn't there? And I'm on it?" Mr. Tweed stood up, no longer able to contain his feelings of betrayal. He paced the small room, the sound of his cane striking sharply against the hard floor with every other step.

Daniel didn't have the heart to tell him that there wasn't actually a list. It was just something Daniel had said on the spur of the moment to try to make him feel better. Tweed's reaction made Daniel immediately regret barging into his offices and accusing him, even if he hadn't actually said the words.

"Need I remind you," Mr. Tweed said, still pacing the room. "Broonburn House—I showed you where to jump the wall to get a peek inside. Tom Shaw's memorial—I led you and the boys to the spot where he died for the service. And now the wind farm—I got you and your father access to the turbine where Sayyid fell to his death."

When he said it all at once like that, Daniel had to admit that Mr. Tweed had done a great deal for him since he'd first arrived in Inverness. But he also had to admit that Mr. Tweed seemed to have a knack for being right in the middle of three major murder investigations in the past two years.

"And to top it all," Mr. Tweed continued. "I…I took you to my golf club!" He finally stopped pacing and faced the door, his back toward Daniel.

"I don't know if that last one's quite—," Daniel started to respond, but then shifted gears. "Look, I'm sorry. There were certain people that made compelling cases. But I should've trusted you. You're my friend, and you didn't deserve that."

"Who?" Mr. Tweed said, spinning around to face him. "Who accused me?"

"Why do you think someone at GlenBreeze Dynamics is involved?" Daniel asked, hoping to change the subject. He couldn't betray Eliza and Samira's trust, and he needed to know: if not Tweed, then who? "Somehow, we've both come to the same conclusion. Someone at this company was involved in Sayyid's death and possibly Lexi Campbell's."

"Lexi Campbell? The Highlands Bulletin woman? She died?" Mr. Tweed asked. He returned to his seat, standing over it, not quite ready to sit down.

"You didn't know? She was in a car crash. My, um, source believes it was to silence her. She was working on a story about the wind farm," Daniel said.

"Hmm, two deaths made to look like accidents. One a construction worker, one a reporter. Do you think Sayyid also knew something he shouldn't have?" Mr. Tweed asked, finally sitting down.

"Possibly. He would have been in a unique position to see how things worked there," Daniel said, not wanting to reveal too much without Samira's permission. "Tell me, though, what makes *you* suspect someone inside GlenBreeze? Do you think it was Mr. Christie, the foreman?"

"Christie's a shifty fellow, but he's too low level, certainly, to orchestrate two murders. No, Reverend, this is all about money."

"What do you mean?" Daniel asked. He was reminded of Eliza MacGillivray saying something similar about Mr. Tweed.

"The money simply doesn't add up, does it?" Mr. Tweed explained. "In the board meeting just then, I brought up, subtly of course, the turbines' construction—specifically the materials used, their source, and cost, et cetera. What your father said got me thinking. How did he put it? Shoddy, cheap construction?"

Daniel nodded.

"So, I did some looking into the company accounts," Mr. Tweed continued. "On paper, the wind farm seems to be right on budget, except for the delays caused by the safety investigation, of course. But if we are using cheap materials, we're certainly paying for them like they're top of the line. So, I ask you, where's all that extra money going?"

"What did the board say?" Daniel asked.

"Well, I couldn't outright accuse them, now could I," Mr. Tweed said with a raised eyebrow. "Subtlety and tact were called for."

"So, you didn't learn anything from them?"

Mr. Tweed sighed and looked away. "No."

Daniel reached into his jacket and retrieved his phone. He scrolled through the photos until he came to the one he'd taken of Sayyid's last letter. "Do you know a Gilbert Ross?"

"Gilly? Of course. We're old mates. Why?"

"I'm not sure yet. His name came up when I was talking to people. Does he have anything to do with the wind farm construction?" Daniel asked.

"Not directly, but it falls under his department, contracts, and whatnot. He's a very busy man. But there's no chance of Gilly being involved in this. He's a shark in the boardroom, but his bite stops there. Come to think of it, he wasn't even in the country when Sayyid died. He was off on one of his holidays to Montenegro."

Daniel frowned and put his phone away. Back to the drawing board.

"In fact, we were planning on lunch after the meeting. When I saw you, I told him to meet me there," Mr. Tweed said, glancing at his watch. "You should join us. Gilly's a good man to know—could open some doors for you, you never know. Plus, you'll see he's a dead end regarding all this, em, unpleasantness."

"Sure, lunch sounds good," Daniel said. "But let's keep this conversation just between us for the time being."

Chapter Forty-Three

Mr. Tweed handed his car keys to the valet. "Wait," he said, reaching into the back seat. He pulled out a dry-cleaning bag and ripped off the plastic to reveal a freshly pressed tweed suit. He handed the jacket and matching tie to Daniel and hung the trousers back in the car. "She's all yours," he said to the valet.

"Well, put them on," he said to Daniel, who was holding the jacket and tie with an expression similar to that of a child whose mother had asked him to hold her purse while she tried on clothes at a department store. "You dress for meals here," Mr. Tweed said.

Daniel slipped on the jacket, which was too long in the arms, and followed him up the stairs to the polished stone and glass entrance of the fanciest restaurant Daniel had ever seen. It was the kind of place that made him feel poor and judged just by walking past it. An attendant in a sleek, black uniform greeted them at the door. Daniel avoided his suspicious eye and stuck close to Mr. Tweed for fear the attendant might shut the door in between them.

"Fraser, reservation for two," Mr. Tweed said to the hostess. "Though we have three now. I hope that won't be any trouble. I think my friend Gil Ross might already be here?"

"No trouble at all, Mr. Fraser. Please follow me," the hostess said and led them into the dining room.

Daniel had to hold his mouth shut to keep from gasping at the opulent décor: soaring ceilings adorned with ornate chandeliers, dark wood paneling along the walls, rich velvet drapes that framed the floor-to-ceiling windows overlooking a gorgeous view of the Ness River. Each table was meticulously set with crisp tartan placemats and napkins, gleaming silverware, and what appeared to be real crystal glassware. And every soul in the room sported a tie and jacket or an elegant dress.

At a table near the center of the room, a man in a perfectly tailored charcoal suit waved at them. His salt-and-pepper hair was encased in a sufficient amount of gel to withstand the strongest of North Sea winds, and his pale blue eyes seemed to twinkle when Mr. Tweed and Daniel pulled up their chairs.

"George, I was beginning to think you'd stood me up," the man said.

"I'm sorry, Gilly. I hope you weren't waiting too long," Mr. Tweed said sheepishly.

"It's my fault. I had something urgent I needed to discuss with him. Kirk matters," Daniel said, knowing that, for Mr. Tweed, punctuality was a virtue that ranked alongside the Ten Commandments, if not higher.

"And you are?" Gilbert Ross asked. He eyed Daniel doubtfully.

"Daniel Darrow. Nice to meet you," Daniel said, shaking his hand before sitting down.

"Nice jacket," Gilbert Ross said.

"Play nice, Gilly. This was an impromptu invite. This is our reverend at Church Street," Mr. Tweed said.

"The more the merrier, I suppose. I didn't know ol' Gorgie was so important down at the kirk. What was so urgent it couldn't wait, eh? Did he forget to pay his dues this month?" Gilbert Ross asked with a laugh.

"It's called a tithe, and no, I'm always quite prompt, I assure you," Mr. Tweed said with a slight note of defensiveness in his voice. "Reverend Darrow needed my advice on his, em, upcoming wedding, isn't that right, Reverend?"

"Um, yes," Daniel said. "I, um, Mr. Fraser, George, has a connection with a florist. It really could have waited. I'm sorry again for making you wait."

"George is proud of his connections. And who said I was waiting?" Gilbert Ross said. He raised a half-empty glass of wine and took a drink. "So, tell me about this lovely young woman you're marrying."

Daniel told him about Ellie—where she worked, how they met. But Gilbert Ross interrupted him. "Yes, yes, let's skip to the good part. Have you made plans for your honeymoon?"

"Honeymoon?" Daniel asked, taken aback. "Um, not really. Ellie and my mom are taking care of most of the wedding planning."

"Except for the florist," Gilbert Ross said.

"Right, except for the florist," Daniel said and shot a glance toward Mr. Tweed. "As far as a honeymoon," Daniel continued, "we've talked about taking a trip to Skye or down south to Bath sometime, so we might just do that."

"Might I make a suggestion?" Gilbert Ross said. Daniel nodded. "Go abroad. Montenegro."

"Here we go," Mr. Tweed sighed, clearly having heard this spiel before.

"Here me out," Gilbert Ross said. "The Balkans are underrated. Montenegro's got beautiful Mediterranean beaches to rival the French Riviera or gorgeous mountains with glacial lakes, if that's more your thing. Plus, it's got the finest casinos in Europe if you're a gambling man or wish to partake in a little side business. Montenegro's not part of the EU, not yet anyway, so the rules are a bit more lax there."

"I don't think the reverend or Ms. Gray would be too interested in those particular aspects, and there are certainly nice beaches closer to home," Mr. Tweed said.

Gilbert Ross held out his hands in a shrug. "A man can make a friendly suggestion, can't he? I take wee holidays there whenever I need to unwind or things get a touch too hot here in Inverness. I can tell you all the best spots if you're interested."

"Thanks, perhaps later," Daniel said. Given the infrequency of very hot days in Inverness, Daniel assumed Ross frequented the Eastern European nation for more than its mild Mediterranean climate. And he was doubtful those reasons coincided with the designs of a honeymoon.

"So, you work with George at GlenBreeze Dynamics? How are things going with the wind farm construction? You know I helped campaign for it in the early days," Daniel said, trying to steer the conversation back toward more pressing matters. Even if Mr. Tweed vouched for the man, clearly not everything about Gilbert Ross was on the up and up. If he wasn't involved in Sayyid and Lexi's deaths, perhaps he could at least point Daniel in the right direction.

"It's coming along. Not as smoothly as we'd all like, but it's coming along, isn't it? But I've had enough of that for the day. The food here is too good to waste on shop talk. Speaking of which, where is that waitress? I'm starving," Gilbert Ross said, glancing around the dining room.

Daniel picked up a menu, afraid to open it for fear he would blow half his wedding savings on this one meal. He winced when he saw that none of the meals even had prices next to them—not even a glass of sparkling water. He decided a salad was his safest bet; how expensive could lettuce be anyway? Then his phone rang. It was Ellie. *Saved by the bell*, Daniel thought. He stood up, apologizing for having to take the call.

"I'm sure glad to hear your voice," Daniel said as he stepped out onto the sidewalk. "I can't even guess how much money you likely saved me."

"You're welcome, I guess. Look, can you meet me at Raigmore?" Ellie asked, her voice full of urgency.

"The hospital? Are you okay?"

"I'm fine. It's Ms. MacGillivray. She's slipped into a coma."

Chapter Forty-Four

Daniel knocked on the door to Eliza MacGillivray's hospital room. "Ms. MacGillivray? Ellie? It's me, Daniel."

"Come in," he heard Ellie's voice call from inside the room.

When he stepped inside, he saw Ellie sitting beside Ms. MacGillivray's bed. Eliza appeared asleep, lying perfectly still. Daniel approached them apprehensively.

"It's okay, you can come inside," Ellie said.

Daniel stood over Eliza and placed his hand over hers. She had no reaction. He glanced at Ellie.

"She's in a coma, but otherwise, the nurse said her vitals are good," Ellie said.

Daniel felt a mixture of sorrow and helplessness well up in his chest. He had been running all over Inverness and the surrounding countryside trying to make sense of Eliza's last premonition, and yet all his efforts seemed to have been in vain. He was simply chasing one dead end after another. He was no closer to understanding Sayyid or Lexi Campbell's deaths, and now Eliza lay in a coma. He said a quick prayer over her and sat down next to Ellie.

"What happened?" Daniel asked.

"She was like this when I came to visit earlier. The nurse said it must have happened sometime last night," Ellie said.

"Do they know what caused it?" Daniel asked. Ellie shook her head. "Do you think *someone* caused it?"

Ellie sighed and looked at Eliza's frail, still body. "I don't know. I don't know what to think. Normally, I would say that's absurd—who could do something like that to another person? But now? After how frightened Eliza was after Lexi Campbell's death? I just don't know."

Ellie turned back to Daniel and held his hand. "I'm scared, Daniel. We've been through some tense situations before, but this feels different."

Daniel had never seen worry like that in her eyes before. He didn't know what to say. Her expression made the feeling of helplessness grow inside him. As much as he tried, he couldn't seem to keep those around him safe. And, if he was honest, Eliza's worsening condition frightened him, too. He worried not only for Eliza, but for Ellie and himself. If someone was targeting people who were asking questions about Sayyid's death, then he or Ellie could very easily be next.

Daniel pulled Ellie into a close embrace. He breathed in the lavender scent of her shampoo and felt the reassuring warmth of her body. For all his recent failings, he could at least hold her now and try to take some mutual comfort in the fact that they were alive and well and together. They had one another and, for this moment at least, that was enough.

"Did you talk to George Fraser?" Ellie finally asked, ending their embrace.

Daniel nodded. "Should we talk about that here?" he asked, glancing at Eliza. "I've heard coma victims can still hear what's going on around them."

"The nurse said it's good for her to hear familiar voices. And I think, if she can hear us, she would want to keep apprized any updates. Knowing Eliza, figuring out who put her in a coma could get her fired up enough to snap out of it so she could go chase 'em down herself!"

"Yeah, that's probably true. She's a feisty old—," Daniel stopped himself with a laugh, in case Eliza really could hear them through her coma. "But I'm afraid I don't have anything useful to share about Mr. Tweed." With an aside to Eliza, he added, "Eliza, if you can hear me, remember you promised not to tell George Fraser about the little nickname I made up for him back when I was trying to remember folks' names."

"You wouldn't believe the nickname he came up with for you," Ellie said playfully.

"What? No. Don't listen to her. You're memorable enough without a nickname."

"He was just too afraid you'd curse him with a bad prophecy," Ellie said.

"No, I wasn't! Well, maybe a little," Daniel admitted.

"I think I might have seen a wee smile on her lips," Ellie whispered.

"Really?" Daniel asked, looking at Eliza's statue-like expression. Ellie simply shrugged.

"Well, back to the topic of Mr. Tweed, or George Fraser; when I confronted him, he seemed truly surprised and kind of hurt that I'd even think of accusing him. And then, before I could even say anything, he surprised me by suggesting someone inside GlenBreeze Dynamics might be involved. So, unless he's just a really good actor, I believe him.

"He told me he thinks someone is secretly syphoning off money from the wind farm construction—charging full price, but using cheaper materials and labor and then pocketing what's left. So, at the very least, even if Fraser doesn't sympathize with the Ghulam family or the other workers, he values his money and doesn't like being cheated out of it. He has, in his own way, as much motivation in finding out who's behind this as we do."

Ellie leaned back in her chair, considering what Daniel had just told her. "Well, Eliza? What do you think of that?" she asked, finally, without really expecting an answer. "What about the man Sayyid had written his complaint letter to? Did you find out anything about him?" she asked Daniel.

"Gilbert Ross. I actually just came from a lunch with him and Mr. Tweed. They're evidently good friends. Tweed said Ross was out of the country when Sayyid died. I tried to ask Ross about the wind farm, but he wasn't keen on talking business at lunch. I don't know if I could afford to find out anything more from him. It was a really pricy place," Daniel said.

While they sat in silence, pondering their next move, Daniel became distracted by Ellie's purse, which was sitting on the windowsill. It was a larger bag than she usually used and had a cheery floral pattern on it, but that wasn't the unusual part. Every few seconds, the bag twitched. At first, Daniel thought it was a trick of the light or a tic in his eye caused by nerves. But the longer he stared at it, the more certain he became that the bag itself was shuddering.

Eventually, Ellie noticed his stare. "Oh my! I forgot," she said and jumped from her chair. She rushed over and unzipped the bag. Two long, furry ears popped out, followed by a fuzzy face with two black eyes and a twitching nose. Ellie pulled the rabbit out of her purse and held it in her arms.

"He's the whole reason I came to visit today. With me working all day, he gets lonely. I thought a wee visit might do both of them some good," Ellie said.

She gently placed the rabbit on the edge of Eliza's bed. The rabbit sat up on its haunches and looked around the room. Its nose twitched furiously, taking in all the unfamiliar smells. Then it sat down and sniffed Eliza's arm. It wiggled its butt and hopped up to her shoulder, then nuzzled the side of her head. Finally, it burrowed its nose in her hair, turned around three times like a dog, and settled in beside the crook of her neck.

"Ah, would you look at that? Now I have to stay a bit longer," Ellie said, fawning over the sight of Eliza and her rabbit. "Keep me company?"

"Of course," Daniel said. He scooted closer to her, and she rested her head on his shoulder. "Oh, I should probably mention that I might have committed us to a florist—for the wedding. I'm not sure." Ellie raised an eyebrow at him. "It's a long story."

Chapter Forty-Five

Daniel and Ellie strolled up to the high brick walls of Inverness Prison. The complex was located rather inconspicuously in the heart of Inverness, surrounded on three sides by single-family houses with well-maintained front gardens. They approached the unimposing pedestrian door and pressed the buzzer. Ellie gave her name and addressed the voice on the other side of the buzzer like an old friend. After passing through a metal detector and an X-ray machine, a uniformed guard waved them in.

"Hello, Ms. Gray. You'll be in the regular visits room today," another guard at the front desk said. "I'll walk you down."

"Ta, George, but I know the way," Ellie said with a friendly wave.

"Aye, but it's my job," the guard said. He nodded to his companion to watch the desk while he led Ellie and Daniel back to the visitors' center.

Elspeth Gray was easy to spot. She sat alone at one of several small round tables. Two or three chairs, each one a bright splash of color in the gray and white, windowless room, surrounded each table. Elspeth sat with her hands folded in her lap, her left hand shielding her right.

"Well, here goes," Ellie said, taking a deep breath before walking over to her mother. Daniel followed close behind.

Elspeth appeared surprised to see them, especially Daniel. "What a pleasant surprise. I wasn't expecting a visit today. Have you come to tell me you've finally set a date for the wedding?" she asked.

"Not yet," Ellie said and sat down.

"Oh, child, you didn't come to tell me about the wedding, did you? What's happened?" Elspeth asked.

"This is why I never play poker," Ellie said with a forced grin. She turned to Daniel. "Would you mind fetching a couple of drinks and crisps from the machine?"

Daniel nodded. He wanted to support Ellie, but he was secretly glad to not be there when she broke the news about Eliza. He'd already shared enough bad news with Ellie's mother to last a lifetime. He lingered at the vending machine, examining each option even though he knew what he was going to buy before he got there. Ellie and her mother liked the same flavor of crisps: prawn cocktail—a tangy flavor Daniel could only describe as like dipping a plain potato chip in a massive dollop of ketchup. He opted for the less adventurous cheese and onion variety for himself.

He returned and unloaded an armful of snacks onto the middle of their table. Elspeth reached for a bag, revealing a burn scar on her right hand—a permanent reminder of why she was in prison. "Ellie's just told me about Eliza, the poor dear. I told her, many years ago, when we were younger than the both of you, to throw that cursed Seeing Stone back into the loch," Elspeth said. She sighed and opened her crisps. Daniel cringed as he watched a puff of red air escape from the bag like a tiny atomic tomato bomb.

"The Seeing Stone?" Daniel asked.

"Aye, that stone has an evil spirit about it. There's a price to pay for the gift of second sight. It took the original Brahan Seer's eye and ultimately his life. I'd hoped it wouldn't ask as much from my dear friend," Elspeth said.

"Eliza's not dead. She's just in a coma. She'll recover," Ellie said, trying to conjure more confidence in her voice than she held in her heart.

"So, you think her sickness is tied to her Seeing Stone?" Daniel asked.

Elspeth nodded. "And now that it's broken, I fear she will meet a similar fate."

"But the clay," Daniel said, suddenly excited. "I got a jar of clay from Loch Ussie. Before she fell into the coma, Ms. MacGillivray said clay from the loch could mend the stone."

"Perhaps, perhaps," Elspeth muttered. She crunched a few crisps, savoring the sweet, salty tomato flavor. "Ellie tells me you have a different theory.

Eliza's illness, that construction worker's death, and the new wind farm—you think they're all connected somehow?"

"We do, and Eliza said as much herself. She was convinced of it after Lexi Cambell's death," Daniel said.

"The Highland Bulletin was one of my favorite programs. I was gutted when I heard about that. But Eliza's reaction? She was truly hysterical when she called me about it. She kept saying she'd be next. I couldn't get her to explain why, though," Elspeth said.

"Lexi was doing a follow-up story about the GlenBreeze wind farm, and she'd just interviewed Eliza," Ellie said.

"She thought that whoever was behind Sayyid's death wanted to silence Lexi too. And since she had talked to Lexi for the story—" Daniel said.

"Eliza thought she would be next," Elspeth said, finishing his thought. She finished the last of her crisps and looked at her red powdered fingers. "I love these things, but they are quite messy, aren't they?" she said, looking around for something to clean her hands with.

"I'll go get some wet paper towels or something," Daniel said. When he returned, he found that the conversation had shifted.

"You still haven't set a date?" Elspeth asked him.

"What?" he asked, confused.

"For the wedding. If you wait too long, you'll have wasted these few warm summer days," Elspeth said.

"You know your daughter said the same thing," Daniel said. He turned to Ellie. "I'm not opposed to getting married sooner rather than later. I could probably book any date we want at a certain kirk on Church Street. I have a bit of sway there."

"I know, I know. It's just..." Ellie hesitated.

"Don't tell me you're getting cold feet," Daniel said.

"No. I want to marry you. That's the one thing I do know. It's just everything with Eliza and..." She looked at her mother. "I want you to be there. With Da gone, I need someone to walk me down the aisle."

"I know, luv, and I want to be there too, but I still have another year on my sentence," Elspeth said.

"Could you get out early for good behavior?" Daniel asked.

"Not that early," Elspeth said.

"I've been working on something," Ellie said. "A supervised release. Just for an afternoon. It's a long shot and a lot of paperwork, but I don't want to set a firm date until I know."

"You never told me," Elspeth said.

"I didn't want to get your hopes up if it doesn't work."

"That's a great idea. Can I help in any way?" Daniel asked.

"Well, if you could write a letter speaking to her character and such, I'm sure something from a minister would help. Perhaps see if Reverend Calder could write one too?" Ellie said.

"Absolutely. I can ask her tomorrow," Daniel said.

"Let's pray it works, then. I would love to see my baby get married," Elspeth said. She wiped a tear from her eye. "And to wear a proper dress, at least for a few hours, instead of these," she said, motioning to her drab prison garb. "And I could finally meet your parents, Daniel."

"I'm sure they would like that. Oh, what time is it? We're supposed to meet them for lunch," Daniel said.

"So soon?" Ellie asked.

"It's all right. Visitation time is nearly up for us today anyway," Elspeth said. Then she motioned for them to lean in close and she said softly, "I'll see what I can find out about Lexi Campbell's so-called car accident and that wind farm. You'd be surprised at the amount of information that flows through these high walls. It's information you wouldn't necessarily hear on the outside. You have to be careful asking around, though. Information can come at a price."

"Mum, please be careful. Don't do anything dangerous," Ellie pleaded.

"Eliza's my dearest friend. She's the only one, besides you and Reverend Calder on occasion, who visits me here. She's worth the risk. I'll, how do you say?" she asked, glancing at Daniel. "I'll keep my ear to the ground and let you know if I hear anything."

Chapter Forty-Six

Two days after Daniel and Ellie visited her mother, Ellie received a phone call from Inverness Prison. Elspeth Gray had put her ear to the prison ground, and the ground had spoken. After the call, Ellie rescheduled her two afternoon appointments at the Kinmylies Veterinary Clinic and drove immediately across town to Church Street. She didn't want to wait for Daniel to try to successfully navigate a bus route to her.

She entered through the kirk's unlocked front doors and walked down the empty aisle through the nave. The afternoon sun filtered through the stained-glass windows into a rainbow of colors over the rows of empty wooden pews. Ellie couldn't help but smile as she imagined herself walking down that same aisle in the near future. She imagined Daniel waiting for her at the front in his black suit, and she in her white flowing dress with her mother at her side. *How is his character reference letter for Elspeth going?* she wondered. When she exited the nave, she turned down the hallway toward Daniel's closet of an office. But before she made it very far, she tripped over a swiftly moving flash of orange fur.

"Whoa, got you," Daniel said, catching her before she hit the ground. "Are you okay?"

"I think so," Ellie said, out of breath. "Where did you come from?"

"I could ask you the same thing. I wasn't expecting a visit, not that I'm complaining," Daniel said with a smile, followed by a kiss.

"I needed to talk to you. My mum called," Ellie said.

"Really? What did she have to say?" Daniel asked, wondering why Ellie hadn't simply called him.

"Can we sit down?" she asked. Daniel nodded and took her hand to lead her to his office. "You should get hazard pay for working here with Sir Walter always underfoot like that, ye ken? That cat nearly killed me."

Daniel paused. His eyes narrowed as he searched up and down the hall for the kirk cat. "Which direction did he come from? Did you see?" he asked. Ellie thought for a moment and then pointed. Daniel shook his head. *That crafty cat*, he thought. *He got through all our best cat-proofing.* "Well, for Sir Walter's sake, I hope Amir's out for the afternoon."

Once they got to his office, Ellie shut the door behind them. Daniel moved a stack of books off the spare chair for her and then wheeled his own chair from behind the desk. He could only get it as far as the side of the desk before it became wedged between the desk and the old pantry-turned-bookshelves.

"So, what did your mom say? I can't imagine it's easy to get an outgoing call from there." Daniel asked.

"No, it's not. I usually have to schedule a time to call well in advance. That's why I was so surprised when the prison's number popped up on my mobile this afternoon," Ellie said. "We weren't able to talk long, but she said she'd been listening for information about the wind farm or Lexi Campbell's car accident."

"Did she hear anything?"

"No one said anything directly, but she was able to put together that Eliza was right—Sayyid and Lexi's deaths are connected," Ellie said. She glanced around the room and lowered her voice, despite the closed door and their close proximity. "She thinks someone paid to have them killed."

"What?" Daniel asked. He leaned back in his chair and bumped his head against the bookshelf. "Beware the hand that offers gold," he said, reciting Eliza MacGillivray's last prophecy. "Who would do that?"

"No one knows. But one of the inmates has suddenly acquired a new solicitor who has managed to get her a new trial to look at overturning her conviction. An attorney who can do that so quickly doesn't come cheap. And the rumor is that this inmate's relative on the outside got a big payday recently."

"Okay, but what does that have to do with Sayyid or Lexi?" Daniel asked.

"The lucky inmate's name is Nora Christie," Ellie said. She crossed her arms, waiting for Daniel to absorb the weight of that name.

"Wait, Christie? As in Keith Christie, the foreman in charge of Sayyid's construction crew at the wind farm?" Daniel asked.

"Nora is his sister," Ellie confirmed.

"You're saying Keith Christie was paid to kill Sayyid and Lexi?"

"And make it look like an accident," Ellie said.

"We've got to tell the police," Daniel said.

"Tell them what, exactly? They're not going to do anything based on the theories of a comatose patient or prison yard rumors. And you've cried wolf with them before," Ellie said.

"Then I'll have to get Keith Christie to confess," Daniel said.

"And how do you expect to do that?"

"I don't know. I can be pretty persuasive, though. I convinced you to marry me," Daniel said with a playful grin.

"I don't think Mr. Christie will be quite as charmed by your cute face as me," Ellie said, rolling her eyes. "This is an actual murderer we're talking about here. Don't forget the rest of Eliza's prophecy—the unsheathed claws, the piercing thistle. No, it's too dangerous. I'm coming with you."

"No, it's too dangerous," Daniel objected.

"That's what I just said!"

"I know. But I'll be careful. And I can take Amir with me for backup."

"I don't like this."

"Neither do I, but I have to do something—for Eliza and Sayyid's family. I can't sit back and let him get away with this. Someone has to stop him before anyone else gets hurt," Daniel said.

Ellie took his hand. "Okay, bring Amir, but I'm coming too. We're getting married, Daniel. You don't have to run off and try to be the hero alone anymore."

Daniel nodded and squeezed her hand. *How did I get so lucky?* he asked himself. "It's settled then—together. Now, let's go find Amir. Assuming he's in, maybe he'll have an idea of how we can get to Christie and get out alive."

Chapter Forty-Seven

As dawn broke over the Port of Inverness, a blanket of mist hung over the harbor. The air was thick and briny, filled with the scent of seawater and diesel fuel. The shrill cries of seagulls and deep ships' horns mingled with the rhythmic clapping of waves against the stony shore. In the distance, the cable suspension towers of the Kessock Bridge appeared to float above the mist and, farther out, several needle-like pillars rose from the waters of the Moray Firth.

Ellie Gray parked her car in a lot just outside the front gates to the Port. She, Daniel, and Amir exited the car and walked with determination toward the dock where Keith Christie's construction crew was due to depart. With each step, though, Daniel felt his courage faltering. He'd faced killers before, but those had been accidental deaths—cover-ups. The man he was walking toward today was a true murderer, killing on purpose and covering them up as accidents. For all Daniel knew, Sayyid and Lexi were not even Keith Christie's first victims.

Daniel took comfort in the presence of his friends on either side of him. He was grateful not to be walking into this danger alone. Together, they would hold the deadly foreman accountable for his crimes and ensure he didn't hurt anyone else ever again. But they had to be careful. Keith Christie wasn't just a killer; he was a hired gun. Christie may have pulled the trigger, but if they wanted to truly find justice for Sayyid and Lexi, they still needed to find out who loaded it.

"Are you sure you know where you're going?" Daniel asked Amir. "I've never been to this part of the Port before.

"Yes. This is where the men told me they depart," Amir answered. He led Daniel and Ellie through a maze of warehouses and cargo containers until they reached a group of men standing near a dock. The men all wore neon yellow or orange waterproof jackets. Some held white hard hats, others steaming cups of coffee. Amir gave a discreet wave as they approached, and several of the construction crew nodded their hellos.

Daniel scanned the area for Christie. He was not hard to spot with his bulky, muscled frame and thick beard, saturated with dew and sea spray. The blue lion tattoo on his forearm appeared to breathe fire with each flex of his muscles as he worked a thick line of rope.

"There he is," Daniel said.

"The one who looks like he could snap you like a twig?" Ellie asked nervously.

"That's why I brought backup," Daniel said.

"You should have brought more," Amir said.

"He's seen us. No turning back now," Daniel said, as Keith Christie looked up and eyed them suspiciously.

"Oi, what do you lot want?" he asked.

"Mr. Christie, you might remember me. I accompanied Mr. George Fraser on a tour of the wind turbines a couple of weeks ago," Daniel said.

"Right, right. You're the, eh, American reverend? Have you brought me another worker to replace the one that had the accident?" Christie asked, eyeing Amir. "Does he have machines training?"

"I work with Reverend Darrow at the kirk," Amir said brusquely.

"So, what's this? You come to recruit me or something?" Christie asked with a laugh.

"No, we came to talk to you about Sayyid Ghulam, the man who had the *accident*, as you said. But it wasn't an accident, was it?" Daniel said.

"What? I've already told the cops all I know about that. Then I put up with those safety inspectors. I've been busting my arse to get back on schedule from all the delays that Sayyid fellow caused me. I don't have time for this," Christie said, irritation and impatience evident in his tone. He turned away and returned to his rope.

"You killed him!" Ellie blurted out. All three men turned to her in surprise.

"That's absurd," Christie said. "I don't know who you three think you are to come here and accuse me. I don't see Mr. Fraser or anyone else from GlenBreeze with you, so I don't have to stand here and take this. Get off my dock now, before you regret it!"

But Daniel, Ellie, and Amir stood firm. "We know you and Sayyid did not get on well. You had arguments. He'd filed complaints about you," Amir said.

"But it was more than that, wasn't it?" Daniel said. "Sayyid knew things he shouldn't have. He knew about the lax safety and cheap materials. He knew you were skimming money from the project, didn't he?" For the briefest of moments, Daniel thought he glimpsed an expression of recognition flash across Keith Christie's face. But it was immediately replaced with a steely indifference that bordered on anger.

"Unless you three have come here to work, I'm done talking to you. My crew and I have an actual job to do today, and I'd hate for any more *accidents* to further delay us. Now bugger off," Christie said.

Daniel, Amir, and Ellie stood in silence as he turned and walked away. "That didn't go quite go to plan," Daniel said.

"Given the look of that guy and the fact that we're still alive, I'd say it went about as well as could be expected," Ellie said.

"We're not done yet," Amir said, gritting his teeth.

"He didn't seem very receptive to our accusations. I thought catching him by surprise might throw him off his guard. I hoped the fear of being found out would lead him to confess or at least give up whoever's paying him. But clearly he's not afraid of anything," Daniel said, disheartened.

"That is where you're wrong," Amir said. "Fear and self-interest consume him. I've met men like Mr. Christie before, on my journey to this country. They act tough and fierce, but it is mostly a mask. Christie is a mouse who only roars like a lion. He is strong as long as he believes he has power over others. Take that away, and he will fall."

"Fear and self-interest," Ellie considered. "So, we must take away his power or offer him a better deal."

"Well, we can't pay him more than what he's stealing from the wind farm. But perhaps we could take away his sense of control," Daniel said. The seed of an idea sprouted in his mind. He furrowed his brow and glanced around the dock, allowing the seed to grow. "Amir, you know the workers pretty well, right? You have a good relationship with them—they trust you?"

"Yes, most of them are my fellow countrymen," Amir said.

"Okay, here's what we're going to do…" Daniel said, lowering his voice so that Amir and Ellie had to lean close to hear.

Chapter Forty-Eight

Daniel squeezed Ellie's hand. "You've got plenty of battery?"

Ellie nodded. "Just don't let this be the last video I shoot of you. I'd hate to have to turn it over as evidence. Getting a new mobile is such a hassle," she said, trying to mask her fear with levity.

"That's why I want you filming. It's hard to make something look like an accident if it's on camera. I love you," Daniel said and gave her a kiss goodbye. *Hopefully not goodbye for good*, he thought.

He walked slowly toward Keith Christie. The foreman had told them he was done talking and had offered a thinly veiled threat if they didn't leave him alone, but Daniel wanted to try to reason with him one last time. If that failed, Daniel would appeal to his heart—see if Christie felt any remorse for what he'd done. *At the very least, I can distract him long enough to give Amir time*, Daniel thought.

"Mr. Christie," Daniel said, with as much authority as he could muster.

"I thought I told you to bugger off," Keith Christie said, without looking up from the ledger he was writing in.

"I know that what happened to Sayyid and Lexi Campbell wasn't your idea. You're working for someone. Just tell me who it is, and I'm sure the police will go easier on you," Daniel said.

"I already told you. I'm done talking to you. Perhaps *I* should ring the cops and tell them there's a pesky tourist harassing me and holding up my work."

"Think of their families. Sayyid had a wife and two small boys. Now they're going to grow up without a father and never know the real reason why. Don't they deserve some justice, or closure at least?" Daniel pleaded.

"I've got myself and my family to think about," Christie said, still scribbling away on his pad.

"I know your sister recently got a new trial to look at overturning her conviction. A lawyer who can do that so quickly doesn't come cheap. I imagine it costs a lot more than what this job pays. One way or another, I'll find out who gave you the money."

Keith Christie put down his pad and turned around slowly. "You leave Nora out of this," he said through clenched teeth. Then he smiled, his thin lips barely visible through his thick, scruffy beard. The sudden shift in emotion was unnerving.

"You've overplayed your hand, Reverend," Christie said. "If you truly had anything on me, you'd have brought the coppers along with you today. Truth is, you're grasping at straws. And I've got no reason to help in your little witch hunt." He looked Daniel up and down and scoffed. "Now, if you'll excuse me, I've got more money to make," he said, tapping his ledger.

With his head held high, Keith Christie turned his back to Daniel and headed off to round up his construction crew. But he only got a few paces before he froze. He peered down the dock toward the boat and then back, left then right. He scratched the back of his head. "Where are they?"

"Did you misplace something?" Daniel taunted. Amir had fulfilled his part of the plan. Now it was time for Daniel to sell his.

"My crew, they—what's going on?"

"Oh, them? While we were having our little chat, my friend, you remember him? You thought he was here to replace Sayyid. He convinced your crew to go with him to the police station. It seems they have a long list of health and safety violations to report," Daniel said.

Keith Christie's eyes narrowed and he balled his fists. He took a menacing step toward Daniel. Daniel nodded at Ellie, who was holding her phone up, recording them. Christie let out an audible huff and unclenched his fists.

"It looks like your job as foreman could soon be over. Who knows, you might be facing some jail time, too. Of course, it takes a minute to get all the way to Burnett Road. I could call and ask my friend to reroute them to a pub or a nice halal deli, if you tell me the truth," Daniel said.

Christie was silent for several long seconds. His eyes flitted back and forth between Daniel and Ellie. He clenched and unclenched his fists. Daniel could see the whiskers on Christie's closed lips move as his tongue rolled over his teeth as he considered his options. Finally, he spoke.

"Tell her to put that away and I'll talk," he said, tilting his head toward Ellie.

Daniel hesitated. Ellie's filming was the only thing that had stopped Christie's fists from colliding with his face. Daniel glanced at the blue tattoo on Christie's forearm. It stood at ease, no longer flexed or tense. Had their plan really been enough to tame this lion?

Daniel decided to chance it. He turned to Ellie, while still keeping Christie in his peripheral vision. "Put your phone away."

Ellie returned a concerned look. "Are you sure?"

"Yeah, it's okay," Daniel said.

Ellie slowly lowered her cell phone, but she didn't return it to her back pocket. She held it at her side with her thumb hovering over the record button, just in case.

"There, now tell me the truth. Why'd you kill Sayyid and Lexi? Who wanted them dead?" Daniel asked.

Keith Christie lowered his eyes and stared at the damp ground. The low bellow of a foghorn in the distance interrupted the quiet of the moment. "I did it for Nora. He said if I helped him with his problem, he'd help me with mine. He promised to get my sister out of prison. But if I didn't do it, he would get her transferred to a high-security prison in the South and make sure she never saw the light of day again. I didn't have a choice."

"Who threatened her?" Daniel asked.

"Are you sure you want to know? Curiosity's what got yer mates killed," Christie said. Though his words were threatening, his voice held more regret than malice.

"Tell me," Daniel said.

"He's a big shot at GlenBreeze Dynamics, the company that owns the wind farm. They subcontract out construction," Christie explained.

Daniel nodded. He already knew that part. "Who?"

"Gilbert Ross."

"Gilly?" Daniel asked, surprised. Mr. Tweed's friend, who liked expensive restaurants and foreign vacations? The man he'd recently had lunch with and told all about his engagement to Ellie and his parents flying over for the upcoming wedding? This whole time, he'd assumed the betrayer with claws in Eliza's vision was Christie, but Christie was just a pawn. Gilbert Ross had bloodied claws and teeth, and he had fooled them all. Daniel glanced back at Ellie and bit his lip. He'd unwittingly told the most dangerous man he'd ever met about the most important people in his life.

Chapter Forty-Nine

"Gilly? Yes, though I'd never dare to call him that," Keith Christie said. "He's the one who hired me as foreman. And I was thrilled to get the job, wasn't I? It was the biggest contract I'd ever won. Plus, I got to work here in Inverness, near my sister. It was only later, when Mr. Ross started poking around my purchasing and hiring, that I began to realize there was more to this job than was recorded on any official paperwork. He was much more hands-on than people I've worked for in the past.

But both the work and paycheck were steady, so I didn't ask questions. Then, when he asked me to engineer Sayyid Ghulam's *accident*, I realized that proximity to my sister wasn't a perk of the job—it was a liability."

Daniel was still trying to wrap his head around the fact that he'd only recently sat down at the same table as Gilbert Ross and Mr. Tweed. The man's nonchalance toward pricy meals and vacations had put a bad taste in Daniel's mouth, but Ross wasn't much worse than Mr. Tweed in that regard. Daniel and Tweed had both been so eager to place blame on a familiar foe, they hadn't seen the threat that was sitting right in front of them.

"But why would Ross want Sayyid dead?" Daniel asked.

"Sayyid was a smart bloke. He figured out Mr. Ross's scheme, but he missed one crucial detail. He didn't realize it was Mr. Ross. He thought I was behind it," Christie said.

"Using cheap materials, but billing the company full price, and then pocketing the remainder?" Daniel asked, remembering Mr. Tweed's suspicion.

"I see Sayyid isn't the only one too smart for his own good," Christie said. "Well, we nearly came to blows over it on several occasions. Of course, I couldn't tell Sayyid who was really pulling the strings, now could I? Mr. Ross had already threatened me, and he was paying me a couple hundred pound extra a week to keep my mouth shut—all off the official books, of course. I warned Sayyid to stay out of it; just take his paycheck and go home. I felt sorry for him, really. He was an honest bloke just trying to keep himself and his mates safe."

That explains Samira's claim that her husband and his boss didn't get along, Daniel thought. Then, as Daniel recalled his last conversation with her, his breath caught in his throat. *Sayyid's letter!* Sayyid had written to Gilbert Ross complaining about Christie. He never realized that his cry for help would end up being his death sentence.

"Well, Mr. Ross found out somehow, and he asked me to take care of the situation before Sayyid could go public with his accusations," Christie continued. "Mr. Ross wanted me to make it look like an accident. He was quite clear about that."

"Ross figured it would be cheaper to have construction delayed for safety inspections than to get caught and have to give back all the money he'd stolen," Daniel said.

"Aye, that's likely. But he didn't have the guts to do the deed himself," Christie said.

"The same thing happened to Lexi Campbell too, didn't it? She was investigating the wind farm and Sayyid's death. She must have found out about Ross. So, he had you silence her, too, before she could report it," Daniel said.

"The podcast woman? Yes, she was poking around here, interviewing members of my crew. I warned her to just let it be. There's no story here, I told her. It's a dangerous job; accidents happen. But she was stubborn. She said she'd go above my head if I wouldn't cooperate. That was her mistake."

"And Eliza MacGillivray?" Daniel asked.

"Who?" Christie asked.

"She was one of Lexi's sources. You poisoned her in the hospital. You put her in a coma."

"I don't know any MacGifly, or whatever her name is. And I can promise you, when I do a job, I finish it. Whoever this woman is wouldn't be in a coma if I'd done her," Christie said almost proudly.

Daniel was both appalled and surprised by Christie's claim. If he hadn't caused Eliza's coma, then what had? Could it have been strictly medical—a natural worsening of her condition? Or did Gilbert Ross have more operatives than Keith Christie?

"We have to go tell the police about all this," Daniel said.

"And cross Mr. Ross? No, thank you. Rich, powerful men like him are untouchable. He knew exactly which buttons to push to get me to go along with his scheme and then take care of any, em, complications. He probably has half the police force on his payroll, too. You may think you're clever, Reverend, puzzling all this out, but I swear to you, Mr. Ross is already several moves ahead. Taking him on is suicide. If you'll remember, the last two people who got close are now dead."

"Gilbert Ross would not be the first powerful businessman I've taken down," Daniel said. "You used to work for Philaguria Energy, right? Did you ever wonder how their old CEO, Alec Harrow, ended up in prison?"

"You?" Christie asked.

Daniel nodded. "It was actually a pretty big story at the time, I'm surprised you didn't hear. But that's beside the point. What I'm trying to say is, we can't let men like Ross off just because they're wealthy. Money may buy him power and influence, but it doesn't make him immune to justice. It just means that we have to have the courage and faith to stand up to him. Have you ever heard the story of Daniel in the lions' den?"

* * *

Daniel walked from the bus stop to the police station on Burnett Road. The rumbling sound of engines and the hissing of brakes from the train station across the road filled the air. He opened the door to the light, yellowish-colored stone building and stepped into a quieter, though no less busy, reception room. The scent of stale coffee and disinfectant hung in the air. Posters promoting police recruitment and safety practices adorned the walls. One bulletin board held photographs of missing persons. Daniel wondered if Sayyid or Lexi's portraits had been up there before their bodies were found—no longer missing, but still gone.

Officers strode in and out, their footsteps echoing off the hard, polished floor. A few civilians sat along a wall, waiting for their turn to speak with an officer. Others milled about or paced anxiously. Behind the front desk, a flustered-looking receptionist fielded calls from an ever-ringing phone and attempted to direct the civilian traffic.

Daniel glanced around the room at the various people waiting. He noticed several unkept, burly beards, but none with an accompanying blue lion tattoo. He checked the time on his phone. He was a few minutes early. Keith Christie would show. *No need to panic just yet*, he thought.

Once he had convinced Christie to come forward, Daniel had wanted to go directly to the police that day. But Christie had protested. "I need to get some things in order first," Christie had said. "If I'm actually going to go up against Mr. Ross, I don't want it devolving into my word against his."

"Whatever you need, we can pick it up on the way. We'll drive you there," Daniel had said, hoping Ellie wouldn't mind having this dangerous man in her car.

"I'll likely end up in a jail cell after the coppers hear what I have to tell 'em—for my protection as much as for what I've done. At least let me spend one last night in my own bed. I want to fall asleep a free man. I never thought to savor a thing like that before," Christie said. He gazed out across the water toward the Kessock Bridge as if he were trying to take a mental picture that would, he knew, have to last him a long time.

Reluctantly, Daniel had agreed to meet him at the police station at ten in the morning. Before leaving him, Daniel had taken down Christie's phone number just in case.

At five minutes past ten the next morning, Daniel began to sweat. At ten minutes past, with still no sign of Christie, Daniel wanted to kick himself for being so gullible. Why would a man risk going to prison for murder when he could simply slip away in the night?

Daniel dialed Keith Christie's phone number. No answer. He weaved through the crowd at the police station to approach the front desk. The receptionist, holding a telephone receiver in one hand and scribbling on a notepad with the other, gave him a *Don't even think about interrupting me* look.

But Daniel's nerves wouldn't allow him to wait any longer. "Excuse me, ma'am?" he asked.

The receptionist rolled her eyes and held up her index finger. Daniel waited. When she hung up the phone, he tried to speak again, but she again held up her finger. She finished writing on her pad and then turned to him. "Now, can I help you, luv?"

"Yes, thank you. I'm scheduled to meet with an inspector this morning at ten—"

"You're late," she interrupted.

"I know, I'm sorry. I was meeting someone here, but I haven't seen him. Do you know if they've started the meeting without me?"

"Name?"

"Daniel Darrow."

"Let me see," the receptionist said as she typed on her keyboard.

As she was looking up the schedule, two inspectors walked quickly past them. Daniel overhead only a snippet of their conversation, but it was enough to make him turn on his heel.

"Neighbor found the body. Went over to complain about the dog barking and found him just lying there," one inspector said. "The responding officer who called it in said it looked like a robbery gone bad."

"Do we have the victim's name?" the other asked.

"Christie something."

Daniel grabbed one inspector by the arm. "Excuse me, did you say Christie? Keith Christie?"

"Aye, that's him. How did you know?"

Chapter Fifty

aniel Darrow sat in his cramped storage closet of an office at Church Street Kirk, attempting to write a sermon for the upcoming Sunday service. But the wedding feast at Cana, despite its miraculous tale of turning water into wine, had trouble holding his attention. It only reminded him of all the unfinished plans for his own wedding and the fact that it was far too early in the day to be drinking.

After the rollercoaster of the past few days, he wanted for nothing more than to call up William MacCrivag and Philip Morrison; they could always be counted on to have a bottle of Scotch at the ready. And he knew they'd be more than happy to slough off the day's responsibilities to enjoy it together. But Daniel knew that a drink wasn't really what he needed. He needed answers.

His mind kept wandering back to the police station two days prior, when he'd overheard the two inspectors mention their most recent case. They'd questioned how he knew the deceased, but wouldn't tell him much about how Keith Christie had died. All Daniel had been able to gather was that a thief had broken into Christie's flat in the middle of the night. There had been a scuffle, and Christie had ended up dead. Police were still looking for the suspected thief.

Daniel had wanted to tell the inspectors why he was supposed to meet Christie at the station that morning, but the shock of hearing about the murder had given him pause. It couldn't be a mere coincidence that his only witness against Gilbert Ross had been killed the night before he was planning on confessing to the police. *No*, Daniel thought, *this wasn't just some robbery gone bad.* Then he'd remembered Christie's speculation about Ross having some of the police on his payroll. So, Daniel had simply told the inspectors that he knew Christie through his work at the kirk—a friend of a friend kind of thing.

An unexpected buzzing from his cell phone interrupted Daniel's musings. It was Ellie.

"Hey, what's up?" he asked.

"I've got some good news and some bad news for you," Ellie said. Her voice was low, as if she were trying not to be overheard.

"Uh-oh, what's wrong?" Daniel asked, hearing the hush in her voice.

"So, you want the bad news first?"

"Um, sure, I guess. Are you okay? You sound like you're whispering," Daniel asked.

"I'm fine. I'm in between patients right now, but the walls in these exam rooms are thin," Ellie explained. "The police are likely done with their investigation into that foreman's death, or at least his apartment—that's the bad news."

"So soon? I haven't heard anything about it online or anywhere. Did they catch the thief? Wait, how do you know?" Daniel asked.

"An officer just dropped off a dog at the clinic for us to board until it can be adopted. That happens from time to time with recently deceased people who don't have any living relatives willing or able to take their pets. They never tell us who the pet used to belong to—something about privacy concerns. But this dog is micro-chipped, so I pulled its records. It's registered to a Mr. Keith Christie," Ellie said.

"Wow, you have his dog? I remember overhearing the inspector say that the neighbor who found his body had gone over to complain about a dog barking," Daniel said.

"I believe it," Ellie said. "It hasn't shut up since it got here. I'm surprised you can't hear it through the phone."

"So, what's the good news? Or was that it?"

"No. I'm glad the dog is safe, but the reason I called was to tell you that it's safe to go to Christie's flat now. The police would've kept custody of it if they still considered the flat an active crime scene. Putting the dog up for adoption means they're done," Ellie said.

"Why would you think I'd want to go to his flat?" Daniel asked. Ellie didn't answer, but Daniel could imagine her left eyebrow arching just over the rim of her glasses in a skeptical look. "All right, you know me better than I know myself. I can't stop thinking about it. There's no way he was accidentally killed in a fight with some random burglar the night before he was going to confess. The police either missed something or are covering it up. But if I could get a look inside his flat…"

"You need his address, don't you?" Ellie asked, anticipating where his thinking was leading.

"If you have it."

"The dog's microchip said 15 Diriebught Road. I don't know if it's current. People don't always update those things when they move, but it's a place to start," Ellie said.

"Great! I may need you to spell that for me," Daniel said as he searched for a scrap piece of paper to write on. "When do you get off today? Do you want to do a little snooping with me?"

"I'm sorry, I can't today. I'm meeting your mum to go over wedding plans, remember?"

"Oh, right. And my dad's golfing with Mr. Tweed this afternoon. Now that I know he's not a murderer, I feel more comfortable leaving my dad alone with him. I just hope he doesn't wear something too embarrassing for Mr. Tweed."

"From what I've seen of your da, he's likely already found himself a matching tweed golfing suit," Ellie laughed. "I don't think you'll run into trouble at the flat, but perhaps you should get Amir to go with you, just in case."

"That's a good idea. I think I saw him around here earlier."

"Be careful and keep me updated," Ellie said.

"You too. Are you sure *you* don't need backup?" Daniel asked jokingly.

"I ken I can handle your mum. Plus, there'll be cakes and wine. Love you," Ellie said.

"Love you too," Daniel said, ending the call. He closed his sermon notebook and crawled out from behind his desk. This was just the distraction he needed.

Daniel followed the sound of piano music down the hall to Amir's office. *There's enough space in there for a piano?* Daniel thought as he knocked on the door. *How did I not think to snag this room for myself before we hired him?* He cracked the door open, and the music stopped.

"Ah, Daniel, I'm glad it's you. I wasn't sure if I should bring this up with Reverend Calder, but I'm having a problem with one of our, ah…members," Amir said before Daniel could even step inside.

Although there had been some initial skepticism among some parishioners, everyone seemed to have warmed to Amir rather quickly. There were certainly fewer complaints about the Sunday music now than during Daniel's brief stint as choir director. Who could Amir be having trouble with?

"Sure. How can I help?" Daniel asked.

Amir simply stood and pointed to a corner of the room. Daniel stepped closer. On top of a wooden chair lay a nest of shredded sheet music. Upon closer inspection, the paper was interlaced with a piece of tartan-patterned scarf, one wool glove, and clumps of short orange hair.

"Sir Walter," Daniel said.

"That cat has bested our defenses," Amir sighed. "We must do something else, or I won't have any music left. We'll have to sing from memory and, well, you know the choir. Not all the songs they have memorized are Sunday morning appropriate."

Daniel laughed. "Okay, we'll try again, but any further cat-proofing will have to wait. You and I have got an apartment to see."

Chapter Fifty-One

"Thanks for coming with me," Daniel said as he and Amir walked from the bus stop to Diriebught Road. "I would've brought Ellie or my dad, but they were both busy."

"Now I see where I rank," Amir said dryly.

"No, that came out wrong. I just didn't want to disturb you again. You've already done so much with this case," Daniel said.

"I'm happy to come. I want to see justice for Sayyid as much as you. But I do wonder how you get any church work done traipsing around the city as you do," Amir joked.

"It's not always easy." Daniel smiled. "Look, I think this is it," he said, pointing to a row of two- and three-story, orange and white brick buildings. The buildings formed a conjoined line down the block with little satellite dishes reaching out from the windows of nearly every flat.

The street was clear with no police cars in sight, so Daniel walked up to number 15 and peeked through one of its two windows. The curtains were partially closed, but he could see enough to tell that no one was home. He checked the door. Locked.

"I do not suppose you have a key?" Amir asked.

Daniel shook his head. He tried the window again. It was locked, too. He moved on to the second window. It shifted slightly when he pushed on it. Daniel squeezed his fingertips underneath the ledge and pulled upward. His fingers strained, but inch by slow inch, the window slid open.

"What are you doing?" Amir asked, alarmed.

"We didn't take two different buses all the way here just to turn back at one locked door," Daniel said as he pried the window open enough for a body to squeeze through. He turned around and saw Amir's startled expression. *I might be getting a touch too comfortable with breaking and entering*, he thought to himself. His old flatmate, Young Hugh Macpherson, would be proud.

"I'll slip in just for a minute and have a look around. If you want to stay out here, you can keep a lookout," Daniel said.

Amir glanced up and down the street. "I think a brown man lingering outside here would be a bit more conspicuous. Let's make this quick," he said. He took one last look down the empty street and then scrambled through the window.

Daniel quickly pulled himself in after Amir. He closed the window and pulled the curtains shut so that no passersby could see in. Muted sunlight filtered through the curtains, but not enough to see clearly, so Daniel decided to chance turning on a light. He spied the shadow of what appeared to be a floor lamp on the other side of the room and carefully made his way over to it. He nearly fell twice, tripping over unknown debris on the floor. Once he found the lamp and flicked it on, he was shocked to see the room's state.

They stood in Keith Christie's complete mess of a living room. The disarray was far more than just the typical bachelor untidiness one might expect from a man who lived alone and worked long, hard hours. Couch cushions lay strewn across the room. The coffee table was upended, its contents scattered on the floor—a jumble of papers, beer cans, and takeout food bags. Shards of glass crunched underfoot, the remains of picture frames and drinking glasses. It looked as if a tornado had torn through the space and left the scattered contents of Keith Christie's life in its wake.

"What happened here?" Amir asked.

"I don't know, but it sure doesn't look like the work of a simple cat burglar," Daniel said. Amir raised a confused eyebrow. "Thief," Daniel clarified. "Look, there's plenty of valuables left out in plain sight." He pointed to a gleaming gold watch lying beside the overturned coffee table. A small shelf beside the front door held several magazines, car keys dangling from a hook, and a clearly visible stack of twenty-pound notes folded in half with a paperclip.

"So, if whoever broke in wasn't after money or valuables, what was he after?" Daniel asked.

"Perhaps it wasn't a thief at all. Perhaps, like the others, Mr. Christie's murder was only made to look like an accident," Amir suggested.

"But why trash the place like this? Why not just kill him and then rifle through a few drawers, steal the TV or cash, or something? That would have been sufficient to stage a robbery. This whole place has been turned inside out."

"Christie did the other murders, so the new killer might not have been as experienced or had the time to plan it out properly?" Amir speculated. "Or Christie was expecting something like this. He knew testifying against Gilbert Ross would be dangerous, did he not? So, he fought back, and the furniture paid the price."

Daniel surveyed the destruction, considering Amir's theories. It did fit Gilbert Ross's pattern of covering up murders under the veil of unlucky accidents: construction accident, car crash, and now a home robbery gone bad. But why leave the police on the lookout for a killer? The first two were much cleaner; there were no loose ends to tie up. Maybe Amir was right, and this new guy simply wasn't as good as Christie had been. But if Christie had truly expected Ross to come after him, then why come home at all? Why not go straight to the police station?

Daniel thought back to the last conversation he'd had with the foreman. Christie had said that he'd wanted one more night in his own bed as a free man. Daniel could see now that Christie had just been pulling at his heartstrings. Perhaps because of Daniel's profession or simply the way he presented himself, Christie had pegged him as sympathetic and had taken advantage of his compassion.

Then Daniel remembered something else he had said, and the puzzle pieces started to fall into place. "Keith Christie's murder wasn't just made to look like a robbery gone bad; it *was* a robbery. And the killer was looking for something specific," Daniel said to Amir. "Christie was worried that if he testified against Gilbert Ross, it would come down to his word against Ross's. And combined with his wealth and influence, Christie was afraid that Ross's word would trump his own. Christie needed proof, and that was why he'd wanted to go home first. That was what his killer was after—whatever dirt Christie had on Ross."

"What could it be?" Amir asked.

Daniel held his head in his hands and closed his eyes. "Let me think." He strained his memory for any clues, but came up blank.

Amir picked the edge of a couch cushion off the floor and then let it go. "Perhaps he had a recording of Ross telling him to kill Sayyid? Or an email? Do you see a computer anywhere?" He moved the pile of papers from the upended coffee table with the toe of his shoe.

"That's it!" Daniel said excitedly.

"What? You see a laptop?"

"No, a paper trail," Daniel said. He remembered, before Christie had confessed, when he'd attempted to brush him off, Christie had tapped on his ledger and said, "Now if you'll excuse me, I've got more money to make." His ledger—that had to be it!

"Christie kept a record of the construction expenses and materials for Ross to report back to GlenBreeze Dynamics. But like Mr. Tweed, um, George Fraser, believes, those numbers didn't add up. If they were secretly using cheaper materials and labor, then there had to be another ledger with the actual figures so that Christie and Ross would know exactly how much money they could siphon away for themselves. We need to find that secret ledger."

Chapter Fifty-Two

With an idea of what they were looking for, Daniel and Amir launched a meticulous search of Keith Christie's flat. They started in the living room, carefully sifting through the wreckage. They checked behind cushions, beneath rugs, and rifled through Christie's extensive DVD collection. Yet, they did not discover anything that resembled a secret ledger.

"It will take forever to go through the entire flat," Amir said as he glanced at the wall clock with an anxious expression on his face.

Daniel knew what he was thinking. Even if no one was coming home to this flat, neighbors would be getting off work before too long, and two strange men walking out of a dead man's home would look mighty suspicious. "Let's split up. You take the kitchen; I'll check his bedroom."

Amir headed to the kitchen to comb through the stacks of dishes and half-opened drawers and cupboards, while Daniel made his way to the bedroom. Christie's dresser drawers were easy enough to search; they were already opened with their contents strewn across the floor. Daniel felt the backs and bottoms of the drawers—no secret compartments. He moved on to the bed and checked under the mattress and behind the headboard. Nothing.

He checked the bathroom, looking behind the mirror and inside the medicine cabinet. He even lifted the cover off the toilet tank, but the elusive ledger was nowhere to be found. Shaking his head in frustration, Daniel reluctantly conceded defeat for now and headed back to the living room. Maybe Amir had had better luck. But when he saw Amir's face, Daniel didn't have to ask if his friend had found anything.

"It was a good idea, but there's nothing here," Amir said. "Our only witness is dead, and this secret ledger, if it ever existed, is gone. Sayyid will never get justice, and Gilbert Ross will go on endangering others for his own profit," Amir said with a heavy sigh. "We should leave here before anyone sees us."

"Wait. Maybe we've been going about this all wrong," Daniel said. "We're assuming the ledger's gone because Christie's killer found it. But what if he didn't? I mean, look at this place. It's a total wreck. Even the silverware drawer's been ransacked," Daniel said, gesturing to the kitchen. "Who hides a secret accounts book in with their spoons and forks? If the killer had to search this hard, it's because he was desperate. I'm betting the ledger was never even here."

Which would mean Keith Christie really did just want to spend one last, peaceful night at home before he went to the police, Daniel thought. But he never got that. His life had ended as violently as he had lived it. If Christie hadn't been a murderer, Daniel would have felt sorry for him.

"So where is it?" Amir asked.

"He had a ledger with him at the dock. Since we were out in the open, I imagine that was the fake one meant for the executives at GlenBreeze Dynamics, so that won't do us any good. But—"

"You think he kept the other records book nearby," Amir said, finishing Daniel's thought.

"I know I would have trouble remembering all those numbers until I got home to record them," Daniel said. "We need to go back to the docks and search that boat, or maybe even the control rooms of the wind turbines themselves."

"I think I know someone who can help us," Amir said.

* * *

Daniel arrived at the Port of Inverness as the last pink and purple rays of sunlight were fading into the calm waters of the Beauly Firth. The day's earlier warmth was beginning to fade, and Daniel was glad for the light jacket he'd thought to bring. It also had pockets large enough to hold two

214

flashlights without looking too conspicuous.

Even in the fading light, the dock was alive with activity. Seagulls circled overhead, their raucous cries echoed off the water as they scavenged for scraps left behind by dock workers who had gone home hours ago—a last meal before the gulls too would leave and settle in for the night. Lapping waves against the hulls of moored boats and the rocky shore created a soothing counter-rhythm to the gulls' cries. Light-sensitive street lamps blinked on like the first stars of the night.

Amir and another man waited beside the entrance gate. "This is Jamil," Amir said as Daniel approached.

"Reverend Darrow," Jamil said as he shook Daniel's hand.

"Call me Daniel," Daniel said. "Thank you for meeting us. Amir told me you could get us onto Mr. Christie's boat?"

Jamil nodded. The flecks of gray in his curly hair shimmered under the bright light of a street lamp. "Mr. Christie only rented the boat, but yes, I will show you onboard," he said and unlocked the gate. As they followed Jamil to the dock, Amir explained Jamil's role in Christie's construction crew.

"Jamil served as the ship's steward when it was more practical for the crew to stay aboard overnight rather than return to shore. He took care of arranging meals, bedding, and housekeeping," Amir said.

"Or would it be *ship-keeping*?" Daniel asked.

Jamil simply shrugged rather than indulge his corny wordplay. "Mr. Christie did not pay me enough for it, whatever you want to call it. The men were filthy after two or three days at sea, and Mr. Christie, he was the worst of them all."

Amir laughed and patted him on the back. "Well, because of his duties, Jamil has his own set of keys for the boat. So, we will not have to rely on unlocked windows tonight."

When they reached the dock, Jamil helped Daniel and Amir aboard. The ship had seemed much larger when Daniel had seen it the other morning from the dock. Now that he was onboard, it felt crowded with all the construction machinery and turbine materials. Jamil hurried across the deck and opened a door that led to the cabins below.

"This is giving me flashbacks," Daniel muttered as they followed Jamil down the narrow metal stairwell.

"Flashbacks?" Amir asked.

"Nothing, never mind," Daniel said, recalling the time he and his onetime flatmate, Young Hugh, had snuck onto a cargo ship in search of a ceramic baby Jesus. That misadventure had ended in an unexpected and icy swim to shore. He was thankful that this time he had a tour guide.

Jamil led them down a short hallway lit with dim safety lights that ran along the ceiling and on either side of the floor. "This is, or was, Mr. Christie's office. He did not like anyone to go inside. He would yell at me even if I peeked in to empty the trash."

Amir tried the door handle. "It's locked. Do you have a key?"

"Of course," Jamil said matter-of-factly. "I cleaned when he was out working on the turbines. Not so much that he would notice, but I had to do something. He was not a tidy man. But if Mr. Christie kept his records onboard, this is where they would be," Jamil said.

As he opened the locked door, a wave of stale air with an undercurrent of decay greeted them. Jamil flipped on the single bare light bulb hanging from the ceiling. The small space was made even more crowded by the voluminous amounts of clutter filling every square inch. Stacks of boxes towered haphazardly against one wall. The floor was strewn with debris—old newspapers, magazines, and random papers mingled with discarded food wrappers and empty beer and soda cans. A desk was crammed against the far wall, its surface buried beneath a hill of paperwork and junk.

The room reminded Daniel of his own office at Church Street Kirk. Like his office, this room had clearly been made into an office space as an afterthought. But unlike his, which was cluttered with books, Christie's office was littered with actual trash. "I feel like we need to put on hazmat suits before digging around in there," he said.

Amir chuckled, while Jamil simply sighed. "I warned you; Mr. Christie did not want anyone in his office, even to clean," Jamil said, shaking his head.

"I am beginning to think the disaster we saw at his flat was not entirely the work of his killer," Amir said.

Neither one of them had yet dared to cross the door's threshold. There was the strange, unsettling feeling of rummaging through a dead man's things. And then there was the sheer scale of the mess. Finding Christie's secret ledger would be like finding a needle in a trash heap.

"Well, we might as well get started," Daniel said. He took a deep breath—the last of the relatively fresh air from the below-deck hallway—and stepped inside.

Chapter Fifty-Three

Daniel started by sifting through a heap of old newspapers stacked in the corner. Their tattered pages tore as he flipped through them, searching for anything that might be hidden within their folds. Amir searched the boxes against the wall. He pulled the top one down, careful not to send the whole pile tumbling.

Not finding anything in the newspapers, Daniel moved on to the metal desk. His footsteps were muffled by the scattered debris beneath his feet. He sat in a small swivel chair with rips in its upholstery and flipped through a stack of magazines about Formula 1 racing, football, boating, and catalogues for machine parts. He slid those aside to focus on an assortment of other papers, but found nothing resembling a ledger or accounts book. He did find several brochures for exotic locales across Europe. Christie was evidently already planning how he was going to spend his cut of the money, or perhaps a safe place to relocate once his sister got out of prison.

Daniel rubbed his temples. The cramped, unclean space and smell of half-eaten, rotting food was getting to him. He turned his attention to a sliding drawer located under the desk. He pulled on it, but it would not budge. "Jamil, do you have a key to this desk drawer?" he asked.

Jamil eyed the desk suspiciously and then shook his head, *No*. Daniel scanned the top of the desk and surrounding wall for a key. "Any luck with those boxes?" he asked Amir.

Amir returned an exasperated look. "The man was a hoarder," he said, "but nothing he kept is of any help to us. It is all junk."

Daniel tried the drawer again. It wiggled this time, giving him hope. He pulled a flashlight out of his pocket and bent down to examine the lock. The keyhole was bent and had deep scratches around it as if someone had attempted to force it open. Daniel looked more closely at the thin gap between the bottom of the desk and the top of the drawer. The lock's latch stood at an angle, not fully engaged, but just enough to keep the drawer from opening. Daniel searched the top of the desk for a pen or anything he could use to pry the latch open. He pricked his index finger on the open blade of a box cutter knife. *I'll have to be careful not to cut off my finger, but that should do*, he thought.

"Amir, can you come hold the flashlight for me? I think I might have found something," Daniel said. "This lock looks like it's been tampered with, but I might can get it open."

Amir gladly put down the box he was going through and held the light, directing its beam onto the drawer. Daniel pushed the small chair out of the way and knelt to be at eye level with the lock. After a couple minutes of wedging and twisting the blade almost to the point of breaking, the latch finally released. Daniel slowly slid the drawer open to find Keith Christie's ledger lying on top of an assortment of other papers.

Daniel felt like a kid on Christmas morning, having just ripped through a well-taped gift. He put the knife down and picked up the ledger with both hands, holding it up proudly for Amir to see. Amir's eyes lit up with excitement and relief. They looked through it together. Christie had kept a precise record of each day's hours, turbine numbers, work crew, materials, and costs. The meticulousness of the columns and daily records they held was a stark contrast to the disorderliness of Christie's office space and home.

"Is this it?" Amir asked.

Daniel flipped through the pages, his initial excitement fading. "It looks like an exhaustive record of the wind farm's expenses, but..."

"But?" Amir asked.

"I'm only seeing one set of numbers. If we were right about Christie and Ross's scheme, there should be two. One set of high, doctored figures for the GlenBreeze Dynamics Board and another account of the lower, actual expenses. I think this is the same ledger Christie had when we confronted him here the other day." Daniel said. To confirm, he walked over and handed the ledger to Jamil, who had remained outside the entrance of the cramped room.

Jamil's brow furrowed as he studied the sheets. He opened his mouth to speak, but then stopped and flipped through several more pages. Finally, he shook his head and handed the ledger back to Daniel. "These are Mr. Christie's accounts, yes. But I don't understand it. I see my crew, the turbines, our hours. Some of the hours seem inflated; if they are correct, then we are owed much back pay. But the stranger part is the materials lists."

"Strange how?" Daniel asked.

"I did not work on the heavy installation, but I did help with sorting and unloading crates. I know the parts, but I do not recognize any of these names or brands," Jamil said, pointing to a column on the spreadsheet.

"This is the fake ledger," Daniel said with a sigh. He tossed it on top of the desk amongst the rest of the trash and useless papers. He plopped down in the desk chair, closed his eyes, and held his head in his hands. "This has all been for nothing. We're no closer to getting justice for Sayyid or Lexi Campbell, and now, because of my meddling, another person is dead. If I hadn't convinced Christie to testify, he'd still be alive."

"Keith Christie was a murderer. If you hadn't meddled, I'm sure his crimes would have caught up with him eventually," Amir said, trying to console his friend. "And now we know Sayyid and Lexi's deaths were not accidents. We know who killed them and why. That is something."

"Yes, but all we have is the word of a dead man. Without any hard evidence, who would believe us? Gilbert Ross will just get someone else to do his dirty work, and people will keep getting hurt," Daniel said.

"There's got to be something else we can do," Amir said. "You said the lock had been tampered with. Do you think Ross knew about the ledger?"

"If he did, he didn't think it was worth stealing. And why would he? It only confirms what he'd been telling the company board all along. I hate to admit it, Amir, but we've failed," Daniel said. He slowly stood from the desk chair with a groan, feeling a decade older than when he'd first sat down. "I'm sorry we wasted your time, Jamil. We should go before you get into trouble for letting us aboard. Jamil?" Daniel asked, confused. Jamil was busy placing old food wrappers and drink cans into a large plastic bag.

"What are you doing?" Daniel asked. "Christie's dead. You don't have to clean up after him anymore."

Jamil paused and glanced around the room. "Old habits," he said. He picked at another candy bar wrapper from inside the desk drawer. "Strange."

"What?" Amir asked.

"This wrapper. It's caught, but there's nothing under the drawer. Where is the rest of it?" Jamil asked. He ran his hand down the underside of the desk drawer and held it up as if to prove his point.

"It's just trash. The sugar, or whatever, probably congealed and stuck to the side," Daniel said, frustrated. He pulled at the wrapper to throw it away so that they could leave. The wrapper slid up, but only an inch. The rest of it was stuck somewhere between the side wall and the bottom of the drawer. Daniel reached under the drawer like Jamil had, but felt only cold metal. So where was the rest of the wrapper?

"Wait a minute!" Daniel tossed out the rest of the clutter from inside the drawer and then felt along the edges. A small notch about the size of a fingertip was located along the back edge—a false bottom! Daniel pulled the drawer out as far as it would go and then lifted.

Underneath the thin false bottom lay a UK passport book, a small flask, a black, leather-bound notebook, and the bottom half of the candy wrapper. Daniel picked up the passport to see Christie's portrait on the front page. The flask was engraved with the same blue lion that he remembered seeing tattooed on the foreman's right forearm. Finally, he reached for the leather notebook and handed it to Amir. After so many false hopes, he was afraid to open it.

"It's a record of expenses like the other one," Amir said after flipping through a few pages.

"Let's see," Daniel said. He retrieved the first ledger and held it open on top of the desk. Amir placed the leather-bound notebook next to it. Both books shared a similar layout: columns and rows of dates, crew, turbines, materials, and costs. At first glance, they looked identical. But when he compared them closely, Daniel found discrepancies.

"Is it just me, or do some of these numbers and material names not match?" Daniel asked.

"No, they do not. Jamil, have a look," Amir said, leaning back so Jamil could see.

"These products I recognize," Jamil said, pointing to the leather notebook. "These are the parts we used for the turbines."

Daniel laughed out loud. It was an inappropriate response, given the deadly consequences of the two records books, but he couldn't help it. Weeks of tense emotion suddenly erupted into physical expression. It was either laugh or cry. After searching for so long and running up against dead end after dead end, they'd finally found it—proof of Christie and Ross's scheme to steal money from GlenBreeze Dynamics. And more importantly, those two sets of lined pages held the motive for the murders of Sayyid Ghulam and Lexi Campbell.

Chapter Fifty-Four

"I'm sorry, this isn't funny. I'm just so relieved," Daniel said, wiping a tear from his eye. "We did it! We found the proof we need to take down Gilbert Ross and bring justice, and hopefully some closure, to Sayyid's and Lexi's families."

Amir smiled and let out a chuckle of satisfaction. "It's too late in the night to tell Samira the good news, but we can go first thing in the morning. Then we will all march down to the police station together."

Daniel sucked in air through his teeth and furrowed his brow. "Can we keep this between us for a little longer? I'd like to get a few more eyes on these books just to make sure they are what we think they are," he said, his initial joy giving way to skepticism.

"Keith Christie was afraid of going against Gilbert Ross, and that fear was obviously well-founded. So, I want to be certain that when we bring accusations against him, they'll stick. In the meantime, we all need to be extra careful and watch our backs. I'm going to stay with my parents at their hotel until this is settled. You two might want to consider something similar. If Ross was willing to take out one of his own, I doubt he'd have a problem doing the same to us," Daniel said.

"Amir, you will stay with me and my brothers," Jamil said, leaving no room for objection.

Amir nodded. "Thank you, my friend. Now, we should leave this place quietly before anyone knows we were here."

* * *

"Where's Mom tonight?" Daniel asked his father as they shared an evening cup of tea in their hotel room. Mr. Darrow was eager to indulge in local traditions, though he had filled his cup half full with milk.

"She should be back soon. She's found a pottery studio somewhere that rents space. You know your mother. Even on vacation, her work comes first," Mr. Darrow said with a shrug. "I just told her that whatever it is she's working on, make sure it can fit on the plane ride home!"

"Before she returns, I have something I'd like to get your opinion on. Did you deal much with international suppliers or companies back before you retired?" Daniel asked as he retrieved Keith Christie's two notebooks from his bag.

"Depended on the job. For big projects, we'd often work with foreign suppliers," his father said.

"What can you tell me about this?" Daniel asked, showing him the fake ledger.

Mr. Darrow studied it for several minutes. "It's an accounts book that a project manager or foreman would keep. Looks like it's for some kind of energy project. Wind turbines?" he asked. Daniel nodded. "I recognize some of these suppliers—pricey, but top-of-the-line stuff. These are the type of materials they should be using on that wind farm here we toured."

"I was hoping you'd say something like that. Now, what about this one?" Daniel asked, handing him the black, leather-bound notebook.

"Hmm, at first glance, I'd say it's a copy, but the suppliers don't match. I'm not familiar with them. No, I do know this one," Mr. Darrow said, pointing to a line in the notebook. "I only remember because we used them once on a job. It was a total disaster. I recommended against it, but the client insisted. He was really cheap and trying to save a few bucks. After the parts failed, it ended up costing him a lot more than if he'd gone with quality materials the first time around. But you get what you pay for. What's this all about, anyway?"

"So, you'd say that the materials in this book are cheaper than the ones listed in the first?" Daniel asked, ignoring his father's question.

"Absolutely. If whoever's in charge of the project is going this cheap, I'd hate to see where else they're cutting corners. Now, I was only a mechanical engineer, so I didn't manage projects, but I would seriously question the integrity of any manager or foreman who'd sign off on this," Mr. Darrow said.

"That's just what I wanted to hear," Daniel said.

"Strange though—the handwriting in both these books looks so similar. And the dates…" Mr. Darrow said, examining both notebooks. "But they can't be the same project."

"You wouldn't think so, would you?" Daniel said, knowingly.

As he was putting away the two notebooks, Daniel's mother returned to the hotel room. She put her purse down and gave him a hug. Daniel noticed that she had bits of dried clay on the sleeves of her shirt.

"Looks like you were busy tonight," Daniel said.

"I didn't realize how late it was until the studio said they were closing for the night. I'm working on something for your bride," Mrs. Darrow said and put her index finger up against her lips. "With the wedding just a couple of weeks away, I want to make sure I finish in time."

"What are you making?" Daniel asked. Knowing his mother, Daniel figured it would either be something practical or completely outlandish. For their twentieth wedding anniversary, she had made matching coffee mugs for herself and his father. The next year, she had sculpted a four-foot palm tree that doubled as a hummingbird feeder. Of course, Daniel's father had loved them both.

"You'll have to wait and see," she said, shaking her finger at his question. "I'm so glad you'll be staying with us. Your father said your apartment was being fumigated? I hope it's nothing too serious."

"It should be fine in a few days," Daniel said. "And the hotel actually had the adjoining room free, so I'll be just on the other side of the wall." He'd had to think of a reason he needed a hotel room on such short notice, and he didn't exactly want to tell them that he feared someone might break in and murder him in his sleep. Bedbugs seemed like an easier story to swallow.

"Oh," his mother said, with disappointment in her voice.

Daniel glanced around the room. There was hardly enough room for the one bed and a small seating area near the window. He didn't know how she thought there'd be enough space for him to stay with them in their room.

"Well, you must stay and watch a movie with us. Your father hooked his tablet up to the TV and downloaded Braveheart."

"Braveheart? Really?" Daniel asked. That was a little too on the nose, even for his father.

"We could split the haggis I've got in the mini-fridge!" Mr. Darrow said with an excited grin.

In the morning, Daniel called to check in on Amir. Amir confirmed he had made it through the night without incident, other than having difficulty sleeping over the noise of Jamil's raucous brothers. Daniel told him that they should only need to keep their heads down for another day or two just to be safe, and then it should all be over. After Daniel's father confirmed what they'd thought about the materials listed in Keith Christie's two accounts books, Daniel wanted to verify the numbers before taking the books to the police. So he left the hotel before his parents could wrangle him into a long breakfast and headed to Church Street.

"I don't understand why we couldn't meet at the clubhouse," Mr. Tweed said when he walked into Daniel's office at the kirk. "There's nothing so urgent it couldn't wait until after a few swings of a nine iron, I say. That's how business is done, isn't it—on the golf course?"

"Believe me, this is not the type of business you want to discuss outside of closed doors," Daniel said, indicating that Mr. Tweed should shut the door behind him.

Mr. Tweed clearly did not like the idea of being holed up inside Daniel's cramped office, but the reverend's cryptic text from earlier that morning and the present call for secrecy intrigued him. He shut the door and leaned on his cane, waiting for Daniel to explain.

"You might want to sit down for this," Daniel said.

Chapter Fifty-Five

Mr. Tweed looked at the old wooden chair in front of Daniel's desk skeptically. It wasn't upholstered, had zero lumbar support, and, next to his towering figure, it resembled a child's seat. He sighed and pulled the chair out to allow room for his knees not to hit the desk when he sat down.

"Now, can you tell me why I gave up my tee time this morning?" he asked.

Daniel opened his bag and pulled out two thin books. He handed one to Mr. Tweed.

"What's this?"

"You tell me," Daniel answered.

Mr. Tweed opened a book and flipped through the first few pages. He looked up at Daniel with one bushy eyebrow raised quizzically on his forehead. Daniel returned a straight poker face. Mr. Tweed returned his attention to the ledger book. He studied it for several minutes before speaking.

"These are the figures for the Moray Firth wind farm. How did you get this?" he asked.

"Before I tell you that, I have another accounts book I want you to see," Daniel said. He handed over the black leather-bound notebook.

Mr. Tweed examined the second book, glancing between it and the first one. "I'm not involved in the day-to-day, but this second ledger is clearly for a different project," he said.

"Compare the dates," Daniel said. "And the handwriting."

"They're…what am I looking at?"

Daniel proceeded to tell Mr. Tweed about the events of the past couple of days: Sayyid's letter of complaint to Gilbert Ross, Ellie's mother's discovery about Keith Christie's sister, Christie's confession and then death, and finally about how he and Amir had found Christie's two ledgers. Mr. Tweed blinked several times, speechless. He looked at the two books and then back at Daniel.

"I see why you wanted me to sit down. That is quite a story. I knew someone was stealing from the company, but Ross? He's my friend," Mr. Tweed said. He shook his head in disbelief. He ran his finger along a row from one ledger to the next. "Still, the numbers don't lie. Just glancing through these, it looks like there's a difference of nearly a million pounds."

"Really? That's incredible," Daniel said.

"I've always had a head for maths," Mr. Tweed boasted. "Oh, you mean the amount he's stolen? Aye, it's quite a sum. At this rate, by the time the project's completed, it could be ten times that much. Have you shown these to anyone else?"

"Just Amir and my father. I needed someone who knew more about the materials and equipment recorded in them. Now that you've confirmed the numbers, I'm ready to show them to the police. But there's just one thing that still gives me pause," Daniel said.

"Oh?"

"All we had implicating Gilbert Ross was Christie's word, and now he's dead. So, what's stopping Ross from simply denying his involvement? It would be easy to say that he didn't know anything about the entire scheme, that it was all Christie's idea. Both ledgers are in Keith Christie's handwriting, after all. Ross could admit to nothing more than exercising poor judgment in hiring a corrupt foreman," Daniel said.

Mr. Tweed considered Daniel's worry for a moment. Then he grabbed the black, leather-bound notebook and flipped hastily to the inside back cover. He flipped it around and handed it back to Daniel. "Do you see that?" he asked, pointing to a string of numbers scrawled onto the bottom of the cover.

"Yeah, I noticed it, but I couldn't figure out what it meant. A product number, maybe?" Daniel asked.

Mr. Tweed shook his head and raised his bushy eyebrows knowingly. "Do you see the two letters at the front of the numbers? That's the clue."

"So, what is it?"

"Hmm, I suppose that would be a bit, em, above your pay grade, as they say. HB stands for the Haller Bank in Switzerland. The numbers are the account."

"Ross needed a place to put all that money that wouldn't raise suspicions here at home, so he funneled it into a Swiss bank account," Daniel said. Mr. Tweed touched his finger to his nose. "Wait, how would you know what a Swiss bank number looks like?"

"Never mind that. What matters is that, like yourself, our unfortunate friend Mr. Christie would not likely have had the know-how or resources to go about setting up something like this," Mr. Tweed said.

"Above his pay grade?" Daniel asked sarcastically.

"Aye, but Gilly—moving money around is like, I don't know. What's something that is easy for you to do? Cooking a hot dog?"

"Sure," Daniel said, trying not to roll his eyes. He couldn't be too offended. He did give George Fraser, or Mr. Tweed, a rather stereotypical nickname behind his back.

"Well, I'm willing to bet that if I did a little digging, that account would lead back to Gilly. Do you mind?" Mr. Tweed asked, motioning to a pen and notepad on Daniel's desk. Daniel slid them over for Mr. Tweed to copy down the Swiss bank account number.

"So, I guess I should take these down to the police station now. You're pretty well-connected in this city. Are there any officers or inspectors that you would trust with a case like this? Keith Christie was hesitant to come forward because he believed Ross had paid off some of the police." Daniel said as he returned the two accounts books to his bag.

Mr. Tweed thought for a moment. "I could give you a couple names, but I don't believe Gilly would do something like that."

"He was willing to have three people killed because they found out about his plans," Daniel said.

Mr. Tweed gripped the handle of his cane and rapped its end against the wooden floor of the office. "It's difficult to believe he's capable of any of this. I've known the man for years, decades. We've invested together and gone on holiday together. I recommended him for membership at my golf club! I feel, I feel…"

"Betrayed?" Daniel asked.

"No," Mr. Tweed shook his head. "Angry." His eyes narrowed. The knuckles grew white on the hand that gripped his cane. "Would you mind waiting just a bit longer before you bring those books to the police? One more day?"

"Why?" Daniel asked. Keith Christie's life had ended less than a day after he'd decided to betray his boss to the police. Now that Daniel had gotten the confirmations he'd wanted, he knew that every minute longer that he held on to Christie's books, he was putting himself, Amir, and anyone else who knew about them in danger.

"I need time to make a few phone calls and trace this bank account," Mr. Tweed said. He rolled his tongue across his bottom row of teeth. "And I need to hear him say it."

Daniel gave him a perplexed look.

"Gilly. We've been mates for ages. It's one thing to lie to the board, but to look an old friend in the eye and lie—that's simply dishonorable. So, I need to hear him say it," Mr. Tweed said.

"I'll come with you," Daniel said.

"No, Reverend, this is something I need to do alone—just Gilly and me," Mr. Tweed said. "I'll confront him tomorrow morning at the GlenBreeze office."

"George, he may be your friend, but Gilbert Ross is dangerous. Just look at what happened to Sayyid, Lexi, and his own partner. I can't let you be his next victim. He's not your only friend," Daniel pleaded.

"I appreciate your concern, Reverend, but I can take care of myself," Mr. Tweed said. He held up his cane by the midsection and flicked the silver-plated handle an inch in the air and then back. "I need this. All I ask is that you give me until noon tomorrow."

Reluctantly, Daniel agreed. "Noon tomorrow. Then I'm taking these to the police, whether you've met with Ross by then or not."

231

Chapter Fifty-Six

aniel held his satchel bag close to his side as he exited the bus at Church Street. The weather that morning was clear and crisp— a far cry from the worry and apprehension that clouded his thoughts. He entered Church Street Kirk and walked straight to his office. He checked the voicemail on his office phone. Empty. He glanced at his cell phone. It was 9:30, and still Mr. Tweed hadn't contacted him.

Daniel couldn't concentrate enough to get any church work done. He paced his office, which was difficult to do given the small space. By the time he'd gotten three good strides, he had to turn back around. Finally, his cell phone buzzed. He scrambled to retrieve it from his pocket and nearly dropped it.

Are you at the kirk? Can you meet in my office?

Daniel hadn't expected to see Amir today, but whatever it was, at least it would take his mind off his present worries. Two and one half hours until he went to the police station. Daniel checked his voice messages again, knowing they would still be empty, before heading down the hall to Amir's office.

He opened the door to find Amir stooped on his hands and knees, peering into a small wall vent. "Hello?" Daniel said. Amir's head shot up and slammed into a music stand. He muttered a couple of sharp words in a language that Daniel did not need translated in order to gather their meaning.

"Sorry, you texted?" Daniel said.

Amir stood up slowly, rubbing his head with one hand. "I don't know how he is still getting in, but he's up to his old tricks again," Amir said. With his free hand, he pointed to a corner of the room where a pile of sheet music sat on top of a wooden chair.

"Sir Walter," Daniel said, understanding why his colleague was on the floor.

"I know the kirk loves that feline, but he is making it impossible for me to work," Amir said.

"Love is a strong word," Daniel said with a chuckle.

"I am serious. I bought replacement sheet music with my own money, and now he's ruined them too," Amir said, clearly frustrated, the bump on the head having done little to soothe his feelings toward the kirk cat.

"I'm sorry, you're right. Sir Walter has always been a mischievous little guy, but this is a lot even for him. He and Mr. Fisher, the old choir director, had a kind of love and hate relationship. But he must have managed some kind of peace because I don't recall Fisher complaining of shredded sheet music." Daniel walked over to the corner where the wooden chair and a pile of papers were located. "Has this chair always been here?"

"I moved it there to get it out of the way the other day," Amir said.

"He seems to have made a little nest of shredded paper on top of it. It almost looks like straw," Daniel said. He had a sudden flash of memory. "Stay here. I'll be right back!" Daniel said and rushed out the door. Amir watched him go, standing beside the music stand, as frustrated and confused as ever.

Over twenty minutes passed before Daniel returned. "Amir, can you get the door?" he called from the hallway.

"What is that?" Amir asked as he held open the door. All he could see of Daniel was legs and the top half of his head, his eyes peering just above a wooden container of some sort. Daniel shuffled in, careful not to knock the doorframe with the sharp, rough corners of the container.

"Where do you want this?" he asked.

"I do not even know what that is," Amir protested.

"I'll put it down over in the corner that Sir Walter's already claimed," Daniel said.

"But—"

"Can you move the chair out of the way? This is kind of heavy," Daniel said. Once the corner was clear, Daniel heaved the wooden piece down with a thud. "Whew," he exhaled heavily. "I don't know how Fisher managed all that on his own."

"All what? What is this? A crate? Are we going to trap the cat?" Amir asked, perplexed.

"Almost done," Daniel said as he left the room again. He returned with a small rectangular bale of hay and placed it inside the wooden bin. "There," he said and stood back to gaze with satisfaction at his handiwork.

"Have you put an animal feed trough in my office? I know I am fairly new to this country, but this is odd, even for the British," Amir said.

"I'm not British. But, yes, sort of. It's from the kirk's Christmas nativity display—the manger," Daniel said.

"You sound as if that should explain things."

"Sir Walter loves this manger. I had to shoo him away when we set it up last Christmas. He ended up breaking the baby Jesus figurine. Now that I think about it, he might've been jealous of the figure. It was a whole thing. Anyway, I think this manger was how Mr. Fisher and Sir Walter managed a truce," Daniel said.

"I don't follow," Amir said.

"After Christmas, we took everything down and put it in the storage shed out by the garden. But the manger's wood is not nearly as weathered as the rest of the nativity set up. In exchange for Sir Walter not destroying his things, Fisher must have left the manger here as a bed for him," Daniel said. "But since Fisher wasn't here when we put it all away this year, I didn't know, and I just stuffed the manger in with everything else."

"So, you expect me to keep a feed trough in my office?" Amir asked.

"It's either that or more shredded sheet music. Sir Walter's—"

An orange blur shot across the baseboard on the opposite side of the room. Before Daniel had time to react, Sir Walter Scott was sitting atop the freshly deposited hay bale. He looked up at Daniel with a curiously affectionate expression on his face and began to purr and rub his furry cheek against

Daniel's hand. The cat then scratched at the hay, forming a round, cat-sized depression right in the middle of the bale. Once satisfied, he spun around three times, lay down, and started licking his paws.

Daniel and Amir stood there speechless until Daniel's cell phone rang. He glanced at the caller ID. It was Mr. Tweed. "Excuse me," he said, hastily pushing the *answer* button.

"George, what's up? Did you meet with Ross? What did he say?" Daniel asked.

"That's why I'm calling," Mr. Tweed said. "Gilly never showed up at the office this morning."

"What do you mean? What happened?" Daniel asked. His mind raced. *Did Gilbert Ross find out about Keith Christie's secret accounts notebook? Did Ross know that he and Amir had taken it?*

"I popped into the office this morning to confront him. I wore my most intimidating tweed, a dark blue barleycorn, and I marched right in unannounced to catch him off his guard. But his secretary said he wasn't in. I demanded she tell me where he went, and she said he never came in. He'd rung her half an hour earlier and instructed her to cancel all appointments on his calendar for the next two weeks," Mr. Tweed said.

"What does that mean?" Daniel asked.

"It means he's gone. He must have gotten spooked and fled the country."

"He was scared of getting caught. That's why Christie's murder wasn't like the others. Ross didn't have time to make it look like an accident because killing Christie was an act of desperation. And when he didn't find the accounts ledgers, he must've thought Christie had already turned them over to the police. That's why he didn't come after me or Amir—he didn't know we had them," Daniel said.

"And I've let him slip away all because I wanted to be the one to catch him in his lies. My pride couldn't take the betrayal. If I'd only gone to the police yesterday like you wanted, he would be in jail right now. But with his means and connections, he could be on a plane to anywhere in the world by now," Mr. Tweed said.

Daniel could hear the despair in his friend's voice. He looked at Amir, who was clearly wondering who he was talking to and what was being said on the other end of the line. How could he tell Amir that they had let Sayyid's killer get away? Dispirited, Daniel leaned against the manger. The hay was still stiff and scratchy, except for the cozy spot Sir Walter had managed to carve out in the center.

Seeing Sir Walter happily curled up in his manger sparked an idea. Even though Mr. Fisher was gone, and despite Daniel and Amir's best attempts to thwart him, the cat kept returning to his familiar spot. Humans, like all animals, are creatures of habit. When pressed, we often returned to old patterns and places that feel safe. *So,* Daniel asked himself, *where did Gilbert Ross continually run to when he felt threatened?*

"I think I know where Ross is going!" Daniel said excitedly. "Amir and I are at the kirk. Come pick us up. We need to get to the airport!"

Chapter Fifty-Seven

Daniel and Amir did not have to wait long before Mr. Tweed's sedan screeched to a stop in front of Church Street Kirk. They scrambled into the back seat and, before Daniel could fully shut the door, the car was pulling away from the curb. Mr. Tweed weaved in and out of traffic. They flew past the train station. Once they hit the A96 out of Inverness, Mr. Tweed pushed the car's engine to its limit. The usually calming shoreline views were a mere blur as they sped toward the airport.

"I think you and Ellie might have had the same driving instructor," Daniel quipped.

"Didn't you know? After her father passed away, I was wee Ellie's instructor," Mr. Tweed said, glancing back at him.

"Keep your eyes on the road!" Daniel shouted as Mr. Tweed turned back around just in time to swerve past a delivery truck.

When they arrived at the airport, Mr. Tweed dropped Daniel and Amir off in front of the terminal. "You two check the flights. I'll park and meet you inside," Mr. Tweed said and then sped away into the nearby premium parking zone.

"What are we looking for again?" Amir asked as he and Daniel searched for the nearest flight information board.

"Any flights with a destination or layover in Montenegro?" Daniel asked.

"How can you be sure Mr. Ross is headed there?" Amir asked.

"A conversation we had the first time I met him. That's where he goes when he wants to blow off steam or when things get a little too hot around here. I didn't get it at first, because Inverness has a pretty mild climate, but now I realize he wasn't talking about the weather. If he's running scared, that's where he'll run to. He actually tried to convince me to take Ellie there for our honeymoon," Daniel said.

They scanned the incoming and outgoing flight numbers. "There," Amir said, pointing to a flight number. "British Airways flight to Podgorica, Montenegro, with a layover at London Heathrow."

"It leaves in thirty minutes!" Daniel said. He looked past the baggage check stations down the long corridor to the security checkpoint. Being a small regional airport, there were no lines. But even without a line, the checkpoint was inaccessible to them. "How are we going to get through there without a ticket? The plane's probably already boarding."

"Anyone need a couple of air tickets?" Mr. Tweed huffed as he jogged toward them. He held up his cell phone with an image of an airline pass on the screen.

"How did you…?" Daniel asked.

"Ross isn't the only one with a secretary. I called on my way to Church Street. When you told me Montenegro, I had him book three seats on the next flight out. I assumed you wouldn't have your passports with you, so these are only good through to Heathrow."

"You never cease to amaze," Daniel said. "Let's go!"

With no luggage to weigh them down, they raced through security and on toward the departure gate. Mr. Tweed's pep was stunning. He led the way down the terminal with the same fervor as he had sped down the highway to get to the airport.

They reached the departure gate with ten minutes to spare before boarding closed. Daniel leaned over with his hands on his knees, out of breath. "Do you see him?" he asked while sucking in oxygen.

"No," Mr. Tweed said, steadying himself with his cane. "Wait. Near the front of the queue. Herringbone driving cap!"

"Huh? The black one?" Daniel asked, spotting a man in a flat driving cap. He held a paper ticket in one hand and pulled a carry-on bag with the other.

"Aye, the *black* one," Mr. Tweed said with a breath of exasperation. "Moonlight Raven—I'd recognize that particular weave anywhere. We got a matching set on a wee holiday to Skye several years ago. That's Gilly!"

"If he sees us, he might run," Daniel said.

"Not all of us," Amir said. "We've never met."

"Right! Okay, Amir, you run ahead and keep him from getting through that departure gate. George, you block him from behind. And I'll, um..." Daniel's mind was racing. They only had a few seconds before Gilbert Ross would be gone for good. "I'll cause a distraction to buy you more time." He looked Amir and Mr. Tweed in the eyes. They both nodded before dashing off.

Daniel made a beeline for the boarding gate desk, swerving around a huddled group of tourists, bumping into a man on his cell phone, and leaping over a stray piece of luggage. The poor desk attendant's eyes grew large with fright as he hurdled toward her. "I'm sorry," Daniel said as he reached over the desk and snatched the intercom handset.

"Hello passengers, can I have your attention? I, um, have an important announcement," Daniel said. The people nearest him stopped what they were doing and looked his direction. But the travelers farther out continued inching toward the gate. He saw Amir gaining ground, but Mr. Tweed was having difficulty jostling through the crowd to get to Ross. Daniel scrambled to think of something more to say. The desk attendant reached over the desk to retrieve the handset. Daniel stepped back as far as the cord would reach. He only needed a few more seconds.

An image of Eliza MacGillivray unexpectedly flashed in his mind. He recalled her vision of him standing on the Kessock Bridge, shouting inaudibly while she fell from the heavens. "As you would know, that which will make you unhappy, I must tell you the truth," Daniel said into the handset. His voice boomed over the loudspeaker. Now, all the passengers waiting in line stopped and turned toward him. And so did two airport security guards.

"My lord seems to have little thought of you, or of his children, or of his Highland home," Daniel said. The security guards were hurrying toward him. "Beware the hand that offers gold, lest it unsheathe its claws," Daniel continued. Now the guards were upon him. "When raven caws, the trusted heart shall pierce as thistle under foot!" Daniel shouted as they ripped the receiver from his hand and tackled him to the ground. As one guard held his arm painfully behind his back, Daniel managed to lift and angle his head just enough to see the front of the line.

Amir stood in front of the loading bridge door, arguing with the ticket checker, who was visibly trying to get him out of the way. Daniel saw Gilbert Ross step out of line in an attempt to slip past Amir and board the plane. But Daniel's distraction had given Mr. Tweed sufficient time to sneak behind Ross and hook his cane around the handle of Ross's carry-on bag. The sudden shift in momentum spun Ross around, and he nearly fell over from the surprise of seeing his old friend staring him down.

Daniel saw them exchange words, but he couldn't hear what they were saying over the bustle from the excited crowd and the shouts from the security guards holding him down. "That was a stupid stunt you pulled," one guard said.

His partner patted Daniel down, looking for weapons. The man's thick cologne was like a fog and burned Daniel's throat. "He's clean," the guard said.

"Right, then. You're coming with us. Don't even think of resisting," the other one said as he loosened his hold on Daniel's arm to allow him to get off the floor.

"I'm not resisting," Daniel said.

When he stood, each guard gripped one of his arms. As they led him away from the gate, Daniel craned his head to see what was happening with Ross. He looked back just in time to glimpse Ross abandon his luggage bag to Mr. Tweed and then slip past Amir and the ticket checker to enter the loading bridge door.

Chapter Fifty-Eight

Daniel sat alone in the stark confines of an airport holding room. Harsh fluorescent lighting cast a cold, hostile glow over the bare surroundings. The room was devoid of comfort or decoration, with plain white walls and a row of hard metal chairs bolted to the floor. The two security guards had left him there, after walking him away from the loading gate, down a long corridor, and into a section of the airport not open to the public. They had taken his phone. The room had no wall clock, so Daniel had no idea how long he'd been sitting there. It could have been hours or mere minutes. He was lost in a timeless sea of frayed nerves and worry.

Would he be arrested? Or deported? What would Ellie think? He imagined her at the veterinary clinic, comforting a customer over a sick pet. Or perhaps she was out dress shopping or tasting more wedding cakes, dreaming of their future together. Would he be able to say goodbye to her before he was forced to leave the country?

The holding room had no windows, but Daniel could hear planes taxiing across the tarmac, landing, and taking off. He knew that Gilbert Ross sat on one of those planes. Though he was missing his carry-on luggage, Daniel imagined him nevertheless tucked away safely in a first-class seat, headed toward Montenegro and freedom. Ross was likely already miles away from Inverness and his crimes and the lives that he had shattered. The thought of Ross getting away, after they had come so close to catching him, tormented Daniel even more than his worry over what would become of him when airport security returned.

The rattling of the door handle brought Daniel out of his rumination. He sat up straight in his chair, steeling himself to face the immigration officer that he imagined to be on the other side. But instead of a dark blue Border Force uniform, a man in a tweed suit of deep blue with specks of gold stepped inside.

"Reverend Darrow, you've gotten yourself into quite a conundrum this time," Mr. Tweed said.

Daniel stood up, hardly able to believe his eyes. "Boy, am I glad to see you! How did you find me? What happened to Ross? Where's Amir?" Daniel asked in rapid succession.

"Whoa, one question at a time," Mr. Tweed said. He shut the door behind him and motioned for Daniel to sit back down. "Amir is fine. He's waiting for us outside. Now, as for how I found you? I am a man of many connections, as you once said. You're not the first person I know that's had some, em, trouble with Immigration before. And since you didn't have any weapons on you or actually hurt or threaten anyone, I was able to arrange a wee chat with you before you're released."

"Really? So, I'm not being deported? Oh, thank you!" Daniel exclaimed. He felt dizzy from relief.

"Don't thank me too soon. Your passport's been flagged because of your disturbance at the gate desk. You'll be subject to enhanced security checks anytime you pass through a UK airport in future," Mr. Tweed said. "That was quite the performance, my boy. Where did you ever come up with that gibberish?"

"Oh, it was just something someone told me once," Daniel said.

"Well, whatever it was, it worked. Stopped the boarding queue long enough for me to get to Gilly, it did," Mr. Tweed said.

"It didn't work, though. I saw Ross slip past you and Amir. He made it through the gate and is probably halfway to Montenegro by now," Daniel said.

Mr. Tweed held up a finger. "Not before a wee stop at London Heathrow. But that's jumping ahead. When I caught Gilly's bag, I finally got the confession I wanted out of him. Oh, the look of surprise in his eyes when he saw me! That was worth every pain I'm going to feel in the morning from racing through this airport," he said, rubbing his knees.

"I told him that I was on to his scheme. I knew about the money he'd been stealing from GlenBreeze and how he'd paid Keith Christie to kill that worker and reporter for getting too close. Gilly denied everything, of course. But the panic in his voice said otherwise. So, I told him I had evidence—his secret Haller Bank account and Christie's ledgers. I told him to turn himself in. A judge might go easier on him that way. I said I'd go with him to the police. Despite his betrayal, our friendship was worth that, at least.

"But he told me I was too late. He'd already directed all his accounts to be transferred this morning and Montenegro doesn't have extradition to the UK, so whatever evidence I thought I had was useless. Then he dropped his luggage, shoved his way past Amir, and ran through the gate door."

"So, we failed," Daniel said. "He killed three people, stole millions, and he gets to just fly away."

"Ah, but you forget; he has a connecting flight in Heathrow," Mr. Tweed said with a sly grin.

"I don't understand. We're still here. We could never catch up with him in time," Daniel said.

"*We* don't have to," Mr. Tweed said. "Gilly isn't the only one with friends in the police force. Before stepping in here, I rang up an old friend, Owen Fletcher."

Daniel responded with a blank expression.

"Sorry, Commissioner Owen Fletcher, of the London Metropolitan Police. We were members of the same golfing club several years ago when I had some business in London," Mr. Tweed said with a wink. "My only regret about letting Gilly get on that plane is that I won't be there to see his face when the bobbies greet him in London." Mr. Tweed stared off past the blank wall and smiled.

Then he tapped his cane twice on the linoleum floor and stood. "Well, let's be off. If we dottle around here any longer, they'll charge me for the whole day of parking!"

Chapter Fifty-Nine

Gilbert Ross sat comfortably in his first-class seat. He stared out the window as the town of Inverness grew ever smaller. He was miles away now, but his thoughts remained fixated on the departure gate. How had his old friend, George Fraser, found out about the wind farm, Keith Christie, the secret ledger, the murders? How had his scheme gone so pear-shaped? It had started out simply enough: find a corrupt, or *corruptible*, foreman, sub expensive building materials for cheap, pocket the savings, and use a work crew who either wouldn't know the difference or wouldn't be in a position to speak up if they did.

And it had worked, hadn't it? Brilliantly, in fact. Everything was going to plan until that one foreign worker started asking too many questions. The foreman was supposed to keep his crew quiet. That's what Ross had paid him to do. And in a way, he had—permanently. Ross chuckled to himself.

Then his expression soured. It was that blasted reverend, wasn't it? No one had suspected a thing until that reverend stuck his meddlesome nose in where it didn't belong. What had he gone on about back at the airport terminal? A lord having no thought of his Highland home, and then some nonsense about a golden hand with claws? No, was it a raven and a thistle? Ross removed his hat and rubbed the rough material between his thumb and forefinger. What was the name of the weave? Night Raven? No, Moonlight Raven. That was it. He and George Fraser had bought a matching set several years ago while on holiday together. *George's reverend must have been the one to turn my once loyal old friend against me,* Ross thought with a grimace.

Never mind. The Highlands were no longer Ross's home, at least not for a while. Ross wondered how long he would have to stay away this time—months, years? *It's fine,* he told himself. He could use an extended holiday. Hell, after all he'd been through lately, he *deserved* one. And he'd squirreled away enough cash to tide him over until this whole wind farm debacle blew over. Ross chuckled at his own pun.

He had lied when he'd told George Fraser about moving his money out of the Haller Bank account that George had discovered. That would be the first thing on his to-do list when he landed in Montenegro—move the funds to an account even George Fraser wouldn't be able to trace. Then he'd be set to wait this out in style.

"Excuse me, sir. Can I get you anything?" a flight attendant asked, interrupting Ross's thoughts. He ordered a Scotch, neat. *That's one thing I'll miss,* Ross thought. Montenegro makes a palatable brandy and a decent beer, but a good Scotch whiskey? He made a mental note to snag a couple of bottles from the duty-free shop on his layover in Heathrow. Once the flight attendant returned, Ross settled in to enjoy his drink and peruse the in-flight magazine. When the captain announced their descent into London Heathrow, Ross sat up and closed his eyes. Just a quick transfer and then hello, warm Mediterranean beaches!

Once the plane came to a stop, Ross stood and reached into the overhead compartment before remembering how he'd had to leave his carry-on suitcase back in Inverness. No matter, he'd buy a whole new wardrobe once he was safe in Montenegro. He smiled, realizing that he was actually looking forward to exchanging his stuffy tweeds for relaxing beach linens.

The line to disembark moved at a snail's pace. Ross glanced at his wristwatch. He tapped on the man's shoulder ahead of him. "What's taking this queue? I'm going to miss my connection." The man simply shook his head and shrugged. Ross huffed impatiently. He had paid for a first-class ticket precisely so that he would not have to endure such inconveniences. His breath caught in his throat when he finally saw the reason for the delay.

Four uniformed London police officers were blocking the arrivals gate, checking each passenger's identification before allowing them to pass through. Ross loosened his necktie and tried to steady his breathing. Why were they here? Who were they looking for? He'd made a clean escape from George Fraser. When he'd glanced back before boarding, he'd seen airport security arrest that meddlesome reverend. No security or flight attendant had ever questioned him.

Ross removed his hat and wiped a line of moisture from his brow. He was sweating, but he felt cold and slightly dizzy. He nearly dropped his hat when he remembered a conversation he'd once had with George Fraser. George was telling him about some business he had in London. Ross couldn't recall the business, but that wasn't the important part of the story. George was bragging about who he'd met on the golf course while there. He was always going on about his latest connections. George Fraser collected high-profile relationships like Ross's ex-wife collected designer purses. Ross recalled that his friend's golfing partner on that particular trip had been none other than the Commissioner of the London Metropolitan Police.

Ross took an unsteady step forward and returned his hat lower on his forehead, averting his gaze from the officers. One of the officers held up her phone. She said something to her partner and nodded toward him. "Aye, that looks like him," the partner said. They walked toward him.

"Gilbert Ross? We need you to come with us," the first police officer said.

Ross stepped back, but the gate door had already closed behind him. He reached for the rope blocking off the arrivals line. His palms were clammy. The two officers took another step toward him. One of them said something, but all Ross could hear was the rapid pounding of his heart echoing in his head. He glanced frantically around him. There was nowhere else to run.

Chapter Sixty

A warm summer breeze blew in from the south through the city of Inverness. It brought with it the faintly sweet scent of blooming heather with strong undernotes of peat, earth, and verdure. Tomorrow's forecast called for rain, but today the sky was a brilliant azure blue dotted with thick white clouds. Sunlight shimmered off the surface of the River Ness as it flowed through the heart of the city, passing under the city's seven bridges on its way to the North Sea. It babbled along past the green fields of Bught Park and Tomnahurich Hill, past the tennis courts and duplexes of Bellfield Park, past the watchful castle towers and the high stone spires and belfries of historic churches, until finally emptying into the open waters of the Beauly and Moray Firths.

Despite the calm, picture-perfect weather, Daniel Darrow was a tangled bundle of nerves and anxious energy. He paced nervously back and forth in the kirk hall near the door that led to the chancel where the choir usually stood. On the other side of the thick wooden door, he could hear muffled chatter and footsteps as people filed into pews. He glanced around the room. The tables were all set with white cloths and bright floral centerpieces. Food and drinks were waiting to be served in the attached kitchen. Everything was ready. So why was he so tense?

"You're going to wear holes in the soles of those shoes if you don't stand still, son. I doubt we'll get our deposit back then," Mr. Darrow said. He wore a sharp black suit with a blue tartan necktie that matched the kilt Daniel wore. He eyed the garment jealously, having waited nearly a month for an excuse to wear one, but the necktie was the closest Mrs. Darrow would allow.

"Yes, there's nothing to worry about. This day will be perfect," Daniel's mother said.

"She's here, right? Y'all saw her?" Daniel asked.

"She's here, and she looks just beautiful," Mrs. Darrow said.

"How long ago did you see her? She hasn't changed her mind?" Daniel asked. He pulled at his necktie, feeling as if it were going to suffocate him.

"Stop fidgeting. You're going to mess it up," his mother said. She slapped his hands away and readjusted the tie.

His father laughed. "We saw Ellie right before we came to check on you. Now, take a deep breath. In and out, slowly—that's it. It's time to get this show on the road."

Daniel closed his eyes and took another long breath to calm his nerves. "Where's Young Hugh? He's supposed to have the ring," Daniel said.

"Your friend is already out there. Strange name, though. Why not just call him Hugh?" Daniel's father said.

"Hugh is his father. Never mind, I think I'm ready," Daniel said. "Wait, my hands are all clammy and sweaty. I don't want to wipe them on my shirt."

"Here," Daniel's father said, stretching out his arm to offer the sleeve of his own jacket.

"Ew, no! That's a new suit," Mrs. Darrow said with an exasperated sigh. She reached into her tiny, bejeweled purse and handed Daniel a tissue. "This thing can't hold much, but I knew I'd need tissues today."

Daniel wiped his hands, swallowed hard, and opened the door. When he stepped into the chancel, the noise from the pews quieted down. When the guests realized it was just him, they resumed chatting. Daniel's parents hugged him and sat down in the front pew. His mother hadn't bothered to return her packet of tissues to her purse and was already dabbing her eyes with one. Daniel took his place next to his friend and sometimes-flatmate, Young Hugh Macpherson. "Thanks again for being here. I know the flight from São Paulo had to have been long. It means a lot to both of us," Daniel said.

"Anything for you and Ellie, mate," Young Hugh said with a smile.

Daniel gazed out at the sea of familiar faces that filled the pews in front of him. It was hard to believe that in just a couple of short years, they had become like an extended family to him. He saw Hugh and Marjory Macpherson, his landlords and Young Hugh's parents, sitting near the front. "Hey, how are you and your folks?" Daniel whispered to Young Hugh.

"Nothing brings people together like a wedding," Young Hugh joked.

"Seriously, though," Daniel prodded.

"We're okay. We had a good talk once I got back. I think they're coming around to the idea that I'm happy, not just flailing about trying to find myself," Young Hugh said with a smile and nod to his parents. "Of course, after today, I'm sure they'll be hounding me to get married and settle down myself."

"Would that be so bad?" Daniel asked. Young Hugh rolled his eyes. "We could go on double dates and have game nights!" Daniel taunted.

"Just kill me now," Young Hugh said. They both laughed.

Returning his attention to the audience, Daniel saw William MacCrivag and Philip Morrison. Mr. MacCrivag caught Daniel's eye and raised a flask to him. Daniel had a good idea what their wedding present would be. Beside Philip Morrison was Edna Caird, whose Highlands tourism business he had taken over from her late husband. Mr. Tweed and his wife, Mary, sat in the next row near Amir and Samira Ghulam and her two young boys. The boys were busy playing some kind of game with their hands, oblivious to the adult world around them. Amir patted the youngest on the head before walking up to Daniel. "Are we ready to begin? Where's Reverend Calder?" Amir asked.

"Sarah's not here?" Daniel asked, a wave of anxiety flushing back over him.

"I thought she would be with you," Amir said.

"She's officiating. We can't do this without her," Daniel said.

"We need to begin soon. People are getting restless."

"It's not like her to be late." Daniel scanned the pews for her and then thought better of it. *Why would she be out there?* "Do either of you have a phone on you?" he asked. "I should call her." Amir shook his head.

"I do, but I don't have her number. I could run down and ask my parents?" Young Hugh said.

While Daniel was considering his suggestion, the front doors to the kirk opened. A beam of sunlight poured in, and everyone in the audience rose. Amir raced over to the piano and started in on the first chords of "Here Comes the Bride." Daniel held his breath. Any second, Ellie would walk down the aisle to be greeted by a sweaty-palmed groom and an empty pulpit.

"Yer bride's gotten shorter and a bit rounder since the last time I saw her," Young Hugh whispered, squinting to see the silhouette that had just entered the building.

"Sit down, it's only Sarah," William MacCrivag shouted from his pew. Daniel put his hand over his forehead to shield the sunlight until the doors closed. Then he waved at Amir to stop playing. Murmuring and the sound of coats and shoes shuffling erupted from the pews as the audience sat back down.

"It's not just Sarah," Reverend Calder said. "So sorry I'm a touch late. I had a special guest to pick up on my way over." She pushed a wheelchair in front of her down the aisle. Inside it sat an older woman wearing a long black Victorian-style gown with a high lace collar and cuffs. She held a large handbag in her lap and, on top of her head, she wore a wide-brimmed lacey hat that obscured her face.

But Daniel didn't need to see her face to know the identity of Rev. Calder's special guest. He knew of only one person that dressed so eloquently out-of-time. When they got closer to the front row, a pair of long, furry ears popped out of the woman's handbag, confirming Daniel's suspicion—Eliza MacGillivray!

Daniel leaped down from the raised floor of the chancel to meet them. "Eliza, I can't believe you're here! How are you feeling? The last time I saw you, you were—"

"Having the best catnap of my life," Eliza said.

Daniel looked to Rev. Calder for clarification.

"The doctor called me this morning. She woke up late last night. They wanted to keep her longer for observation, but our Eliza can be quite persuasive when she wants to be," Rev. Calder said.

"She means crabbit. I raised quite a fuss until they let me out of there. I couldn't miss the wedding, could I? I did prophesy it, after all," Eliza said. "Sarah, be a dear and park me near the front row. My eyes aren't what they used to be."

Rev. Calder laughed and did as she requested.

"Did you see Ellie?" Daniel asked.

"Aye, she's waiting with Elspeth outside. She looks simply stunning. I asked them to give me a minute to get Eliza situated," Rev. Calder said. "Now, are you ready to get married?"

Chapter Sixty-One

The heavy wooden doors of Church Street Kirk creaked open, letting in the late afternoon sunlight. Two figures appeared in silhouette, arm-in-arm. At the front of the church, Rev. Calder nodded to Amir at the piano to begin playing. The audience rose, and Daniel stood stiff as a board beside his friend Young Hugh.

"Now that would be your bride, ye ken?" Young Hugh whispered. Daniel nodded without looking away, his eyes fixed straight ahead.

Elspeth Gray walked her daughter slowly down the center aisle of the kirk. Ellie's cinnamon hair was done up and shimmered in the light. She held a small bouquet of white roses mixed with purple Scottish thistles. Rev. Calder had described her as stunning, but the word didn't do her justice. *More like radiant*, Daniel thought. But more than her beauty, he was overcome with a surprising feeling of calm the nearer she approached. When she smiled at him, all the butterflies in his stomach suddenly fell silent. He knew with absolute certainty that this was exactly where he was supposed to be—standing beside her, hand-in-hand.

Ellie's mother sat down beside his parents. The audience sat down, as well, and Rev. Calder began speaking. But Daniel didn't hear a word she said. His attention was wholly on Ellie, butterflies having given way to a gleeful lightheadedness. Amir began playing another song, and Ellie leaned in and whispered, "You look very handsome in your kilt."

"Thanks. You're...I don't even have the words. Stunning," Daniel whispered back. Then something caught his eye. Her necklace looked strangely familiar. "Is that Eliza's Seeing Stone?" he asked.

Ellie smiled and glanced down at the smooth donut-shaped stone that hung from a new silver chain. "Your mother surprised me with it last night. A while ago, she'd asked me about the jar of clay you had them collect from Loch Ussie, and I told her about the broken stone."

"So that was the secret pottery project she's been working on," Daniel said.

"Something old, something new, right?" Ellie smiled.

The music ended, and Rev. Calder addressed them. "Do you have the rings?" she asked.

Daniel turned to Young Hugh, who held out two empty hands. Daniel's face turned whiter than the roses in Ellie's bouquet. "Where is it?" he asked through clenched teeth. Young Hugh replied with a blank stare. "Hugh!" Daniel whispered, his panic turning to frustration.

Young Hugh smiled and winked at Ellie. Daniel turned to her. *What was going on?*

"Eliza," Ellie said.

"Oh, aye, sorry," Eliza MacGillivray said. She patted the bottom of her large handbag. Her rabbit peeked its fuzzy head out, black eyes darting around the room, nose twitching nervously. Eliza patted the bottom of the bag more forcefully. The rabbit popped out and hopped in a slight zig-zag pattern toward Ellie. Ellie bent down, gave it a pat on the head, and untied a ribbon from around its neck. The rabbit darted back to Eliza and leaped straight back into her bag.

A tiny velvet pouch hung from the center of the ribbon. Ellie handed it to Daniel. He opened it skeptically and then let out an audible chuckle when he saw what was inside—two wedding bands.

"I had to do something to keep him from missing Eliza too badly while I rabbit-sat. So, we learned a wee trick," Ellie said.

Daniel smiled and shook his head in mock exasperation. He handed the rings to Rev. Calder. Her expression told him that she had also been in on the stunt. Young Hugh leaned in and whispered in Daniel's ear, "Too late to back out now, mate."

* * *

The fiddle and accordion players began softly tuning their instruments in a corner of the kirk hall. Plates soiled with icing and cake crumbs filled the kitchen sink and spilled over onto the counter. Daniel Darrow sat at a table with his parents and Elspeth Gray. He loosened his dress shoes and exchanged them for a comfortable pair of sneakers he had earlier stashed in the hall.

"I still don't know why you insisted on bringing those. They don't match at all," Mrs. Darrow said.

"This is your first ceilidh. Believe me, by the end of the evening, you'll understand," Daniel said.

"Where is Ellie? My chaperones look like they're growing impatient," Elspeth Gray said, nodding towards a burly-looking man in a blue suit standing guard at the front door and a woman at the side door in a matching uniform. "I was hoping to get at least one dance in before they take me back."

"Eliza said she needed some air. I think Ellie took her out to the garden. I'll go check on them," Daniel said. He laced up his sneakers and headed outside.

Ellie was sitting beside Eliza on a bench under the tree in the middle of the kirk garden. The last of the sun's rays painted brilliant splashes of pink and purple across the horizon. Daniel stood for a moment, admiring the way the light made Ellie appear to glow in her white dress. He caught the tail end of their conversation as he approached.

"I couldn't possibly. It's yours, Eliza. I only borrowed it for the wedding," Ellie said. She held the newly repaired Seeing Stone between her finger and thumb. Two seams of a slightly darker color were visible where Daniel's mother had fused them back together with the clay from Loch Ussie. She had also added a clear glaze to strengthen it.

"No, I've had my time. The Stone has chosen you. The Seer's burden is yours to carry now," Eliza said.

"Hi, sorry to interrupt," Daniel said. "I think they're wanting to start the dancing soon."

Ellie nodded. "Eliza, do you want me to take you back inside? The ceilidh's about to start."

But Eliza was staring at the base of the tree. "Now what's that cat after now?" she asked, protectively clutching her handbag.

Sir Walter sat at attention, staring up into the tree branches, cackling and making high-pitched mewing sounds. Daniel followed the cat's gaze until he saw two birds perched on a high branch—a pitch black raven and a marble gray dove. The raven stood its ground and cawed back at its feline tormentor. The dove took flight, soaring up over the roof of the kirk. Daniel watched as it doubled back around the steeple and then flew north toward the Moray Firth.

"Did you see that? A raven and a dove. How strange. What do you suppose it means?" he asked Ellie. But Ellie didn't respond. She clutched the Seeing Stone and stared off into the distance at seemingly nothing. "What are you looking at?" Daniel asked, trying to see what had caught her attention.

"It's no use, luv," Eliza said. She reached up and placed her hand on Daniel's arm. "She sees beyond what our mortal eyes can see now."

"Ellie? Are you okay?" Daniel asked.

After a few seconds, Ellie blinked several times and shook her head. She released the stone that still hung on the silver chain around her neck and turned to look at Daniel and Eliza. "I just saw the most amazing thing. You wouldn't believe."

About the Author

Daniel K. Miller holds advanced degrees from the University of Edinburgh and Duke University. His short fiction and nonfiction have appeared in various literary journals. He lives with his wife and a motley assortment of horses, cats, and wildlife. *Den of Lions* is his third novel.

AUTHOR WEBSITE:
  www.danielkmillerauthor.com

SOCIAL MEDIA HANDLES:
  @danielkmillerauthor

Also by Daniel K. Miller

Fire on the Firth (Level Best Books)

Loch and Key (Level Best Books)